"Just when you think you have this maze of double-dealing figured out—surprise, it isn't what you think. All the elements of a classic espionage story are here. The novel moves with relentless momentum, scattering bodies in its wake."

—*Kirkus Reviews*

"The golden age of the spy novel is not over, not with the master (Matthew Dunn) and his top notch agent, William Cochrane."

—*Iron Mountain Daily News*

"Dunn's exuberant, bullet-drenched prose, with its descriptions of intelligence tradecraft and modern anti-terrorism campaigns, bristles with authenticity."

—*The Economist*

"Matthew Dunn's third Will Cochrane novel is a complex work with a twisting and turning plot that moves ever forward, loaded with the double—and triple—crosses that readers who follow the author have come to expect. . . . Should be added to the must-read lists of all fans of espionage thrillers."

—Bookreporter.com

"Dunn is a born storyteller . . . I know of no other spy thriller that so successfully blends the fascinating nuances of the business of espionage and intelligence work with full-throttle suspense storytelling."

—Jeffery Deaver, author of *The Steel Kiss*

"Dunn's Spycatcher series features MI6/CIA task force operative Will Cochrane, who lacks James Bond's gadgets but relies on encyclopedic knowledge, physical prowess, and an off-the-charts degree of self-sufficiency that even Jack Reacher would envy. . . . The author's prose is lean and compelling, and the pace is frantic."

—*Publishers Weekly*

"[Dunn has] a superlative talent for three-dimensional characterization, gripping dialogue, and plots that feature gasp-inducing twists and betrayals."

—TheExaminer.com

"The general is a terrific villain—strong, sly, scheming, sick, smart, and really, really evil. And as Dunn spins out the story, the whole scenario seems to become more and more believable. The adventurous episodes and personal battles between Cochrane and the general are extremely involving. While reading them, the reader starts thinking, 'I wonder if Dunn actually was involved in a battle just like this.' I'll bet he was. And on top of all that, there is a fascinating shocker at the climax."

—*National Book Examiner*

"Great talent, great imagination, and real been-there done-that authenticity make this one of the year's best. . . . Highly recommended."

—Lee Child, author of *Night School*

"You can thrill to the high-pressure intrigue as CIA and MI6 agents bumble into each other, unfortunately rubbing out the wrong principles in their haste to save their ideals. . . . *Sentinel*'s characters are thoroughly and irresistibly believable."

— Examiner.com

"*Spycatcher* makes a strong argument that it takes a real spy to write a truly authentic espionage novel. . . . [The story] practically bursts at the seams with boots-on-the-ground insight and realism. But there's another key ingredient that likely will make the ruthless yet noble protagonist, Will Cochrane, a popular series character for many years to come: Dunn is a gifted storyteller."

—*Fort Worth Star-Telegram*

By Matthew Dunn

A SOLDIER'S REVENGE

THE SPY HOUSE

DARK SPIES

SLINGSHOT

SENTINEL

SPYCATCHER

Novellas

SPY TRADE

COUNTERSPY

Coming Soon in Hardcover

ACT OF BETRAYAL

MATTHEW DUNN

A SOLDIER'S REVENGE

A WILL COCHRANE NOVEL

WILLIAM MORROW
An Imprint of HarperCollinsPublishers

A SOLDIER'S REVENGE. Copyright © 2016 by Matthew Dunn. All rights reserved. Printed in the United States of America. No part of this book may be used or reproduced in any manner whatsoever without written permission except in the case of brief quotations embodied in critical articles and reviews. For information, address HarperCollins Publishers, 195 Broadway, New York, NY 10007.

First William Morrow premium printing: July 2017
First William Morrow hardcover printing: October 2016

ISBN: 978-0-06-242720-5

William Morrow and HarperCollins are registered trademarks of HarperCollins Publishers in the United States of America and other countries.

16 17 18 19 20   QGM   10 9 8 7 6 5 4 3 2 1

To my children

PART I
THE SETUP

PROLOGUE

New York City, Waldorf Astoria Hotel, 8:03 A.M.

I opened my eyes to find my hands were caked in blood, and I had no idea why.

More blood stained the Egyptian cotton sheets on top of me.

I swung my feet out of bed and onto the deep-pile cream carpet, hands motionless in midair. A nosebleed in the night was a possibility, though that hadn't happened since I was ten years old. Thirty-five years ago. Urgently, I checked my body—all six foot four inches. Some of my scars were courtesy of my service as a paratrooper in the French Foreign Legion. Others from being an American and British spy. None of the scars were ruptured.

On my right arm was a tiny cut. Maybe I had scratched the area and broken skin while sleeping.

It was the only laceration on my flesh, but that wouldn't account for the quantity of blood.

A warm breeze came through the open windows and swirled around the room, which was furnished with art deco paintings, velvet drapes, upholstered furniture, and a television atop an oak cabinet crammed with fine wines and single malts. A corridor led to the closed bathroom door. The bedroom windows had been shut when I went to bed.

Nothing made sense.

The bathroom door had been open last night. Perhaps I'd stumbled in there half asleep to relieve myself, shutting the door on my way out. I didn't know. But I was awake now and my mind had finally kicked into gear.

I opened the bathroom door and turned the light on.

The sight that greeted me was like a heavyweight punch to the face.

In the bathtub was a smartly dressed woman— short brown hair, Caucasian. She'd been shot twice in the back of the head at close range with bullets that were sufficiently powerful to leave savage exit wounds.

Her face was an obliterated mess. Within the confines of the tub, her limbs were contorted, her body twisted, the result of a sudden jerk of movement during instant death.

I stayed still, silent, because I'd had too much experience of death to express my emotions. But internally, adrenaline and panic were kicking in big-time.

I looked everywhere for something to tell me what had happened.

Judging by her attire, the woman could have been one of the hotel's hundreds of wealthy guests or numerous management staff. One of her hands was resting on the side of the tub. She wasn't wearing wedding and engagement rings, but normally did. Neither had previously been taken off for some time, judging by the buildup of fat around the place where they should have been. They were gone now.

On the floor beneath her hand was an MK23 pistol with a sound suppressor attached. It was a weapon used by specialists. It's a good gun—zero recoil. Why was it there? Who had left it there? The woman had bruises on her wrists, and one shoe heel was broken off. It was clear to me that she'd futilely fought before death and was placed here while alive, held down, and shot dead. How could I have slept through this? Had I been drugged? This body had been killed and placed here for a reason.

To implicate me.

After washing the blood off my hands, I examined everything in the crime scene—little bottles of Ferragamo perfumed soap on the side of the bath, mostly unused, those open done so by me the night before; blood on walls, floor too, and underneath the woman's fingernails.

A bloody handprint was on the wall of tile. I held my hand against it and saw its shape and size exactly matched my own. Next to it were five red fingerprints. I dashed into the bedroom, opened my pen, and poured ink into a cup. After dipping one set of fingers into the ink, I pressed them against a sheet of hotel paper. In the bathroom, I held the sheet next to the fingerprints on the wall. A perfect match. It was my fingerprints on that wall.

My life was ruined by the scene in the bathroom. Torn apart, turned to shit.

But ruined by me? I wondered if I'd gone insane. My recollection of how I'd spent the evening before might have been a deliberate false memory. I hadn't spent a quiet night of solitary reflection in my hotel room, making plans for my future. Instead, perhaps I'd met the woman in the hotel bar and asked her up to my room to join me for a drink. And then? Then she said something that set me off. A naïve or sarcastic comment that triggered memories of past traumas. It wasn't the woman's fault; she was just in the wrong place at the wrong time. Regardless, my ordinarily superb moral compass was sent into a helter-skelter spin of confused anger and revenge against the person I'd become. After a life of protecting people and getting no thanks in return, I'd gotten pissed off by something the woman in the bathtub had said. Maybe I shot her. Simple as that.

That would make me a good man turned crazed lunatic. A person pushed over the edge. A man who needed to be put behind bars forever, while receiving treatment for a brain that was firing on the wrong cylinders. The death penalty might be a better way out.

I picked up the pistol, checked its magazine, pulled back the workings, and sniffed the barrel.

At least one bullet had recently exited the handgun. Eight bullets remained in the gun. I hadn't smuggled a pistol into America. This was not my weapon.

I had to hand myself in to the police. I would tell them I didn't think I'd killed the woman, and certainly had no recollection of doing so, but there was every possibility that I was a lying madman. The chances that I would be found not guilty were slim to nonexistent. Detectives would probe into my background and would get just enough information on my exploits to conclude that their prisoner was a man who'd been instructed to kill far too many times. Motive: acute mental disorder brought about by cumulative traumas. Victim: a random member of the human race. And while I was investigated, I'd be kept in a cage with no chance to establish the truth.

Thing was, though, I knew my own mind.

I kill people who need to be killed.

I didn't shoot the woman.

I couldn't trust the police to help me understand what had happened here. For them it would be a no-brainer. I would be guilty as charged.

There was no one I could trust.

I needed to move quickly. After dressing in jeans, boots, T-shirt, sweater, and jacket, I grabbed only essential items and shoved them into a small backpack, together with the pistol. I removed my cell phone battery and smashed the phone into pieces, collecting all debris and dumping it into a shower cap. When far away from here, I'd dispose of the destroyed phone.

And getting away from here was now my absolute priority.

But I hesitated.

I touched the fresh cut on my arm as I looked at the woman's bloody nails. She'd scratched me, I was sure. I put the tips of my fingers against hers. I knew I shouldn't have done so, but I was convinced my DNA was already all over the scene. Almost certainly my prints were on the gun. I kept my hand against hers because I needed the faceless corpse to know that someone really cared about what had happened.

I hated leaving her.

The vast hotel lobby had a marble floor with potted plants and rows of golden pillars that were illuminated by huge crystal chandeliers. Numerous guests were checking in or out or heading to breakfast. It was a civilized place. I was innocent of what had happened in room 1944, but I felt like a guilty murderer. This wasn't the place for me. Getting out of here was all that mattered.

The concierge glanced up from his computer, smiled, and walked from behind his desk directly toward me. He was carrying a clipboard and a small parcel.

He blocked my path, held up the parcel, and said, "This came for you in the early hours. Hand delivered. We were going to run it up to your room today. Still can, if you like. Or you can take it now."

Nobody apart from hotel staff knew I was in the Waldorf. The parcel was a small cardboard box, though big enough to contain a bomb that would obliterate me. I wondered whether I should take the parcel far away from here and dump it in a deserted field. But somebody had dragged a woman into my room, shot her, and exited without killing me. He'd have killed me then if he wanted.

I opened the box.

Inside was a hardcover encyclopedia. I flicked though the first pages. Printed in 1924 by a publishing house I'd never heard of, almost certainly the book was long ago out of print. As I rifled through the book I came across the brief handwritten note.

> *The classifieds section of the Washington*
> *Post. Not available online; only print copies.*
> *Tomorrow's edition.*

"Just need you to sign for this." The concierge handed me his clipboard and pen. "Hope you're having a great day," he added, his smile broadening.

I took the clipboard and wrote my name.

Will Cochrane.

ONE

The Romanian cleaner was crying as she jogged down the nineteenth-floor corridor alongside the Waldorf's head of security. She didn't know the man by her side. He was serious, an ex-NYPD cop, she'd heard, and had the demeanor of someone who'd been waiting for a moment like this so that he could kick into action and do something other than hushing rowdy guests. She was in her cleaning apron and flat shoes. He was in a dark suit and had an earpiece, making him look like the Secret Service men she'd seen in movies.

They reached the room where the Do Not Disturb sign had hung on the door all day. It was only ten minutes ago that the cleaner had knocked on the door again, heard no response, and entered.

That's when she'd screamed.

The head of security told her to stay in the

corridor, used a universal swipe card to enter the room, and walked into the bathroom.

The ex-cop had never seen anything like this.

As the Amtrak train turned on a bend in the tracks, Philadelphia became visible in the distance. I'd disappear in the city for one night. Spending any longer here would be suicidal. Nowhere was safe.

I'd pretended to sleep for most of the journey in the full train car, head bowed low, jacket hood up, and arms folded as if I was hugging myself warm rather than keeping one hand close to the murder weapon I'd taken from the bathroom. A tired kid called Andy was sitting next to me. Mom was sitting opposite her son, her accent from North Carolina, I was sure; a patient woman who spoke to Andy in a noncondescending yet commanding tone.

Next to her was a jerk called Kevin, who was almost certainly hated by the U.S. Marine Corps, though he was a marine. Regulation marine haircut, a new tattoo on his sinewy forearm, and a mouth that blathered in all directions to other travelers. He was getting promoted to corporal, he told everyone, because he knew his shit. Discipline—he pumped his chest as he looked at Andy—was his savior. The Corps, God, America, ten Buds, and warm thighs made him tick, ooh-rah, y'all—in that frickin' order, you get?

Single Mom clearly didn't take to Kevin. "Please, young man. No language like that in front of my son."

The marine wasn't bothered. "Ma'am, your son

hears worse at school. And he'll hear a darn sight worse when he's grown some balls."

I opened my eyes.

No doubt Andy's mom was worried. Kevin had a grin on his face and an unstoppable tongue. Mom glanced at the rear of the car, probably wondering whether she should grab her son and leave.

I leaned forward, silent because I didn't want to draw attention to myself. But I stared at Kevin.

The action worked. It got the marine's attention away from other passengers.

Kevin said, "Guys like you don't know what it's like to be in the Corps."

I didn't. But I did know how to do a HALO parachute jump from thirty thousand feet, run across snow-covered mountains with an orange boiler suit on and a hunter-killer squad with dogs on my trail, twist a man's neck until his body becomes limp, and make a car explode.

Kevin had the look of a man who thought he'd won the day. That was all I needed. He was pacified. Calmer. A guy who thought he dominated everyone around him with his masculinity. I wanted that for the sake of the folks next to me. The alternative would have been to punch him in the throat and leave him gasping for breath. I've done that many times to men far bigger than Kevin. But I didn't want to draw attention to myself. More important, the kid next to me didn't need to see the results of that action.

The train stopped. I watched Single Mom and her son exit, then picked up my things and stared at Kevin. I smiled as I towered over him. He was silent. I knew why. He now realized he was out of his league. I got off the train and walked through the station.

The Waldorf Astoria's room 1944 was officially a crime scene.

The hotel's head of security was loitering in the corridor. In the room were two forensics officers, head to toe in white coveralls, masks over their mouths, rubber gloves changed each time they touched something. It was only ten minutes ago that they'd let Detectives Józef Kopański and Thyme Painter back into the room.

Always in a bleached shirt and immaculate suit when working, Kopański—a rangy man with silver hair and not an ounce of fat on his imposing frame—had a face that was half handsome and half mutilated from nitric acid, and callused hands, the size of shovels and as strong as clamps, that could quickly put any bullet where it needed to be. Joe Cop Killer, his colleagues called him behind his back but not to his face, a nickname derived from the time he'd entered a house alone and with pinpoint accuracy shot a dangerous sheriff who was strung out on meth and was pointing a gun at his wife's head.

Compared to Kopański, whose parents were impoverished immigrants, Painter's background couldn't have been more different. Her parents were investment bankers and she was a graduate of Stanford. She'd had options on Capitol Hill, but went to West Point and graduated at the top of her class. Three years later, she was a helicopter

Night Stalker for the 160th SOAR. Her career ended when she'd offloaded five DEVGRU SEALs in Afghanistan and saw that another chopper on her six had been locked on by a SAM. To save the other helo, which contained more SEALs, she'd flown into the path of the missile. Doctors saved her life but not her leg. She joked that the stress of having an artificial limb kept her weight down.

Both single, Kopański and Painter formed a tireless unit who broke more murder cases than the rest of Manhattan's precincts combined.

The forensics team told them that the blood prints in the bathroom matched prints elsewhere in the room, meaning it was almost certain that the guest staying in 1944 was the murderer; the prints would be sent off for analysis along with all other samples.

Kopański moved left and said nothing as Painter leaned in from behind him and placed her face by the bloody handprints on the bathroom wall. She moved from one place to another, silent, shooting only the quickest of occasional glances at Kopański to let him know she was on the case and getting signals, as she called her methodology. She saw a powerful man, grip as strong as Kopański's, holding the victim with one hand, pumping bullets into the back of her skull with the other.

Painter touched Kopański's shoulder.

The big Polish American sensed the killer in the room, an electric feeling of immediacy that heightened every nerve-shredding instinct. He had been here. He'd kill you now if he still were. The murderer had washed in the bathroom, cleaning himself up after the death of an innocent woman. Killers are two a dime, serial killers a slight notch up only because their deranged personalities and get-away-with-it track record hold fascination. But this killer was different—he'd killed with brutal efficiency, yet had been sloppy by leaving his prints and DNA all over the crime scene.

According to the hotel, the room occupant was an English guy called Will Cochrane.

Both detectives wondered if he was a pro who didn't care whether the world knew he'd gone mad.

The taxi dropped me outside the Holiday Inn Express in Penn's Landing, Philadelphia. When the car was out of sight, I turned away from the hotel, walking through the city, which was wet and cold despite the last vestiges of summer lingering in the air. I stopped by an ATM, withdrew the maximum limit allowed by my bank, and moved on until I found a cheap hotel on Spruce Street, near the center of the city. After paying for a room up front in cash, I went to my room and held my head in my hands while sitting on the bed. It seemed only minutes ago that I'd sat on my Waldorf bed and stared at my bloody hands.

Traveling between New York and Philadelphia had kept me preoccupied with the urgency of fleeing and hiding. My next destination was eight hundred miles southwest, the home of twin ten-year-old boys. They were the reason I was in the States. Their parents were friends of mine and had been murdered. I'd planned to adopt the boys and start a new life in America. After months of preparation, today I was supposed to visit a law firm in NYC to sign adoption papers. I'd intended to have a new life, give the boys the security and love they so needed, start working as a teacher at their school, and be a parent. Their father was a former SEAL who'd worked with me. Many times he'd saved my life. It was my duty to look after his remaining family.

I opened the encyclopedia and reread the note. Tomorrow I'd get a copy of the *Washington Post* and scan the classifieds section. Focus on that, I told myself. The note had been written by the murderer, of that I was in no doubt. I'd know what my opponent was made of in a few hours. If he revealed his hand and implicated himself, I'd mail the *Post* and encyclopedia to the feds, telling them I was an innocent man who couldn't give himself up just yet.

I clung to the hope that it would pan out that way.

TWO

At seven fifty-five the following morning, Painter and Kopański walked quickly across the Waldorf Astoria's palatial lobby, focused but tired. The night had been intense and sleepless.

Despite the early hour, the hotel was brimming, much as it would have been when the occupant of room 1944 escaped. But today, approximately forty people in the hotel weren't guests or staff; they were journalists, some homegrown, broadsheet and tabloid, others representatives of foreign press organizations. All of them were heading to the lobby-level Empire Room, where Lieutenant Pat Brody of the Office of the Deputy Commissioner, Public Information, was about to read verbatim what Kopański and Painter had written an hour earlier.

Kopański had wanted to stage the NYPD press briefing somewhere more public in the hotel. News coverage of the briefing needed to show the hotel in order for the crime to become real in people's minds and for potential witnesses to unlock vital information hidden in their memories.

Journalists agreed, though for different reasons. This was hot press material, not because there was yet another killing in New York, but because it had taken place somewhere as swanky as the Waldorf. They wanted the Q&A to be held in front of the hotel or in the lobby. Understandably, hotel management didn't take kindly to the prospect of their hotel being advertised as the site of a brutal crime. They insisted on a discreet meeting room so the press briefing wouldn't scare off guests.

Brody took the podium. Journalists were in their seats in the Empire, lined up, chomping at the bit. Painter and Kopański stood at the back of the Edwardian room, eyeing its crystal chandeliers, drapes surmounted by gold swags, ceiling spot lamps, and brown carpet in the pattern of a maze.

"Ladies and gentlemen, good morning." Brody was in uniform; he had been on the force for twenty years.

Murmurs from the press.

Brody read out the detectives' script: short sentences, written with precision by the detectives so there could be no misinterpretation.

"The night before last, a murder took place in room 1944 of this hotel. The victim was shot twice in the back of the head with an MK23 pistol. Probably the pistol was sound suppressed, though we can't be sure at present. The murder weapon was not left at the scene. The identity of the victim is still unknown, though we're certain she's not a hotel guest or member of staff. We're running traces on her DNA and fingerprints in our national databases. We'll know soon who she is. We have one suspect: the occupant of room 1944. An Englishman. Forty-five years old. Estimated height six feet, four inches. Athletic build, according to this hotel. Short-cropped, graying blond hair. One eye green, the other blue. We've got information packs for you all at the table by the door. In there are hotel scans of the suspect's passport when he checked in and his photograph. Also a description of the clothes he was last seen wearing. You have our permission to replicate and print anything in the pack. We have an ongoing murder investigation. It's complex. Motive is unclear. Details about victim and suspect are needed. Rest assured: the detectives in charge of the investigation have moved very fast. The city is on alert, and all East Coast police and sheriff's departments are cooperating in the manhunt. Are there any questions?"

The questions fired at him were all the same.

"Who are the detectives in charge?" asked a reporter from CNN.

Brody looked at the two cops at the back of the room. "Our best."

"And the suspect?" From NBC.

Brody replied, "William Cochrane. We want to interview him. If anyone sees him, telephone the police. Don't engage with him, talk to him, or assume he's innocent. In fact, assume he's extremely dangerous."

* * *

It was mid-morning as I walked through central Philadelphia, having checked out of my hotel sixty minutes earlier. People around me were dashing for cover from the wind and rain, and vehicles with headlights on were splashing through puddles. I was wearing jeans, boots, and a Windbreaker, and had my small backpack slung over one shoulder. I wanted to blend in, but felt as if everyone was looking at me. When operating as a spy, I'd been on the run in many overseas locations. This was different. I had no place to run to. No place of safety to reach.

At a newsstand, I bought a copy of the *Washington Post*. The woman's body in room 1944 would have been discovered the previous day, I knew. The issue was how quickly the police would make my name public. I entered a small café near the entrance to the sprawling outdoor Italian Market, ordered a coffee, and sat in the corner of the room. Also here were a young couple browsing their iPads, a street vendor who was standing by the counter and chatting up a pretty waitress, and an old woman.

The *Post* on the table, I turned to the classifieds section. My eyes locked on an ad that made no sense. Its heading was HONOR OUR FALLEN HERO. In the text below were only numbers.

7(9), 18(47), 2(3), 91(78), 45(102), 29(271),
77(59), 1(33), 531(84), 531(85), 4(26), 1(32),
11(84), 243(301).

I glanced at the other occupants of the café. They were all still preoccupied with their drinks and activities. I pulled out the encyclopedia and a pen. I wanted the newspaper to make sense of all this shit, even if I knew that answers could make matters infinitely worse.

My guess was that the numbers in the ad were page numbers, with the number in parentheses referring to a word on the page. I set to work, heart racing yet mind focused. Within two minutes, I knew my instinct about the code was probably correct. On page 7 in the encyclopedia, the ninth word was "I've." I continued cross-referring the numbers in the ad with pages and words in the book.

The code was simple, but without the old encyclopedia in hand as the key to match the code, it would be impossible to break. And its creator was very clever, because there was no mention of me, nor anything else incriminating.

He was taunting me.

With the header in place, the ad read:

Honor Our Fallen Hero. I've waited. Now you have my cold dish. More tomorrow.

The message was clear.

Honor our fallen hero. Was this a reference to me? Did he see me as a onetime hero who was now on the run because of him? And if so, how did he know I was once a hero?

I've waited. Now you have my cold dish. This was about revenge. And, like all revenge, best served cold.

Tomorrow there would be another message in the *Post*.

Someone had set me up for murder. But why and who?

I looked up. The iPad couple was separated. Girl still at the table, her device open on a Fox News headline. And my face on the screen. Her guy on his cell in the street, looking anxiously at his girlfriend while talking rapid inaudible words, clearly calling for help. So it was out there. I was now a hunted man and I had to get out of there—fast.

I left cash on the table for my drink and exited the café. The moment I'd seen the dead woman in the bathtub, I knew that the media would be all over the story because of the venue. And the publicity on news networks and their online portals wouldn't end today. Tomorrow the print newspapers would be running their headlines, keeping the story alive.

I passed the young man on the phone, not too close but near enough to catch his reaction and to hear his voice. The man was a rabbit in headlights when he saw me looking directly at him. There was no doubt about what was going on here.

I walked away from him, keeping a steady pace down Ninth, dodging shoppers idling under the awnings of cafés and restaurants, cheese sellers, bakeries, and butchers. A group of European tourists were being led in the center of the street by an American guide holding a stick in the air and looking miserable in the wet weather. They stopped by a fishmonger. I attached myself to the rear of the group, turned to look back up the street, and saw two cops on foot walking diagonally from one side of the street to the other. They were a hundred yards away, hands on holsters and radio mics.

The tourist group moved on, me with them, hoping that the guide was going to announce that they were done with the market and needed to now walk quickly to another part of Philadelphia. Instead, the guide instructed everyone to take an hour's break to browse and shop. Quickly, I moved to the head of the group before it dispersed, putting tourists between me and the cops. I walked fast, praying to God that the cops didn't spot me and order me to freeze.

If that happened, South Ninth Street would become chaos.

I reached the end of the market and stopped, lifting an orange from a display and sniffing it while looking back down the street. The cops were visible, now two hundred yards away and stationary while one of them was speaking on his radio. A false alarm, I hoped they were telling their base. But the sound of police sirens told me that was not how it was being perceived. NYPD had moved faster than I'd expected, getting the media involved so quickly. I had to assume that the murder investigators would take today's sighting as a genuine lead.

I needed to get the hell out of Philly.

THREE

Thyme Painter and Joe Kopański entered the Manhattan Midtown North Precinct's interview room and sat opposite Marty Fleet from the U.S. Attorney General's office and a guy in his fifties called Phil.

Fleet was a thirty-six-year-old lawyer, good-looking, with expensive clothes, dentistry that made his permanent smile gleam, hair coifed in the style of a 1920s golf pro, and the ready charm prevalent among those who don't need to worry about grubby matters such as job security, bills, and bad genes. A Yale graduate, he was on the fast track to one day potentially become the "AG," as Fleet referred to his boss. But despite appearances, he wasn't a country-club WASP. His parents were blue-collar workers. They'd killed each other in a drunken argument when he was sixteen. His older sister had to look after him. Ten years later, she'd suffered a terrible climbing accident, leaving her wheelchair bound and brain damaged. Fleet had looked after his sister ever since.

There was more to Fleet than met the eye, but he could still be ruthless and Machiavellian. The detectives had to be careful around him.

"I saw this guy Will Cochrane on the news this morning." Fleet's smile almost drew the detectives' attention away from his flickering eyes, which were mentally undressing them. "I decided the AG's office should be aware if New York's finest know which side's up on this."

"Meaning?" Painter held his gaze.

"Meaning, tell me what you think you know."

"We're detectives, *meaning* it's foolish to start an investigation thinking you know what's happened." Kopański wanted to cut the crap. "Who's Phil, and why are you both here?"

Phil said nothing.

And Fleet didn't fully answer. "Phil's an associate, and we're here to get some nuts-and-bolts data on the Waldorf murder."

"Why?" Painter was trying to get the measure of the man in the room who was silent. He was portly, balding on top, wearing a suit, with half-rim glasses on a chain resting on his chest, and was watching the detectives intently. "Is there something about our case we should know about? Victim, suspect, circumstances? If there is, you'd better spit it out."

"Nuts-and-bolts data," the lawyer repeated.

"You've read the news. The public statement was prepared by us. That's the data."

Fleet sighed. "Come on, Thyme, Joe. We've done this too many times to put up barriers. There's a reason we're here, and I'll come to that, but I just want inside track."

Kopański didn't buy Fleet's we're-in-this-together tactic. "Prints taken from documents William Cochrane signed when he checked into the Waldorf, and from elsewhere in his hotel room, exactly match those all over the crime scene. Ditto DNA we got from a leftover sandwich he dumped in his room's trash and from the neck of a bottle of mineral water. We don't know who the woman is. We're running her autopsy results through local and national databases, plus we're hoping her family or friends get in touch with us."

Painter added, "Nothing on motive, though that will become clearer when we've ID'd the victim and find out who this guy Cochrane is. I've put a call in to Scotland Yard. Their Met Police is investigating. Nothing back from them yet. What I can say is . . ." Painter frowned. "The crime scene is odd."

Fleet said, "Odd?"

"Odd because the killing was clinical and absolute. Two bullets in the back of the head to be sure of death. A professional killing. And yet, the scene was sloppy. A pro wouldn't have left so many traces, unless . . ."

"Unless?"

It was Kopański who finished the sentence. "Unless he didn't care. The victim may have been a casual encounter, a colleague, a lover. Doesn't matter. What does is that Cochrane's mind broke in that room. Gun's pulled out, he holds her down in the bathtub, she struggles but ain't going anywhere, double tap in the back of the skull, job done."

Painter added, "And then he realizes what's just happened. Instinct's done its bit; now it's time to face the music."

Kopański. "But if he gives himself up, that's him in a box for the rest of his life."

"Too much time to dwell on the demons."

"Impossible to clean up the hotel room, but he doesn't worry about covering his tracks."

"He didn't know it was going to be today, but he suspected a day like this was going to happen sometime soon."

"It was his way out. Escape from whatever shitty life he's had."

"So he just leaves, thankful the nightmares in his brain are soon going to finally be over."

Fleet asked, "You think he's going to take his own life?"

Both detectives nodded while Kopański asked, "What has any of this has got to do with the attorney general's office?"

Fleet pointed at the man next to him. "Philip Knox. Central Intelligence Agency."

The detectives said nothing as Knox placed his spectacles on the tip of his nose. "Cochrane's ex-MI6. MI6 is Britain's spy agency, equivalent to the CIA. He was their lead field operative for fifteen years."

"How do you know this?" Kopański didn't like Knox one bit.

The senior Agency man replied, "For the last five years Cochrane was a joint asset with us."

"Doing what?"

"That's confidential, *Detective* Painter." Knox smiled. "I can tell you he was the West's prime operative used for our most complex and risky operations. The Brits put him through a twelve-month highly classified training and assessment program—only him. All previous applicants had failed the course or died on it. Somehow, he passed. He's a very resourceful man. Joined the French Foreign Legion straight from school. Served as a paratrooper before passing selection into special forces. Was handpicked to do deniable black ops work for French Intelligence."

"Black ops?"

"Assassinations." Knox continued. "After five years in the army, he went to Cambridge University and gained a double first-class degree. Then he was approached by MI6. Other than what I've just told you, we restrict this conversation to matters pertinent to your investigation. Ask me relevant questions. I'll answer what I can."

The detectives took it in turn to pose their questions.

"Is he still MI6-CIA?"

"No, he retired a year ago after his cover was blown by one of our own."

"Firearms trained?"

"To the highest standard."

"A killer?"

"Define."

"Does he enjoy killing?"

"He hates it. Or, at least, he did. But he's exceptionally good at it."

"How far did you push him?"

Knox paused before answering the question. "His CIA and MI6 controllers are dead. They'd be able to answer your question with accuracy."

"But you'll have some idea. Was he driven too hard?"

"With his blessing. He wanted to get the job done."

"No matter what?"

"Precisely."

"Skills involve disappearing?"

"The very best skills, but this will be a test for Cochrane. Even operatives as capable as him can't survive for long if there's no purpose and they're unloved."

"Unloved?"

"Being out of service and wanted for murder."

"You think he's snapped?"

"Yes."

"Why?"

Knox answered, "Because he's no longer serving the greater good. All the bad stuff we made him do will be catching up with him."

Painter asked, "What resources does he have? Fake ID? Local assets who can help him? Exit routes out of the country? Anything that will hinder our investigation?"

"Nothing."

"Nothing?"

"We fucked him on that because he's no longer one of ours. He's alone. *Very* alone."

"And that's how you treat your former employees, is it?"

Knox smiled.

Painter: "Any idea why he was in New York?"

"None whatsoever. Possibly freelance work."

"The identity of the victim?"

"No idea." Knox cleaned his glasses. "Don't underestimate what you're up against. No matter who's the smartest woman or man in the room, he's smarter. He doesn't relate to people like us. He's a dog. We were his master. We don't love him anymore, and we kicked him out of our backyard to fend for himself. Now he can be who he really is."

"A scavenging mutt?" Kopański's dislike of Knox was increasing by the second.

Knox laughed. "In time, exactly. Here's my number." He handed across a card. "Call me anytime. And keep me posted on progress. I'd like your cell numbers."

After the detectives handed over their business cards, Painter said to Fleet, "There is every chance this will escalate, possibly spilling over into other states. If Cochrane commits crimes outside of our jurisdiction, this could get messy."

Fleet was nonchalant as he answered, "If that happens, we wheel in the feds."

"No way."

The lawyer sternly responded, "That's how it works."

"Not if you make an exception," interjected

Kopański. "Whatever happens, it started on our patch and we're the investigating officers. We need primacy throughout, regardless of jurisdiction."

"Joe, you know I can't—"

"Of course you can. You have that authority."

Fleet was about to kick back.

But, to his surprise, Philip Knox gestured for him to cool it. "I don't see why that would be a problem. In any case, these are the best NYPD detectives. Why make their life harder?"

Fleet was deep in thought. "Okay, but don't piss off other state PDs."

Painter smiled. "And we'd like the primacy authority in writing from the attorney general."

Fleet sighed. "Okay, okay. I'll fax it over to you later today." He was actually glad that Painter and Kopański had made a stand on this point. They *were* the best NYPD detectives.

Kopański leaned forward, looking directly at Knox. "Cochrane's presumably armed, carrying the pistol that he used to kill the woman. Maybe he's got other weapons. Tell me something: If we trap him, will he shoot back at us?"

The CIA officer checked his watch, glanced at Fleet, and replied, "I'm not sure. But I can say with conviction that if Cochrane shoots at you and your colleagues, you'll all be dead."

FOUR

In their remote rural house twenty miles outside of Roanoke, Virginia, retired academics Robert and Celia Grange were enjoying their last day with twins Tom and Billy Koenig.

The boys' father had been killed a year before while on active service with the CIA. A few weeks later, their mother was murdered for reasons that were connected to her husband's death. Initially the boys had lived with their aunt Faye. But Faye couldn't cope, struck down by grief over the death of her sister. With no other surviving family members to care for the boys, their great-uncle and -aunt had stepped in. The boys had lived with them ever since.

But both were in their seventies. It would have been an almighty struggle to raise the boys through adolescence. To their relief, three months ago Will Cochrane—a man who'd served with the twins' father—came to them and said he wanted to adopt the ten-year-old boys. He'd bought a home near their school, had secured a teaching post there, and was resolute that he could give them everything they needed.

After signing the legal documents prepared by a New York law firm, today he was collecting the boys.

Though the Granges would still see them frequently, it meant today was tinged with sadness.

Robert was standing outside his home, looking at the valley below. So often the boys had played down there, fishing in the river, running through the woods pretending to be explorers. Part of him wished that could continue. But he was in no doubt that their future with Will Cochrane would be better. He was a fine man and would make an excellent father.

On the outskirts of Edinburgh, James Goldsmith left the rural farmhouse that he and his wife, Sarah, owned and got in his car. As the solicitor drove to the nearest village to buy groceries, he wondered if his bank account had enough funds to make the purchase. The couple's financial situation during the last three months had been dire. It had started with him receiving a letter from the tax authorities stating they were investigating the possibility he owed eighty-seven thousand pounds in unpaid taxes. Then Sarah's bank account was hacked and five thousand pounds were filtered out. And at a time when they were on their knees, Sarah read

James's bank statement and erupted with rage when she saw that he'd apparently spent thousands on a night out in strip clubs. He hadn't.

The only glimmer of hope was when she received a call from a headhunter offering her the chance to secure a senior management position in a global law firm. She was away now, being interviewed for the job. If she got it, their financial worries would be over. Trouble was, it would mean they'd have to move. James knew that was the only option, but he loved it here. This was their new life, away from the stresses of the one they'd had in London.

Even if Sarah got the job, he didn't know what the future held. Sarah was still fuming at him. The only updates he was getting from her were via text messages, and even those were terse. She'd told him not to bother her while she was doing everything she could to solve their money problems.

As he drove along a narrow country lane, he mused that at least nothing else could go wrong.

He turned a corner, too late spotted a pony standing immobile in the middle of the lane, swerved, and crashed into a stone wall. He was dazed by the violent impact, and sat for a moment before he could summon the energy to climb out of his battered car.

Shaken, he bent to examine the front of their only vehicle. It had to be a write-off. He had no idea if the insurance company would pay out on the damage.

He laid his head against the car and whispered softly, "No, no, no."

* * *

Major Dickie Mountjoy, a punctilious retiree who'd left the Coldstream Guards four decades ago though had never allowed the army to leave him, was sitting in his ground-floor apartment scrolling back and forth between BBC1 and 2 for news about the queen's inspection this morning of the Coldstream Guards parade.

In South London's tiny yet beautiful West Square, the major shared the converted Edwardian terraced town house with three other occupants. In the flat above him was Phoebe, a thirty-something seller of art, who loved champagne and nights out at middleweight boxing matches. She wrapped the old man around her finger, and occasionally could get him to smile at the absurdity of his comments. More important, she kept an eye on him to see that he was okay. Mrs. Mountjoy had died three years ago. He was alone.

On the third floor was Phoebe's boyfriend, David, a middle-aged mortician, divorced, with shoulder-length hair, flabby and unkempt, with a passion for Dixieland jazz and cooking.

Neither had anything whatsoever in common with the old man, who always wore immaculately pressed garments, as he had when he had been an off-duty major partaking of a glass of port in the officers' mess. With silver hair trimmed to military precision, a pencil-thin mustache, a slight build but back always ramrod straight despite his aching limbs, the major spoke to his neighbors as if they were the personification of ill-discipline and slothfulness.

They were never offended, because they knew his comments—delivered in the bitten-off style favored by British army officers—were merely his attempt to bring order to the world. They also knew he had a heart of gold.

The other occupant of the building lived in the top-floor apartment, within which was a décor not to the tastes of a guardsman who kept his home as pristine and functional as his previous quarters in Wellington Barracks. Nevertheless, it captivated Dickie every time he went in there. Though a modest two bedrooms in size, it was cleverly designed to invoke the sense that one was in the presence of a part-oriental, part-Renaissance fairy-tale cavern.

The occupants of the West Square property were a ragtag group of disparate friends, glued together by a shared sense that every now and again they needed each other.

But aside from Dickie, no one else was in the building right now.

He was about to turn the television off, but stopped as credits rolled on the cookery program and an announcer stated that next up was the news. "About bloody time," Dickie muttered to himself. To his consternation, the news show didn't open with shots of the queen standing on a platform as massed ranks on foot and horseback moved with collective precision in front of her. Instead, the opener was about a murder in New York City.

Disgusted with the show's scheduling decision, the retiree painfully stood up and entered his kitchen to make a cup of tea. He could hear the TV in the background as he prepared his drink, and he was only half listening—something about one of New York's most iconic hotels, a woman shot in a bathtub, a manhunt.

The news reporter said the suspect was English.

Dickie stepped into the kitchen doorway to look at the TV. A photograph of the murder suspect was shown full screen, with the announcement that the wanted man was Will Cochrane.

Dickie dropped his cup and saucer, felt giddy, staggered, and reached out to grip a side table so that he didn't collapse. "Not now," he muttered. "Those poor boys—please, God, not now."

The man on the screen was the occupant of the top-floor apartment above him. A killer on the run and one of his closest friends.

FIVE

Thyme Painter walked as fast as her artificial limb would let her along a corridor in the police station. Her cell phone in hand, she entered the office she shared with Józef Kopański. Joe had two phones against his ears and another on speaker on his desk. He was talking fast to various law enforcement officials up and down the East Coast. Painter moved her hand back and forth across her throat as if she were slicing it open. Kopański ended the calls and looked at her.

"Sightings in Philly." Painter gestured to her cell. "Captain from Philly PD just called."

"Credible sightings?"

Painter nodded. "Yes. A couple had a news picture of Cochrane on their iPad. Cochrane was sitting right next to them in a café."

"We need to move."

Painter summoned two of the precinct's best uniformed drivers and gave them precise instructions. She and Kopański grabbed their bags containing clothes and other essential items for last-minute excursions, and three minutes later they were in Kopański's unmarked vehicle. One squad car was ahead of them, its lights flashing and siren screaming at all other drivers to get out of their way as they raced out of Manhattan toward Philadelphia. The other squad car was behind them, also using its emergency features and driving no more than five feet behind the rear of the detectives' vehicle. The journey to Philly was ninety-three miles and ordinarily would take nearly two hours by car. Painter was adamant they needed to be there in one hour.

As Kopański expertly gunned through gears, Painter was on her radio mic telling the officers in the cavalcade that she would rather they all died in a 120-mile-per-hour crash than fail to get to Philly on time.

"Where the hell is he?" exclaimed Robert Grange as he paced back and forth in their Virginia home. The twins Billy and Tom Koenig were sitting on a nearby sofa, in coats, suitcases at their feet, their expressions expectant and confused.

Celia placed a hand on Robert's forearm. "There'll be an explanation. Will's probably just running late."

"Late?" Robert was fuming. "The boys need the opposite of late. This is hardly the best start for Mr. Cochrane. I'm beginning to wonder if we made the wrong decision."

"Calm down, my dear."

"No, I won't calm down!" Robert stopped, seeing that the boys' eyes were watery as they watched his indignation. He composed himself and smiled. "Don't listen to your granduncle, my boys. William will be with us soon. He's not very familiar with the roads around here, so I bet he's gotten lost. He'll call."

There was a knock at the door, prompting Celia to exclaim in relief, "Here he is."

But the person at the door was Faye Glass, the twins' aunt. A rotund woman with marble-white skin, except where it was dark under her eyes, she was wearing a skirt that had been unstitched and restitched many times to accommodate weight loss and gain, and a pink cardigan that she loathed the look of but that felt nice. Today her beautiful straight hair was coiled like a resting snake atop her head. She wore an expression of anger and urgency.

"You've seen the news, Aunt Celia?"

They hadn't switched on a TV all day, having been too busy packing the boys' belongings.

"You haven't," said Faye, seeing the boys were all ready to leave. "I'd better come in."

Billy and Tom were sent upstairs, confused. They played with identical teddy bears Will had bought them. Inside were recording devices. Pulling the string on the bears' backs activated the device. Pull it again, and the bear would play back the message.

Tom recorded a message. "Is something bad happening?"

Moments later, Billy's bear said, "Has our new daddy had an accident?"

"Why did he do this?" asked Celia in a hushed tone to Faye and Robert. "It doesn't make any sense."

"We don't know him well enough to know what makes sense." Robert's sharp mind was working fast. "Suspect, not murderer?"

Faye nodded. "That's how the networks are describing him."

"At the behest of the police." Robert wanted to calm down. "He's on the run?"

"Yes."

"Suggests culpability."

"Or fear." Faye was as sharp as her uncle. "He's running because he has no choice."

"He told us he was once connected to the military. Do you think the murder is something to do with his past?"

Faye replied, "I don't know. So far no one does."

Celia sensed confrontation. "We know *what* has happened. We don't know *why* it's happened. But we do know we have to pick up the pieces."

Robert waved his hand dismissively. "Why hasn't he called us?"

"Why would he?" Celia was the smartest of the family.

Robert snapped, "To tell us he can't be a father to the twins because he's gone crazy and killed a woman! We need to keep this from the boys for as long as possible." Robert placed his arms on Faye.

"Faye, my love, can you come and stay with us for a while?"

"Why?"

"Because it may well be you're the only one young enough to look after the boys. But I know you can't do that alone. We have to pull together now, until we find out what we're dealing with."

I'd been watching Amtrak's neoclassical Philly station for fifteen minutes, looking for signs that law enforcement were all over the place. There was nothing unusual, but I could tell from the number of people entering and exiting the place that the station was jammed with commuters. And I had to go in there to find out the time of the next train south and to buy a ticket. Doing that was immensely risky.

But I had no choice.

I entered the vast hall. It was a modern interpretation of how stations looked in the nineteenth century. Big lights resembling lanterns were hanging from the ceiling. The walls on either side of the wide marble concourse must have been at least thirty feet high and were covered with massive windows that were letting in feeble gray light from the rainy sky. Symmetrical benches were on either side of the hall. Men, women, and kids lounged on the seats. And in the center of the concourse people were moving.

I estimated there were at least 320 people in here.

On the plus side, some of them would be preoccupied with their travel arrangements.

On the minus side, others would be bored while waiting. Many of them would be people watching.

With my head low, I walked alongside a wall. All the training in the world doesn't give you the ability to turn invisible, so this was all I could do. Stay away from the center of the hall, avoid eye contact with anyone, and take a chance.

I purchased my ticket. The next train south was due in thirty-three minutes.

I walked casually to the platform to wait.

Half an hour to wait? Jeez.

I felt like everyone was looking at me.

And there was nothing I could do about that.

Painter and Kopański arrived in Philly, together with their two uniformed NYPD escorts. Their vehicles screeched to a halt in the parking lot of the Philadelphia Police Department headquarters on Race Street. They'd made the journey in sixty-seven minutes.

Captain O'Shea met them in the lot and ignored the pleasantries. "I've put extra uniforms on the streets. But I can't afford a shootout. The governor's in town to commend my men on their anti-crime work. It's being televised. A gun battle is the last thing I need."

Kopański said, "We want to capture Cochrane quietly."

"What's his plan?"

"We've no idea. In all probability he hasn't got one."

"Coming here was random?"

"Looks that way." Kopański wondered how the

senior district commander was going to react to what he was about to say. "Detective Painter and I have been given authority to operate in other states on this case. But we're not here to throw our weight around."

O'Shea eyed Kopański. "Just as well. But you want to get him quiet?"

"Yes."

The captain's cell rang. He listened to the caller, hung up, and said to the detectives, "He's just been sighted on a platform in Thirtieth Street Station. Next train in's headed to Baltimore. I can flood the place with uniforms."

Both detectives recalled what Knox had said about everyone dying if Cochrane opened fire.

Painter said, "You don't want a serious situation today. Plus, the station has too many exits. Cochrane will probably escape if he sees uniforms. Let me and Kopański deal with this. But if we can borrow three of your officers, that would be useful. When's the train due to arrive?"

"Fifteen minutes."

I boarded the train. My gut was in knots of anxiety. I felt like I was on a covert job.

I had to put fear to one side. My absolute priority was staying alive. I knew that if the shit hit the fan, I'd stop anyone who tried to capture me. That wasn't bravado. It was what I'd been trained to do. For some reason, I was exceptionally good at it.

That was no consolation. If I went up against Philly PD, I'd win the battle but not the war.

And it was highly probable they knew I'd just gotten on the train.

The two NYPD squad cars and Kopański's unmarked car stopped outside 30th Street Station. Inside each car was an officer from Philly PD.

Kopański said to the Philly cop in his car, "You and your colleagues use our cars to parallel the Amtrak route." He tapped the radio set he'd been loaned by O'Shea. "I'll let you know any updates."

He, Painter, and the NYPD cops entered the station.

The train had been moving for ten minutes.

Windows in the train car were steamy because of the cold air outside. I was exhausted, yet alert. I stood in the aisle; the car was packed due to the cancellation of a previous train. Passengers were irritable, swaying with each movement of the train. Most of them were likely fantasizing about getting back to their homes for dinner.

My back hurt, and my stomach muscles felt like a rolling pin was being moved over them.

Every smell hit my nostrils—musk, a man wearing too much Dior Sauvage eau de toilette, the stench of saccharine candy, and vomit from a child who'd overindulged in Philly's finest cheesesteak. Most people were silent or talking in whispers. But a huge woman with a shock of frizzy hair was louder, berating her husband about the stupidity of going to Philly in this weather. I listened to everything around me, in case someone said, "That guy over there—doesn't he look like the man on the news?"

But people didn't notice me. They were consumed by their own thoughts. For now, I was anonymous.

My train ticket was to Roanoke, Virginia; from there I'd travel twenty miles to see the twins, the Granges, and Faye Glass. By now, they'd know I was a wanted man. They deserved to hear from me that I was innocent, but I had to stay on the run to clear my name and find out who was the real culprit. Then, I would return to them and take the boys to their new home. In the meantime, I had to make sure they were okay. The Granges' age worried me; so too did Faye Glass's state of mind. Almost certainly she had PTSD thrown into the mix of grief. After all, this was a woman who had discovered her murdered sister's body.

I tensed. Something was happening at the head of the car, though I couldn't see what. Two men were speaking, their voices authoritative yet unclear in the clatter of the train. Passengers were trying to move, as if to make space for the men, though it was a devil of a job given the crammed conditions. Then I saw them—a uniformed cop and a tall man who was undoubtedly a plainclothes detective. They were issuing commands to passengers, looking at the faces of males, talking to them before moving on.

I turned and pushed my way toward the other end of the car, muttering in an American accent that I needed the bathroom. People were cursing at me in annoyance. I entered the next car, desperately trying to recall what time the train arrived at the next stop and whether I'd have time to jump off there before the cops behind me completed their search. Whether the presence of the police on the train was random or connected to a reported sighting of me didn't matter.

I just couldn't allow them to get anywhere near me.

Kopański moved as quickly as the packed train would allow him to, the NYPD uniformed officer by his side. They'd reached the station with only minutes to spare to board the train from the crowded platform where the man resembling Cochrane had been seen.

Painter's decision not to send Philly cops to 30th Street Station had been justified by what the detectives had seen when they arrived at the Amtrak hub. The crowds there and the number of exits would have probably resulted in Cochrane vanishing if they'd swamped the zone with uniforms. But the train was a closed environment. If Cochrane was on here, Kopański would find him. He moved onward, his hand close to his gun.

I kept my head bowed low as I squeezed my way between passengers in the next car. But then I stopped dead, as if I'd been poleaxed.

Ahead of me were another uniformed officer and a female detective.

Thyme Painter studied the faces of every man around her. She and her uniformed colleague had started at the rear of the train, Joe and his colleague the front. She was getting toward the center of the train and knew that Joe would be doing the same from the other direction. She grabbed the uniformed officer's arm, twisting him away from the man he was talking to. The cop followed her gaze. At the far end of the car a tall man was staring right at them. No doubt, he looked exactly like the man in Will Cochrane's passport. Both officers pulled out their guns and barked at everyone to get down.

I spun around and ran, forcing people out of my way, knowing that my situation was desperate. People around me were screaming, darting looks at the encroaching cops and at me. I yanked on the emergency Stop lever. Nothing. I did so again. The train kept moving. Damn. The cops had predicted this possibility and told the driver to ignore emergency activations. God knows how they'd managed to get the driver to agree.

I put more space between me and the female detective, but now could see the tall male detective coming from the other direction, shouting orders at people, a large pistol in his hand. Some people were dropping to the floor; others remained upright or in seats. A gunfight remained way too risky. But I was trapped. I clambered over bodies to reach the door.

Locked.

The window could slide open, but was not large enough for my big frame to squeeze through. That left only one option, though I had to decide whether it meant the big male detective and his male colleague or the easier option of the woman and her male colleague. I decided on the former, but had to move quickly before the four cops converged.

"Officers," I called out as I raised my arms in the air and moved toward them.

The male detective and the cop pointed their weapons at me halfway down their car, their safeties off though fingers not on triggers.

"I'm guessing you think I look a bit like that guy in the news." My accent American, I tried to look nervous. "It's been worrying me all day that I look like him." I kept walking toward them, passengers climbing over each other to get out of my way and the line of fire.

"Stay where you are! Get on your knees." The detective had his gun pointed at my head.

I ignored him, hoping my actions would seem like they belonged to a dumb nervous idiot who'd never confronted armed police before.

"I said, stay where you are."

"I haven't done anything wrong. But I'm putting myself in your hands so you can clear this up and find the real murderer."

"Hands behind your head! On your knees!" The cop next to the detective crouched, ready to fire.

"Steady, Officer." The detective was motionless. "Think about collateral."

I was now five feet from them. I put my hands in front of me. "Here. You can cuff me. I'm no trouble."

Four feet.

The detective took two steps forward.

"On your fucking knees."

"Okay, okay." I lowered myself, hands again held

up. The action seemed to settle the concerns of the uniformed cop, who moved closer.

It all happened in less than two seconds.

I sprang forward, grabbed the detective's gun, twisted it so that the detective's wrist was in agony and he was unable to resist, kicked him in the stomach with sufficient force to lift him off his feet and send him crashing into the other cop, then stamped on the uniformed officer's belly and chest.

Neither could do anything other than writhe in pain.

I glanced back down the car and saw the female detective and her colleague desperately trying to force their way through the panicking passengers. I pushed my way toward the front of the train, brandishing the handgun I'd taken from the hotel room, people around me screaming and hugging each other. I spotted the conductor who'd come through the train earlier, in a car full of people who were oblivious to what had happened farther back in the train.

Feeling shitty for doing so, I placed my gun against the conductor's temple, dropped my fake American accent, and told him to walk fast to the front of the train and the locked compartment containing the driver.

"Open the door."

The man tried to object.

"Open it or I'll shoot your kneecaps."

The conductor's hands shook as he picked out the correct key from a bunch and unlocked the door.

He was about to open it, but I stopped him from

doing so. "Back there are four cops, two in uniform. They'll be heading this way fast. For the safety of this train, I need you to stop them."

"Why would I?"

"Because if I spot the cops, I'll put a bullet in the head of the driver. Then I'll fiddle with the controls to try to stop the train. Thing is, I know nothing about trains. I'm likely to crash the thing."

The conductor nodded and headed off.

I entered the driver's cab and placed my gun against the driver's neck. "Stop the train and let me off."

The driver tried to turn to face me.

I shouted, "Eyes front. Do it now."

"It's not that easy"—the driver's voice was trembling—"to make an unscheduled stop. There are safety issues if—"

"Stop this fucking train or I'll pull the trigger and do this myself."

The driver's face was sweaty as he brought the train to a screeching, grinding halt. He leaned across and opened his door. "There, it's stopped. Please, mister, don't . . ."

I jumped onto the gravel and raced as fast as I could into the stormy afternoon.

The four cops got off the train seconds after Cochrane had alighted. Cochrane was sprinting into the woods. Kopański and the uniformed cops immediately dashed after him.

Painter was on her radio to the three drivers of their vehicles. "We're near Chester. Pick us up.

We'll give you a precise location once we get a landmark." She called Captain O'Shea.

Kopański and his colleagues raced into the woods, guns in hand. They'd lost sight of Cochrane, but he was only a hundred yards ahead of them when they'd last seen him. They were spread apart, but not too much in case Cochrane got the drop on one of them. If that happened, they'd need to work as a team to restrain him or put a bullet in his head.

The trees were dense, visibility made worse by rain and black clouds.

While running at full speed, Kopański called to his colleagues, "You spot him, you shoot him in the leg."

Dodging between trees, I was running as fast as I could, changing direction, not daring to look back. The last time I'd seen the three cops was when they were sprinting over the field adjacent to the train, just as I'd entered the forest. They were on my heels. And I was in no doubt they'd shoot me in the back rather than let me escape.

I had no idea where I was. Had no plan. Nothing was in my head apart from putting distance between me and my pursuers. My backpack bounced against me. Breathing was fast and excruciating. My legs were in pain. My eyes were wide as I searched for a way to shake off the cops.

I exited the forest. No cover ahead of me. Just open land, a road, and beyond that, houses. Double back into the forest and try to lose them there? Or risk going ahead?

I spotted a car driving to the left of me. One driver inside. No one else. The road was fifty yards ahead of me. If I moved like fury, there was just enough time. I ran across the open grass, all the time expecting a bullet to enter my spine.

I reached the road, stood in the center, and faced the oncoming red vehicle. Whipping out my gun, I pointed it at the driver when he was ten feet away from me. Fear was all over his face as he screeched to a halt, right in front of me.

I ran to his side, gun trained on his head, opened his door, and barked, "Slide across to the passenger side. Now!"

"Please don't—"

"Now!"

He did as he was told.

I got in the driver's seat, put my foot to the floor, and said, "If you stay still and do nothing, you'll live."

Kopański and his colleagues ran out of the forest. On the road ahead of them, they saw Cochrane enter a red car and race off.

"Get the plate number!" Kopański ran full tilt toward the road, his colleagues by his side. They reached the road just in time to read the plate. One of the cops raised his gun to fire at its tires, but Kopański put his hand over the man's gun. "He's got a hostage. Too dangerous."

Cochrane made a turn and vanished from view.

The detective asked, "Where are we?"

The New York cops had no idea.

Kopański ran to the nearest house and banged

on the door. An old lady answered. Twenty seconds later, he was back on the road and on the radio to Painter. Gasping for breath, he gave her the plate number and added, "We're on West Sixth Street in Trainer. Pick us up here. And we need a helo in the air."

Painter told him that she'd already got O'Shea to get one close to their zone.

Everywhere around me was alien.

The car owner was in his mid-thirties, Caucasian, dressed casually.

"What's your name?" I asked.

"Pete . . . Pete."

"Okay. Listen, Pete. Stay calm. I don't know this area. I'm betting you do. I need to get onto a major highway. You're going to direct me."

"Don't hurt me!"

"I won't if you do what I say."

Pete pointed. "Take this turn right. It'll take you to I-95."

"It'll take me south?"

"South and north. Depends which on-ramp you take."

"I want south. You're going to get me there."

The car was a performance-model BMW. But its color meant we'd stick out like a sore thumb.

Within five minutes we were on 95. Signs told me it would take me to Baltimore. I doubted I'd make it there.

The three NYPD cars picked up Kopański and his colleagues on West Sixth Street. In his unmarked car, Kopański took over driver duties. Painter was by his side, the Philly cop now in a squad car.

As the detectives and their two squad car escorts raced in the direction they'd last seen Cochrane, Painter spoke on her radio to the Philly cops, "Cochrane was heading south. We have to assume he's still headed in that direction. What's the quickest route?"

The Philly cop radioed back, "I-95."

"All right. Get us onto 95."

"Will do," the officer replied.

Another voice came over the radio, giving his Philadelphia PD call sign. "We've got a visual of you."

Painter glanced up. The police helicopter was close by. Into her mic, she said, "We've lost him. Our best hunch is he's southbound on I-95. Go ahead of us and focus on that area."

The chopper veered off in the direction of the main highway.

The Philly officer in the lead car was giving his driver directions. Within minutes, the convoy was on I-95, at breakneck speed as they wove in and out of different lanes.

I rapidly changed gears, glancing in my wing mirror, driving way over the speed limit.

"Where are we going?" asked Pete.

"Anywhere but here," I answered.

Pete was a mess, and I didn't blame him. My gun was on my lap, pointing at him. I wouldn't use it. But if he tried to reach for it, I'd be quicker. The gun would be pointing at his head and I'd make sure he was certain I was prepared to pull the trigger. I felt sorry for the guy. He was in the wrong place at the wrong time.

But it was the right time for me.

I changed lanes at speed, annoying other drivers who beeped their horns at me.

"Fuck," I muttered. I could hear a helicopter. Had to be cops.

Things had just gotten a whole lot worse.

"We got him." The voice on the radio belonged to the helo pilot. "Good call to check the 95. He's heading south, as you predicted."

Painter tried to decide what to do. If she ordered that a police barricade be constructed ahead of Cochrane, traffic would grind to a halt. Cochrane would drag his hostage out of the car at gunpoint and flee on foot. Or he might start shooting. There'd be casualties, and some of them could be civilians. The chopper could hover low over the highway, trying to block his path. But that could panic him into swerving and causing an accident. If he was able to get out of his car, the same thing would happen. Gun to his hostage's head. Escape the highway on foot.

She said to Kopański, "Joe—I'm thinking we play this cool."

"Me, too." The detective was keeping pace with the squad car in front. "Let's tail him. Hope he leads us to a place where he abandons the car and hostage. Then we take him down."

Painter got on her cell to O'Shea and gave him updates. "We've got to be very careful. Can you get on the phone to all police commanders and sheriffs between here and Baltimore? I don't want one of their patrol cars spotting Cochrane breaking the speed limit and trying to pull him over. He needs to be left untouched."

O'Shea agreed to get on it.

The helicopter pilot said, "He's slowing down. He's hit a bottleneck. Traffic's clearer after that. Ah—I've got a visual of you guys. You're about eight hundred yards behind."

Kopański said to Painter, "I can't see a good outcome from this, as things stand."

Painter agreed. With the helo sticking to Cochrane, the hostage's life was in serious danger. "It's damn risky."

"I don't see any other choice."

"You're four hundred yards behind him." This was from the chopper pilot. "He's halfway through the bottleneck."

The convoy was moving at ninety miles an hour in the fast lane.

Within seconds, Painter said, "There, that's him."

They had Cochrane in their sights. But in a moment, he'd be clear of the traffic and racing ahead.

"I say we do it." Kopański followed the squad car as it moved into the center lane.

Painter spoke into her mic. "Kopański and I are going to take over the lead. I want the squad cars to drop back by one mile. And I want the helo to return to base."

The chopper pilot said, "You're kidding."

Painter replied that she was not.

Reluctantly, the pilot complied, turning his helo around and heading back to Philly. The squad car in front swapped lanes, slowed down, and let Kopański's unmarked vehicle stay on Cochrane's tail. Within one minute, the squad cars were out of sight. And that meant that Cochrane could now see no evidence of police pursuing him.

It was the right call to make, but the detectives knew that they were taking one hell of a gamble.

What was going on? The helo had vanished. And now I couldn't see the squad cars behind me. A police barricade somewhere up ahead? I thought it unlikely, as logistically it would be difficult. Plus they'd be worried I'd put a bullet in Pete's head. But the police wouldn't back off completely. I was wanted for murder. And I'd added assault on police officers to my charge. No. I was still being followed. By officers in unmarked cars. Possibly two of them were the detectives on the train.

I had to make a quick decision.

As signs told me I was passing Newark, Delaware, I glanced at Pete. "Listen carefully to me. No matter what happens, I'm not going to shoot you. Nor will I hurt you. Do you understand that?"

Pete seemed like he didn't know how to reply.

"I need to hear that you understand exactly what I've just said."

Pete looked confused. "I understand."

"Do you know who I am?"

Pete's voice shook as he said, "Don't make me answer that. I don't want to know anything. It's best if I—"

"Who am I?"

"The . . . the guy on the news. English. Man who shot a woman in the Waldorf."

"That's what they say I did. The truth is different. I'm not a murderer. But there's no doubt the police will do everything they can to get me." I sped up. "I have an idea how you and I need never see each other again. It involves you doing exactly as I say. At the end of it, you'll be tired. But that'll be the worst of it. Then you'll walk away."

I told him what I had in mind.

"Brake lights. No cars ahead of him. What's he doing?" Painter placed her hand on the dash as Kopański urgently braked to slow to Cochrane's speed.

"Maybe he thinks he's still being followed and is trying to clock us."

Painter spoke on her radio to the squad cars. "He's slowing down. Where are you?"

They told her they'd just passed a turnoff to Newark.

"Good, you're about a mile behind. But slow to thirty."

She watched Cochrane's car further reduce speed.

Then it veered onto the hard shoulder and stopped.

"Shit!"

It happened so quickly.

Cochrane and the passenger jumped out of the car, Cochrane's gun pointing at the man's head. From behind, Cochrane wrapped one arm around the man's chest and placed the muzzle against his temple. They stepped over the guardrail and ran backward, into a field, Cochrane keeping his body flush against the hostage's. And they kept running, Cochrane supporting the man's body so he didn't trip.

Kopański stopped his car by the abandoned vehicle. The detectives got out, sidearms unholstered.

Painter was screaming into her mic. "Get here now! He's on foot with the hostage!"

Cochrane and his hostage were fifty yards away.

Cochrane was looking straight at them.

Still moving as fast as possible.

Kopański made ready to leap over the guardrail.

But Painter said, "Wait for the squad cars."

A hundred fifty yards. Beyond accurate pistol range.

Two hundred yards.

Cochrane released the hostage. The man was stock-still in the field, Cochrane's gun still trained on him.

Then Cochrane turned and bolted.

Now, nothing was going to stop Kopański. He jumped over the guardrail and sprinted. Sirens were drawing closer, no doubt his colleagues. But for now he was on his own. Kopański was athletic for his age and had chased down many perps. But Cochrane was faster, dashing off the field into a suburban area.

He was at least three hundred yards ahead.

Zigzagging to make himself an even harder moving target.

Kopański fired a warning shot in the air, anyway, hoping it would make Cochrane stop.

He didn't.

Cochrane turned into a side street, disappearing from view. Kopański ran to the spot he'd last seen him.

But now Cochrane was nowhere to be seen.

The detective stopped, gasped for air, and said, "Shit!" He got onto his radio mic. "I lost him."

SIX

In northeastern Israel, on Kibbutz Dalia, Michael Stein kicked man-high sacks of soap powder in the commune's factory. His job was to work an assembly line for eight hours each day, bagging up powder, ensuring conveyer belts didn't jam, and ultimately making sure the bags were full for distribution to Israelis and Arabs across the Middle East. The factory was the biggest exporter of soap in the region. Its product transcended racial and religious antipathies more than any number of political summits and any amount of back-channel diplomacy. That's why Michael lived and worked here. It seemed to make more difference to the Levant he so loved than all his years of being a Mossad assassin.

Now retired from that world, Michael, who was in his mid-thirties, had recently turned up at the gates of the kibbutz with his beloved mongrel dog, Mr. Peres, and asked, "Do you have room for us?"

Michael and his loyal companion lived in a little house on the site. People here knew he had once been a member of Israel's Sayeret Matkal, a special forces unit comparable to the U.S. Delta Force, but didn't know about his subsequent work with Mossad.

They didn't need to.

For Michael, his years in the secret world were a bad taste in the mouth compared to his prior military service. Five months ago he'd had a lifestyle volte-face, thrown in the towel of being a Mossad combatant, sold his apartment in Tel Aviv, and decided to kick bags of soap.

Strikingly handsome, and with the face of a man ten years younger, the tall, athletic Israeli had blue eyes and shoulder-length blond hair. His looks caught the attention of the single ladies on the kibbutz. But at this point in his life, women didn't particularly interest him. He'd stripped his life back to simple essentials, a monklike existence.

There was one woman, though, who he allowed near to him. Her name was Joanna and she was a friend.

Knowing he was about to break for lunch, she came to him now holding a copy of the *Jerusalem Post*. She was the only person he'd told about his life in espionage. Perhaps he shouldn't have done so, though he'd felt it was important to have a confidante, and Joanna listened very well without judgment. One of the things he'd told her about was his last mission. It had taken him to Beirut,

London, and the French city of Rennes, where he'd initially tried to kill an English spy before deciding to work with him. He'd given her the name of the spy. Today, that man's image and name were headline news in many foreign newspapers. She handed the paper to Michael as he brushed dust off his blue overalls and shook his hair to rid it of more of the stuff.

He read the front page carefully, betraying no signs of emotion. Joanna liked that about him. He seemed collected, thoughtful, and poised, though in what direction she couldn't tell. But she worried that the paper would take him to a place that wouldn't be good for him.

Michael handed her the newspaper back and said, "I need to leave for a while."

Joanna placed her hand on his arm. "To do what?"

He pointed at the picture of the man in the paper. "Will Cochrane saved my life. He's a good man. Something's not right about this. I need to try to help him."

The subterranean White House Situation Room was at capacity. The president was at the head of the rectangular wooden table. His chief of staff was by his side. Facing them were the secretary of state and other officials from the State Department. Philip Knox of the CIA was the only non-politician in the room.

The senior CIA officer felt smug being in the seat of power. It was where he felt he belonged.

The chief of staff said to Knox, "You called this

meeting because of Will Cochrane. We want a damage assessment."

Knox raised his pen. "If there's one employee we don't want going rogue, it's Will Cochrane. He's cracked. So here's the problem." Knox smiled. "We made him this way."

The president asked, "A killer?"

"Too highly trained."

The chief of staff added, "And with too many secrets in his head?"

"Yes." Ink from Knox's pen dripped out on the sheet of paper in front of him. "The Brits trained him. We used him. And boy, did we use him."

The chief of staff said, "So what that he was a former special operative? All that means is that he's going to be harder to take down."

"Take down?" Knox looked at the politician over his half-rim glasses. "And how do you expect police to take him down?"

"If he's compliant—shot in the leg; cuffs behind his back. If he wants trouble—shot in the head."

Knox nodded. "It won't be that easy."

The chief of staff looked exasperated. "Police officers are trained for this."

"Not as well as Cochrane."

"He's not bulletproof."

"No, he's not." Knox grinned. "He can be killed. But it's a question of where and when."

The president interjected. "Now hold on a minute. Are you suggesting a shoot-to-kill policy? I can't authorize that."

Knox lied. "I'm not suggesting that."

"Then what are you suggesting?"

The CIA officer chose his words carefully. "I'm suggesting his capture be dealt with as delicately as possible. Excuse my language, Mr. President, but I don't want the son of a bitch opening his mouth and telling people what we made him do. He could bring us all down. We used him. He did what we wanted him to do—no matter how tough or unpalatable. That has to be kept secret."

The chief of staff said, "Cochrane doesn't strike me as someone who'll open his mouth if he's arrested."

Knox agreed, but said, "We can't take that risk. Maybe Cochrane won't say anything. But in a court of law, a defense lawyer will explain his background as a means to partially mitigate Cochrane's actions."

"It will be a closed court hearing."

"But if even just five percent of his background is leaked, the press will be all over it."

The president asked, "So what are you suggesting?"

No way was Knox going to share his solution. "There is nothing that can be done other than letting the NYPD do its job. But we have a serious vested interest in this case. Cochrane is a hero. The American public will think we let him down. They'd be right. We wring guys like him dry and toss them aside. What the public doesn't understand is that our heroes are pawns. The executive is all that matters, right?"

The president nodded. "I wouldn't go on the record with that, but yes, damn right."

"The thing is, though, American citizens will

argue that Cochrane signed up to protect ordinary folks, not just those at the top table. They'd say that a man of his incredible achievements should have been highly decorated, not thrown onto the scrap heap and left to go crazy. They'll start pointing at other American heroes who we've treated badly. If we're not careful, Cochrane's case will be held up as a prime example of how we crap on our military, even Special Forces."

The president was deep in thought. To Knox, he said, "You have my authority to keep a very close eye on Cochrane's case. What's the best outcome?"

Knox didn't hesitate. "The best outcome for everyone in this room is that the police kill Cochrane. And all the world ever knows about him was that he was a cold-blooded murderer."

SEVEN

Phoebe and David were cross with Dickie Mountjoy. The old man was having one of his obstinate moods. They were in his apartment in London, having come downstairs after hearing him bashing, crashing, and cursing at the top of his voice. Though once a seasoned traveler, Dickie hadn't ventured out of London for years and his out-of-date experience showed as he tried to remember what to pack in his suitcase.

"Where are you going?" David asked for the sixth time in as many minutes.

"I need more shirts." The retiree went into his bedroom and returned with the garments, rolling them into tight tubes, which he then inserted into the case on the living room floor, alongside other rolled garments.

"They'll crease like that," said Phoebe.

"Doesn't matter." Dickie had his hands behind

his back as he surveyed the contents of his bag. "I'll iron them when I get there."

"You shouldn't be traveling at your . . ." David glanced at Phoebe, nerves taking hold of him. "Your doctor said—"

"My doctor isn't my commanding officer. He's an interfering busybody who needs a bit of life under his belt."

"That doesn't mean he doesn't know what he's talking about." Phoebe placed an arm around Dickie's back. "What's wrong, sweetie? You don't break routine, remember? This isn't like you."

Dickie walked away from her and picked up his passport. "Routine's for the barracks. But that's not where soldiering begins and ends. Now and again, we have to go out and fight."

David was exasperated. "For you that was decades ago. Now . . . now you're an . . ."

"Old man?" Dickie tucked the passport into the inner pocket of his overcoat. "Maybe, but I'm not one of your corpses on a mortuary slab just yet. Still got blood pumping in me."

"Where are you going, Dickie?" Phoebe's tone was now forthright.

He looked at his neighbors, and for the briefest of moments his bottom lip trembled, before he coughed, straightened his back, and replied, "I'm going to help our boy Cochrane. And to do that I need to go the United States of America."

Demijohns of apple, gooseberry, and plum wine were carefully lifted by James Goldsmith out of the boiler room and placed on the kitchen table.

James was still alone in his rural house outside of Edinburgh. Most likely Sarah would be home in a couple of days. That still seemed like such a long time to James. He knew his emotions were frayed because their financial situation was still so dire and he and Sarah were at the lowest ebb in their marriage. Right now the one person he wanted around was his beloved wife. To take his mind off matters, he was keeping busy doing anything. Outside, the hills were a fierce swirl of sleet, rain, and high winds. He'd tried to take his beagle, Tess, for a walk, but only managed to get a few hundred yards before muttering, "Fuck this shit," and returning home. Even the ordinarily hardy Tess seemed grateful for the decision. Now she was in her basket next to a fire, watching her master remove air traps and corks and lower a hydrometer into the wine to test for alcohol content.

"Wine's not yet at the right strength, my girl," he said to his dog as he noticed the flotation levels of the hydrometer. "A bit more sugar and another couple of months in a warm place will sort them out."

After completing the task and returning the demijohns to the boiler room, he briefly considered catching up on the world's news, though quickly discounted the notion. One of the joys of his new lifestyle was the recognition that what was happening elsewhere didn't make a blind difference to his day-to-day life. He and Sarah had a TV, but they only used it to watch DVDs. In his capacity as a solicitor, he used the Web, but he was taking a few days off and the Web reminded him of work. It was the last thing he wanted to view right now. In any case, the only news he wanted was from his wife. Her job was their only way out of their debts, though he remained utterly conflicted on that option given it would mean leaving home. Still, he had to man up on that. He had to man up on a lot of things, he'd already decided.

He called the garage to check up on the status of his crashed car. For now, he had the use of a car on loan, though only for a week. After that, goodness knew what he'd do. He was cut off here, miles from anyone. And he didn't have the cash to buy another vehicle.

He prepared himself a late breakfast of bacon, sausages, and beans. It was a bachelor treat, as Sarah liked him eating only healthy food because of his weak lungs. He wondered how he could occupy himself for the remaining twelve hours of waking time. He'd do a meal plan, he decided; something very special for Sarah for her return home. She deserved that after being away for so long, and because he had no idea how to dig his marriage out of the financial crap he and his wife had found themselves in.

He tried calling her on his cell, but it went straight to voice mail. He sent her a text, but it went unanswered. It would just be good to have an idea when she would be home, if he could make her something special to eat without her throwing it in his face. He hadn't called her at her hotel, because she'd left James strict instructions not to disturb her while she was trying to rescue their situation. But now he felt an overwhelming need to hear her voice, to tell her that he loved her, to say he couldn't wait until she was home.

He looked at Tess. "What do you think, my girl? Give her a call and risk her wrath?"

Tess rolled in her basket, exposing her belly.

James smiled, though he felt lost and alone. He breathed in deeply and called her hotel, asking to be connected to Sarah Goldsmith's room.

At the other end of the call, the receptionist typed fast on a keyboard. She stopped, telling James to hold, then she started typing again. She spoke inaudible words to a colleague before returning to the call. "Sir, your wife never checked in."

James frowned. "What do you mean?"

"We had the reservation all booked. We were expecting her. She was a no-show."

"No-show?"

"Didn't turn up. Happens all the time. Probably she decided . . ."

James hung up, his mind racing. Was she cheating on him, staying with a man? Revenge for her assumptions about his alleged night out in Edinburgh's strip clubs? His hands shaking, he sent her another SMS.

WHAT THE HELL'S GOING ON? I JUST TRIED YOUR HOTEL. THEY SAY YOU NEVER CHECKED IN.

The headhunter who'd set up her job interview would know where Sarah was. Maybe the explanation was simply that she'd turned up at the hotel, didn't like the look of it, and decided to stay in a nicer place. Yes, that was probably the answer. Nothing worse than that.

He went to the tiny office she used when she worked from home. Though James would constantly rib Sarah about her meticulous filing systems, now he was grateful for her organizational skills. It took him only one minute to find letters from the head-hunter, stored in a labeled drawer. He tried calling the number shown in the company address block on one of the letters. The voice mail said the office was currently closed. Silently cursing, he took the letter to his own ramshackle office, powered up his laptop, and entered the company's Web site, hoping other contact numbers might be listed on the site. A message popped up on his screen saying the Web site domain no longer existed. He tried again, same message. Now he was starting to feel scared. The first contact with the headhunter had been the recruiter calling Sarah. The second, third, and fourth contacts had been via letters. Neither Sarah nor James had met the London-based man.

James's breathing was wheezy, always a sign he was panicking. He sucked on his inhaler a couple of times to try to settle his lungs. Not knowing what to do next was sending him into a tailspin of bewilderment. He was anxious and very concerned for Sarah's welfare. But if there was a perfectly normal explanation for all this, Sarah would crucify him for interfering at such a crucial and delicate juncture of her job applications. It could be the final nail in the coffin if he did anything that might derail her efforts.

Then again, he was her husband and had a duty

to her. He wouldn't be able to live with himself if he backed down from that duty simply because he was too scared to check on her. He had to put his mind at rest, and to do that he had no other option than calling the law firm she was being interviewed by.

For thirty minutes, he was on the phone to them. They had 126 offices spread across the globe, each operating with different management structures and to all intents and purposes autonomous businesses within a worldwide brand. He was transferred to the head office, then to regional offices, then back to the head office in London. Finally, he was connected to the firm's global head of human resources.

She said to him, "Mr. Goldsmith—I can tell you with certainty that we have no record of a Sarah Goldsmith being interviewed by our company, or an authorized representative of our company, for any position in our firm. Something is not right. If I were you, I would alert the police."

The inhaler was now a permanent fixture in his mouth as the dread consumed him. This wouldn't be an elaborate ruse by Sarah, covering her tracks of infidelity. His wife had far too much integrity to cheat behind his back. Many times, she'd made it clear that she would rather get divorced than sleep with another man while married. And there was the crucial matter that she loved her husband dearly. His biggest fear was that she'd fallen victim to an elaborate fraud, something far more complex and clever than the scheme that had earlier this year drained five thousand pounds out of her current account.

He googled her name, unsure what he was looking for, yet beside himself with trepidation. He opened the BBC News site.

And that's when he saw the headline.

SUSPECTED MURDERER WILL COCHRANE ATTACKS POLICE ON AMTRAK TRAIN

Disbelief hit him as he read the news story that contained updates about the murder in the Waldorf Astoria, the manhunt in the U.S. East Coast, the incident on the train, the fact he was being pursued though his whereabouts were unknown, and the unrecognizable female victim in the bathtub.

The woman in the bathtub.

James spat out his inhaler. "No, no, no, no!" he cried. His hands shook as he called the Scottish police emergency number. "Not Cochrane." Tess was by his side, barking. "Anyone but Cochrane," James said, before speaking to the police operator.

"My wife . . . wife . . . her name is Sarah Goldsmith. She's in New York City, supposedly for a job interview. I think she's been murdered. She's been murdered by her brother.

"His name is Will Cochrane."

EIGHT

Thyme Painter and Joe Kopański were in Baltimore, grabbing breakfast in a diner a few minutes after it'd opened, at 6 A.M. They'd had no sleep and had come to Baltimore because everything suggested Cochrane was heading south. The night had been frenetic, with the detectives coordinating the manhunt and issuing instructions to local police units. But they'd found nothing. Cochrane had vanished.

Now there was nothing else that could be done until Cochrane was spotted again. They were exhausted, famished, and pissed off.

Kopański asked, "Why didn't Cochrane kill me on the Amtrak?"

Painter thought about this. "His mind might be broken, but maybe cop killing is a step too far for him. Soldiers, covert operatives, police officers—they're a brotherhood. If he kills one of them, he's killing his own. It would really be crossing the line."

"Still doesn't reassure me. He put me on my ass. I've never come up against something like that."

Painter touched his hand. "If you'd opened fire in the train, it would have turned into a bloodbath. You made the right call."

Kopański looked at her hand. "I think you're right. He doesn't want to kill cops right now. My worry is, what happens if that changes?"

Painter's cell phone rang and she recognized the number as belonging to her Manhattan precinct. The officer at the end of the line said she had an important call to transfer from a firm of family attorneys in New York.

"Yeah, patch it through."

Painter listened without speaking as the caller introduced himself as head of the firm. He said he'd been remiss in not calling earlier; he had been upstate on an urgent matter and had only just returned to the office at this early hour to catch up on what had been happening during his absence. He'd discovered that two days ago a man called Will Cochrane had been due to visit his offices to sign adoption papers. The matter was being dealt with by one of his junior attorneys, and unfortunately the employee hadn't put two and two together and realized that the man who skipped his appointment was the same man being sought for questioning in relation to a murder. For that significant lapse, he was sorry. He gave Painter details about the intended adoption before concluding, "Ma'am, if any of the police officers Cochrane attacked last night had been killed, I'd have no hesitation in sacking my employee for being so dumb."

Painter hung up and told Kopański about the call. "I'm thinking two options: first is Cochrane stays away from the Granges. That's no use to us, unless we—"

"Entrap him by—"

"Luring him there on a false pretext."

"Which is illegal."

"And unethical." Painter added, "We could get the Granges' cooperation. But a man like Cochrane would see through that. Second option is that Cochrane's headed to the Granges' without the need for entrapment."

"To explain his side of the story."

"Or do something far worse." She bowed her head, deep in thought. "It looks like that's where he's headed. Our job is to find him between here and there. But we'd better send a couple of Roanoke detectives over to the Granges to warn them about the situation and to camp in their home."

"I agree. But having two cops in the house for days, maybe weeks, can be frightening for young minds. The twins will be unsettled."

Painter smiled. Her tough companion, as ruthless as they get when he had the bit between his teeth, now and again surprised her. "The issue is whether the Granges will cooperate with us. Even with detectives there, if Cochrane calls the Granges they might try to warn him off."

Kopański said, "We could get Marty Fleet involved."

Painter eyed him. "Get a warrant from the

attorney general's office to monitor the Granges' phones and e-mails?"

"Yes."

"Is that what you want?"

"I don't like it, but we've got no other option."

His colleague agreed. "Cochrane's desperate. He'll be forced to do things he ordinarily wouldn't." Her phone rang again; it was NYPD forensics. Painter frowned as she listened. "Nothing? That can only mean she's foreign, but that's needle-in-a-haystack territory unless someone comes forward with information." When the call ended, she said to Kopański, "Forensics has been thorough. They've run the victim's DNA through our national databases three times, plus have been cross-referencing them to the archives of hospitals on the East Coast, in case for some reason her details weren't transferred to the main database. Nothing. We have to assume she's not an American national. Forensics is going to start liaising with foreign counterparts, starting with Europe, to try to identify her that way." Painter stared out the adjacent window. Outside it was lashing rain and looked bleak. "The hostage said that Cochrane claims he's innocent of the murder."

"Most murderers say stuff like that."

"What if he's telling the truth?"

"Well, if he's innocent, he's digging himself into a deeper and deeper hole."

She pointed at the dreadful weather. "If we don't get him, it'll only be a matter of time before he dies from exposure to the weather."

NINE

After Marty Fleet ended his call to Detective Kopański, he spooned pureed food into his wheelchair-bound sister's mouth. The thirty-eight-year-old had glossy straight auburn hair that Marty had washed, blow-dried, and combed an hour earlier. They lived in Chevy Chase, outside Washington, D.C., in a big apartment building that had great views of the city and had been selected with care by the lawyer because it had excellent wheelchair access and elevators to the twenty-second floor where they lived.

Her brain damage meant that while she would forget what had happened an hour ago, she still retained enough clarity to occasionally look at Marty with a heartbreaking expression that said she knew exactly what he was saying to her. He spoke to her constantly when in her presence. He believed it might keep her brain alive.

"I've got to head off to work in thirty minutes. Before then, I made this specially for you, Penny. A new experiment: bacon, eggs, waffles. Let me know if it tastes like puke."

Penny smiled. It was one thing she could do very well, and it made Marty's toil to look after her worth every effort. He did have help, in the guise of a home health aide who attended to Penny when he was at work, but when he returned, he always sent the aide home and took over her duties.

"NYPD and Virginia State police are very close to catching Will Cochrane, but we had a serious incident on a train last night. He disarmed a detective and uniformed cop, put them on their asses, jumped the train, and escaped. My best detectives think it's a warning, that he's likely to turn cop killer very soon if we push him into a corner. Trouble is, we have to corner him. My officers want me to get the AG to issue a warrant to bug a house where Cochrane has family connections."

Penny emitted a sound.

"That's what I think. Still, we have no choice. It's a shitty part of the job." Marty continued feeding his sister her breakfast. "This is the first time I've been in a legal case involving a man with Cochrane's background. See, he was a covert operative, worked for us as well as the Brits. The CIA pushed him too hard. I'm dealing with a dick there called Philip Knox. He doesn't seem to care about what's happened to Cochrane's mind, though I can tell he and everyone in the Agency highly regard Cochrane. But they keep hanging guys like him out to dry. They squeeze them for everything they've got, then abandon them. I believe there's something wrong with that."

Penny responded in her way.

"Yeah. None of it makes any difference. Most likely Cochrane's going to get the death penalty."

I clambered out of a hedgerow three miles beyond the outskirts of Baltimore.

I'd stopped for an hour—the rest being not sleep, but rather a change of consciousness; eyes open, mind for the most part powered down but aware of sounds, images, and smells around me. During the preceding hours, I'd covered thirty-three miles on foot, my route erratic, zigzag, sometimes doubling back before moving off on a new tangent, all in open countryside, over fields, forests, rivers, under a cloudy, moonless night sky.

Several times I'd crashed into trees and other foliage, tripped on uneven ground, stopped with my hands on my knees to catch my steaming breath, before moving onward at a pace that alternated between a fast walk and a run. It was only when I was convinced I wasn't being pursued, had put enough ground between me and the Amtrak train, and simply didn't have the energy to put another foot forward, that I allowed myself the luxury of rest.

Shivering as my body heat began to evaporate and sweat made my skin cold, I'd sat alone, my hands and head smarting from grazes and cuts from branches and twigs. Now I had to get into

Baltimore, because out here I was too visible. But I worried about my physical appearance and my hunger.

I reached a river that flowed through woods and crouched for ten minutes, motionless, as I observed my surroundings. No other creatures were moving, the air and trees also still above water that was shallow yet running fast over boulders. There was significant risk in doing so, but I had to do something about my disheveled and grimy appearance.

Stripping naked, I stood in the river using water and clumps of grass to clean mud off my outer garments and boots, and thoroughly rinsing my underwear. I washed, grime and blood flowing down my body and into the river. The developing beard on my face was a good thing, but I needed to clear it and my hair of grease. Nothing in the wild could do that, only a man-made surfactant; which is why I'd stolen a small bottle of Ferragamo soap from the Waldorf.

After I was clean, I wrung out my underwear and put it back on. I dressed in the partially wet outer garments, donned my boots, jacket, and backpack, and walked to Baltimore.

TEN

In a boardroom in the headquarters of the Central Intelligence Agency, Philip Knox presided over a meeting with the heads of the Agency and the NSA, and their deputies.

The room, functional and businesslike, contained TV monitors that could be linked to any other senior intelligence chief in the United States and its allies, as well as Capitol Hill. Knox was acutely aware that he was not the most senior person in the room, though right now he held most sway on all matters Will Cochrane.

He began his address as if he were a judge summoning up his findings after being presented with the case for the prosecution and defense. "Mr. Cochrane is no longer one of us." He paused to see if there was any dissension on that point, while observing his colleagues over the top of his half-rim spectacles. The room was silent, watching him. "Perhaps we should conclude that he was never truly *one of us*."

"Now, hang on . . ." the head of NSA interjected.

But Knox held his hand up and continued. "We would do well to think that way in order to distance ourselves from his circumstances."

"Circumstances?" Knox's boss in the CIA ordinarily wouldn't have broken ranks with one of his own, but this was a place where opinions were allowed to be expressed openly and loyalties were momentarily shelved.

"Yes." Knox picked up a pen and jabbed it in the air toward each member. "At what point must we worry about this?"

His senior responded, "People like you created the monster."

Knox said, "Yes and no. But this is now about national security."

"No, it's not. It's about a man on the run."

Knox didn't reply.

"Our best operative is scrabbling about the East Coast, hunted."

"And rightly so." Knox wondered if the others in the room had the balls to enact what he was thinking. He decided no one but him did. "He butchered a woman."

"Maybe he didn't."

"Do you honestly believe that?"

No one answered.

Knox stared at them. "Cochrane's got brutal capabilities. A woman was murdered in his hotel room. Clinically dispatched. That leaves *us all* in no doubt that he's the killer. Why? Open to discussion. Circumstance? Who gives a fuck after the fact?"

Knox's boss was more tentative when he asked, "Do you have any ideas about what should be done?"

Knox weighed up his response carefully. This was the reason for today's meeting. But he was taking a professional risk with what he was about to say. "I told Marty Fleet of the attorney general's office that I thought it was a good idea that the two NYPD detectives maintain the lead in capturing Cochrane, even if he commits crimes in other states. Why give it to the feds, I asked him, when they won't do a better job? That was true. These detectives are the best for the job. But there's another reason I want them right at the front of the game. I need to have at least one cop constantly involved in the investigation." He looked at the head of the NSA. "I believe it's in all of your interests not to ask me why I'm requesting this. But it would be extremely helpful if you could supply me with a cell phone that intercepts every call and SMS sent from and received on the phone belonging to Detective Thyme Painter."

This early in the morning, I briefly felt anonymous and secure. I was on the outskirts of the city, navigating on foot solely by the sight of skyscrapers in the center of the metropolis. There was no need to get too close to the center, but drawing nearer to the tall buildings would bring me into areas containing shops and other much-needed amenities.

I had to see the twins. It was vital the boys heard from me that I didn't murder the woman in the hotel. I felt truly awful for letting them down. I wanted to tell them to stay strong until I could pick matters up where they left off and start our new life together. But I couldn't investigate the murder victim and what had happened in the Waldorf. Only the cops could do that—though, armed with new information, I hoped I could read between the lines and establish a line of inquiry that would be invisible to detectives.

And then, that would be the end of the road.

I'd hand myself in. If I hadn't already died from exposure.

As I walked fast, head low and hands in pockets, residential suburbs became industrial zones, before transforming into the cheaper end of the commercial district. People were around me, most of them looking dog-tired and irritable as they shuffled off to work. They didn't care about me. But if they'd bothered to look, I was betting they'd think I was just some guy who'd finished a night shift on a construction site.

I spent two hours in the area, buying a bus ticket, food, today's edition of the *Washington Post* from a convenience store, and a new set of clothes from a men's store.

In forty-five minutes, I'd be making the five-hour bus journey to Roanoke.

On a park bench, away from the busier areas around me, I checked the newspaper's classifieds section, cross-referencing it to the encyclopedia given to me by the Waldorf's concierge. As promised, there was another entry in coded numbers. The message read:

HOW ARE YOU TODAY? A BIT TIRED AND FORLORN? FORGIVE ME IF I SEE THE FUNNY SIDE OF THAT. YOU ARE A MURDERER NOW. THIS IS WHAT HAPPENS TO PEOPLE WHO GO CRAZY. BUT I SUPPOSE YOU THINK YOU CAN SURVIVE A BIT LONGER. ALL A MAN LIKE YOU NEEDS IS TO AVOID IMPETUOS- ITY AND RETAIN A BIT OF CASH IN YOUR POCKET. SORRY ABOUT THAT. MORE TOMORROW.

I frowned.

Sorry about that?

That sentence gave me a sinking feeling.

I walked to an ATM across the street. I wanted to withdraw my permitted maximum of five hundred dollars. I reckoned my dwindling savings could keep me on the streets for another week or two. After that, prison could take care of me.

The latest message had been a taunt, but cleverly written so the author didn't implicate himself. This was his dish served cold. But revenge for what? This was eating away at me. After fourteen years of working in MI6, I'd made infinitely more enemies than friends.

There was a legion of people who wanted me dead.

I entered my cash card and keyed in my details.

Insufficient funds. I tried again. Same response. I checked my balance. Zero.

Shit.

For the first time since waking in the Waldorf, genuine panic struck me with such force that I had to grip the side of the ATM to avoid crumpling to my knees.

Had the cops done this to my account? Taken everything away from me so that I couldn't move? I doubted that. The police thought I was a desperate killer. Doing this to me would make me even more desperate. In the law's eyes, I would become an even bigger danger to American citizens.

No, this was the work of the man or people who'd orchestrated this nightmare.

That was the other thing that kept me moving.

I wanted to come face-to-face with him.

When that happened, I'd show him what I was capable of.

ELEVEN

Technically, Billy and Tom were playing outside of their great-uncle and -aunt's home. But once out of eyeshot of Robert and Celia, they gave up any pretense of looking happy. Instead, the ten-year-old twins sat together and spoke in the way that young children do when they're confused by events around them and unsettled.

Below them was the beautiful valley that so often had been the place of their adventures, where they could let their imaginations roam as they pretended to be Native Americans hunting for fish or other wild creatures, soldiers in a jungle, Hobbits looking for Treebeard, anything that engaged their fertile minds.

Now the valley with its river and woodlands didn't register. The boys were lost in thought, their eyes burning, feeling that everything was being churned up.

"Uncle Robert and Aunt Celia are acting a bit strange," Tom declared.

Billy nodded while circling his finger in the ground. "I think they must be mad at Uncle Will for being late. Aunt Faye is mad, too."

"Why is he late?"

"He's lost, remember?"

"He should ask a policeman to help him."

"Probably that's what he'll do."

It came from nowhere, but suddenly Tom burst into tears, his body shaking. "I miss Mommy and Daddy."

Billy started crying, too. He hugged his brother. "Me, too . . . me, too."

"Daddy shouldn't have been in the . . . in the . . ."

"SEALs." Billy always remembered the name of Roger Koenig's former unit by associating it to the sea mammal.

"And the other thing he did. The secret stuff. I think that's why Mom was killed. Somebody bad came looking for him."

No one in their family had told the boys what had really happened. Roger had already been dead when Katy Koenig was brutally stabbed to death by an assassin. He'd been working on a highly classified mission as a CIA paramilitary operative in Beirut when men shot him in cold blood. Katy was murdered by the same men back in the U.S., simply to send a message to Will Cochrane that more of his beloved friends would die if he didn't back down from seeking revenge for his dear friend Roger's death.

Billy stood up, not caring that he had bits of

gravel and soil stuck to the skin below his shorts. "Is Aunt Faye here to look after us until Uncle Will arrives? She seemed so sad when she looked after us before."

"She was Mom's sister. That's why." Tom tried to rally his immature brain into some semblance of adult insight. "Maybe she's here again to learn how to look after us again. Uncle Robert and Aunt Celia are helping her."

Billy agreed. "I hope Uncle Will gets here soon. I can't wait to see our new home."

The boys were no longer crying. Tom suddenly felt a moment of hope. "He always buys us toys. Do you think he's got us some new ones in the house?"

Billy's thoughts were now on the same topic. "Maybe some new DS games. If he's got a Microsoft account, he can download some games on our Kindles."

"If not, we can show him how to get an account."

In tandem, the twins looked at the valley and beyond, genuinely trying to spot him driving up the solitary road that led to the Granges' property.

"He'll be here soon."

The matter was settled. Will Cochrane would be arriving any moment, ready to be their guardian and guide them through life.

Both boys' faces lit up when they saw a police cruiser in the distance.

"He's here!"

"The police found Uncle Will!"

The tall sixty-three-year-old gentleman—a slender figure with silver hair, green eyes, a smooth visage that suggested refinement and vast intellect, and a voice that was soft and beguiling—was today jettisoning his usual formality of wearing a suit during the working week and tweeds on the weekend. Right now he didn't need to be anywhere other than on the deck of his large berthed yacht; the sea air was balmy enough for him to be wearing slacks and an open-collared shirt.

But he was still working, always did, sitting at a table with numerous cell phones, a laptop, and a copy of the *Washington Post*. He was deep in thought, his fingertips pressed together, around him Long Island's Montauk Yacht Club and its dozens of moored luxury vessels, possessions of the wealthy who frequented the harbor for onshore rounds of golf while their wives flocked to the Hamptons to spend thousands on designer clothes and jewelry.

He wasn't like them, though his fortune was now considerable. Wealth brought many advantages, but he had little interest in whether he could buy the latest Ferrari or upgrade his Andreas L motor cruiser to a Sycara V. What mattered to him was that money bought people and power, though his hand was for the most part invisible and unknown in the work he did.

His business was influence—steering political decisions in new directions, assisting major corporations with acquisitions they previously deemed impossible, deflecting potential damage and making it a potent force for his customers, arranging the disgrace of the most stubbornly resolute opponents.

To do this, he would use whatever tactic was

required. Instead of specializing in a particular field, he had a general knowledge. If a problem presented itself, the man would close his eyes and let thousands of thoughts race through his mind; then, when he had logically deduced the correct solution, he would open his eyes and smile.

His current vocation was in many ways as far removed as it could be from his previous job of battlefield surgeon, a role that had taken him to nasty parts of the world where he would act as God in a makeshift operating theater strewn with wounded soldiers and their screams. That said, it was his role as a surgeon that had prepared him to be so formidable in his current line of work. A surgeon must find the correct solution to the manifold conditions that can afflict the human body in war. In business, he was no different, though he used his skills to punish and damage, not heal.

His name was Edward Carley.

It was soon going to be lunchtime. His crew was inside the vessel, cooking him salt-baked cod, parsley sauce, mange-tout, and herb mashed potatoes. As usual, he'd be eating alone. His wife had died a few years ago of a condition that even he couldn't reverse, and neither of them had ever had children. His work as a colonel in the army had precluded any inclination to settle down to a domestic family life. He didn't mind that he'd be partaking of his meal in solitude. He was at his most content when left in peace to collect his thoughts.

A guest arrived on his yacht, one of his associates, though the man had absolutely nothing in common with his employer.

His name was Viktor Zhukov, a medium-height Russian with jet-black hair. His body was lacerated with scars and was as strong as high-tensile steel. Most of the scars came from his brutal training and deployment in Spetsnaz, Russia's special forces. The rest were gained in the streets of Moscow, St. Petersburg, and other cities where he'd turned his skills to crime and had gained a reputation as a murderer. It was a reputation that was thoroughly deserved and had brought him to the attention of the man whose yacht he was now standing on. Carley had given him a new identity so that his criminal record was clean. Carley controlled Zhukov with brutal efficiency and respected his track record. He had never failed to complete a job, no matter how distasteful.

As usual, Zhukov was in the black suit he wore when managing his legitimate trading company in Washington, D.C.

"Good morning to you, sir."

Carley barely glanced at him. "My offer to put a scalpel to your mouth and correct your lisp still stands."

"But it gives me . . ." Zhukov struggled to find the word.

"A degree of distinction?"

The Russian thought about the phrase before nodding in approval. "*Distinction*. I like that."

Carley's expression was cold. "All matters are in hand. You've been observing?"

"For days."

"Confident?"

"Certain."

It was all Carley needed to hear. Zhukov was not a liar or egotist. If he said he was certain of success, he meant every word.

Carley said, "I'm extracting the men and women who've helped you so far. They must leave America and lie low for a few months. Their equipment will be left behind at your safe house. A new team is flying in this afternoon. You remain in charge. Brief them on what you know. They know barely anything about me. Keep it that way."

"Understood."

Carley's mind was thinking on multiple levels, and not just about this job. Tonight he was dining with an influential senator who'd turned to Carley for help because the politician had been accused of embezzling money out of a joint U.S.-Chinese oil deal. "As far as Cochrane goes, we've put him on the run and shut down his revenue stream. That's only the beginning. Tomorrow we escalate matters. I will send him another message in the *Washington Post*. You will do your task to the best of your abilities. That will keep him alive, because he won't put a gun to his head if you're successful. We will kick him out of purgatory and kick him into hell."

Zhukov didn't understand the English word *purgatory*. But he understood everything else. He had to, because even Zhukov wouldn't dare to misunderstand Carley's orders. He knew enough about the man to be terrified of that happening.

Enough, including one stark fact.

Edward Carley had been dismissed from the army after being diagnosed as a full-blown psychopath.

PART II
THE DESCENT

TWELVE

Though it was dark in the cabin of the British Airways flight over the Atlantic, too many passengers were still pressing their call buttons and requesting drinks. In the confines of economy class, Dickie Mountjoy was apoplectic that people didn't just shut up and sleep, instead of behaving like spoiled kids crying out to their parents for more drinks. He hadn't been on an airplane since he was in the army. It seemed to him to be a place where people were trapped; there was a clear division between the passengers who needed and the crew who sometimes gave.

Next to him was a thirty-year-old American woman called Barbara who'd introduced herself to Dickie after she'd boarded and had told him that she was returning home to New York to be reunited with her boyfriend after a period of cooling off.

Beyond saying he didn't know what cooling off meant, Dickie had said little else, eaten his meal, and was now trying to rest. But the infernal pinging kept him awake and irritable, with at least four hours left until touchdown.

"Are you okay? You're sweating." Barbara was looking at the old man with concern.

A talkative passenger by his side was the last thing he needed. "I'm all right, missy. Just don't like being shoehorned into a box that's flying at thirty thousand feet."

"Scared of flying?"

"No. Just bored."

"That doesn't explain the sweat on your face. Here." She reached above him and directed the ceiling fan so that it blew cool air on his face. "Any better?"

"Now you've just made it windy in this awful place."

"Where are you headed to in the States?"

Dickie wished she'd shut up. "New York. Same place as you. Don't intend to stay long."

"Have you been before?"

"Never been to America in my life."

Barbara smiled. "New York City's cool."

"Cool? What do you mean?"

"Hip. Happening. A great place to hang out."

"Oh, for the love of God."

"You might find you like it there."

Dickie withdrew from his jacket pocket a cutout segment from his copy of the *Telegraph* newspaper. "It's full of murderers! Look." He thrust the article describing the Waldorf killing under her nose. "People get shot in hotel rooms. Nowhere is safe."

Barbara glanced at the article. "Yes, I know about that. Everyone does. They're still hunting him. He's English as well. And there I was thinking all you Englishmen were civilized." She held her hand to her mouth as she saw that Dickie was wincing in pain, his teeth gritted and his face pouring more sweat. She asked, "What's wrong? What's wrong?" Dickie didn't reply, just looked like he was in agony.

Turbulence struck the plane and the seat belt lights immediately came on just as she undid hers and unsteadily tried to move along the aisle to seek help. A voice announced that everyone had to stay in their seats. Barbara ignored the instruction as she tried to find a flight attendant. But they were at the far end of the plane, also buckled up in their seats. Panic hit her. Uncertain what to do, she returned to Dickie and was relieved to see the man was breathing deeply, his expression now calm, though his face was still wet. "Are you okay?"

Dickie tried to look reassuring. "Better do as they say and sit back down. Nothing to worry about, my love. Feel completely better now. Bet it was just cabin pressure playing havoc with my insides."

Michael Stein entered the Arrivals area of Washington's Dulles airport and recalled the last time he'd done so, as a Mossad assassin tracking down a Hamas terrorist.

He had looked no different back then from how he looked now—the persona of a carefree traveler, a satchel slung over one shoulder, his expression inquiring and happy, as if everything around him was a first-time experience and full of wonderment. The difference was that now he was traveling under his real name and could tell the truth that his vocation was factory worker. What he lied about to the immigration officer was that he was in D.C. to visit the nearby Alexandria Archaeology Museum, among other historic points of interest. The truth was wholly different.

He was here to meet an extremely dangerous man.

The two male detectives from Roanoke Police Department had been selected for the job because of their proficiency with close protection and firearms. In the Granges' isolated home, they spoke to the retirees and Faye for an hour, warning them that if Cochrane called them they were to alert the detectives immediately.

They'd brought camp beds and personal belongings, so they could stay somewhere in the house until Cochrane was captured or dead. There was no negotiating this point, they added sternly. Lives were at risk, and on that point the police had primacy to do whatever was necessary.

Celia and Robert reluctantly agreed, advising them that they had no need for their makeshift beds. There were perfectly adequate spare bedrooms they could use.

The detectives said that the squad car containing two uniformed cops that had brought them here would be parked one mile away at the end of the lane that led to their property. When their shift ended they would be relieved by another car and officers, but there would always be a police presence in the valley. Now and again, they might drive up to the house to check on everyone, so the residents were not to be alarmed if they saw a police car approaching.

The more senior of the detectives said, "That way you have four armed men all over this place if Cochrane comes here. But here's a thing. You might not want Cochrane to be caught. If you try anything stupid, we'll know."

The detectives started making checks of the house and its surroundings.

Celia, Robert, and Faye remained in the kitchen, deep in thought.

It was Faye who broke the silence. "They don't trust us."

"They don't." Robert walked to the window and watched one of the detectives walk along the side of the valley rise. "But maybe they're right to stay with us. We don't know Cochrane's intentions."

"Meaning what, Uncle?" asked Faye.

Celia answered for him. "There is a strong probability that Will is guilty and is now in an unhinged state of mind. Who knows what he'll do? We're the only people he knows in the States. Even if he doesn't know why, he will probably gravitate toward us. And we have the boys to think about."

"And protect."

Faye couldn't prevent anger welling up inside her. "Whether he murdered her or not, Will Cochrane is most certainly connected to what happened in that hotel room. He . . ." She stopped when she saw the twins standing at the base of the stairs. "We told you to stay in your rooms until we called you. This is a grown-up conversation."

Shock was evident on the boys' faces.

Billy asked, "Uncle Will killed someone? Is that why the police came? Is that why Uncle Will's not here?"

Faye glanced anxiously at Robert and Celia. "I don't think we can keep this from them any longer."

"I agree." Robert walked to the twins and put his hands gently on their shoulders. "Everything is going to be okay. We think there's been a mistake. Here's a deal—we'll tell you what we know once we've worked out *how* to tell you what we know."

Faye said to the boys, "How about I take you out to dinner tonight?"

Billy nodded.

Tom replied, "I want to stay here. I have a head-ache."

Faye gave him some aspirin, while saying to Robert, "Maybe it makes sense to speak to them individually."

Robert said to the twins, "Can you leave us to finish our grown-up chat? Go back to your room and play with your toys? Maybe you could record some nice messages on the teddies that Uncle Will bought you. You could tell him that you hope he's okay and gets here soon. That would be nice for him."

The boys did as they were told, though their expressions remained confused and uneasy.

Faye said, "When we tell them, we should immediately reassure them about their future. Tell them that whatever happens, they'll be looked after by us."

Celia looked sternly at Faye. "*Us* means you as well, Faye. You've got to ask yourself about *your* future. If Will can't clear his name, you're the only relative young enough to look after the boys. But you've got to get over this . . . this . . ."

"That's enough, Celia." Robert studied Faye. "But my wife's right. I know it's tough, but somehow you need to overcome your grief about your sister's murder. Billy and Tom need you now more than ever. Do you think you have what it takes?"

Faye's anger faded as she remembered being in floods of tears washing dishes while the twins were in her care. But that was months ago. Was she stronger now? She thought she might be. She hadn't cried in weeks, and before that the episodes of gut-wrenching sorrow had become more sporadic. But it remained a question of trust. Could she trust herself to once again carry the enormous burden of parenting? She guessed it didn't matter. She had Robert and Celia as backup in the house if she had another meltdown.

Faye said, "Why don't I take Billy out for dinner tonight in Roanoke? I can talk to him there. And you can cook Tom a nice meal and talk to him here."

The Granges nodded. "Perfect."

Two hours later, the two detectives finished their rounds of the property. Both were uneasy. The Granges' house was miles from civilization.

They had at least eight acres of land. Worse, there were no distinct borders with the wooded countryside beyond. The only consolation was that the mile-long drive that led to the main road at the bottom of the valley was the only way a car could get in or out. But to their knowledge, Cochrane didn't have a car. And the house itself was big. Six bedrooms. Three doors to get into the house. The ground-level windows were old; their locks would be easy to jimmy open.

The senior detective said to his colleague, "This is bad. On or off duty, we keep our guns on us at all times."

THIRTEEN

In the National Zoo, the light was beginning to fade as early evening descended, accompanied by renewed rain. Most people were leaving quickly to seek shelter or head home.

Philip Knox remained where he was, his raincoat and umbrella an indication that he always came prepared and was never surprised by a switch in weather.

He was sitting on a park bench, staring ahead while listening to the sound of water pounding his umbrella. Very deliberately, he'd been in the same spot for sixty minutes, watching others around him, but most important, making himself visible to one man. He couldn't see that man, but he knew he'd be watching both Knox and his surroundings. The man was cautious and would only approach when it was safe to do so. Now, there was no one to be seen. This was a good thing.

The man now approached from behind the CIA officer and sat on the bench next to him. He was forty-one years old, tall, muscular, and had hair that was long and tied into a ponytail, a hairstyle left over from his infiltration of an eastern European arms cartel.

Knox looked at him. "Hello, Simon. Everything okay?"

Simon Tap didn't immediately respond, just sat looking ahead at the park, rain washing over his uncovered face. A minute later he asked, "What is it this time?"

Knox chuckled. "No time for small talk?"

"No," responded the former Delta Force operative who'd subsequently spent three years in the CIA's Special Operations Group, before being kicked out for coldly executing five Taliban men in Afghanistan. "Just get on with it."

"Very well. I need you to stick very close to certain police detectives. And armed with what information they give you, I'd like you to be one step ahead of them."

"You want me to locate a criminal they're hunting?"

"Clever, Simon." Knox handed him what looked like a cell phone, though it was twice the size of a standard phone. "The NSA gave me this. You won't be able to communicate using this, but it will be able to hear every call and read every SMS, incoming and outgoing, in her phone."

"Her?"

"Detective Thyme Painter of the New York Police Department. She and her partner—Józef

Kopański, usually known as Joe—are leading the manhunt for a man called Will Cochrane."

"The guy on the news, the one who killed a woman in NYC."

"The very same. Now, I've met Detectives Painter and Kopański and subsequently did some checking up on them. They're the best detectives in New York; probably the whole East Coast." He handed Tap photos of the cops, adding, "Painter has an artificial leg, makes her walk awkwardly. And the reason half Kopański's face looks the way it does is because he pissed off a perp who was holding a bottle of nitric acid. They'll stand out."

Tap's frame was motionless as he asked, "You want me to grab Cochrane and wait for cops to arrive?"

Knox skirted the question. "I will pay you two hundred thousand dollars."

"Lot of money compared to the last jobs. You sure you can cover that up without the Agency knowing a large chunk of their cash has gone missing?"

Knox smiled. "If you knew the size of the annual budget under my control, most of it deniable and unaccountable, you'd possibly have an argument to state that I'm underpaying you." His tone turned serious. "You've never let me down before. Will you do it?"

Tap shrugged. "Can't promise I'll get him without good police data from"—he held the device—"this. But if I get good leads, I'll close him down. It'll be a walk in the park once I have him in my sights. Then I'll call it in to the cops."

"Actually, Simon, if you don't mind, I'd rather you didn't."

Tap was quiet.

"I told Painter and Kopański that the Agency couldn't interfere in their police matter. It was a lie. See, the thing is, it's better for everyone if Cochrane doesn't remain on the run. But it's also better if he's not incarcerated. He's got too much stuff in his head. Too many things he might spill to get a reduced sentence. Because—"

"He was a covert operative."

Knox always admired the rapid thinking of the asset he'd used many times without the Agency knowing. He liked to think of Tap as his cutthroat razor—for the most part delicate and precise, but extremely capable of creating an awful mess if needed. "I need Cochrane permanently removed."

"Then my price has just doubled."

Knox had anticipated this and had ensured he could squirrel four hundred thousand dollars out of his slush fund without anyone noticing.

Tap asked, "Does NSA know why it made this gadget for you?"

"It believes we're merely keeping tabs on the investigation and that if we hear anything from the cops that they don't understand but we do, then we can subtly steer the detectives in the right direction. NSA thinks their tool is to help capture Cochrane."

Tap was deep in thought. "If I kill Cochrane close to cops, what will they think has happened?"

The CIA officer shrugged. "I'll muddy their thinking—tell them that there are a vast number of foreign people who want payback for Cochrane's service to the West. He killed some of theirs. They decided to end his life while he was on the run and vulnerable." He added, "We have a deal?"

"It'll be done."

Knox's tone was earnest and urgent as he replied, "Don't get close to him."

"I can handle myself."

"With most people, yes. But with this one things are different. He'll easily kill you if you're in close proximity to him. Trust me on that. Get a rifle, or whatever works for you, and take his head off from a distance."

FOURTEEN

My bus was on route 81, about an hour away from Roanoke. The entire journey south, I'd had my jacket collar and hood up, pretending to sleep. I wished I really could have got some shut-eye. I was dog-tired.

The bus was at full capacity. Most people were dozing. Thankfully, the interior was in darkness. I was in an aisle seat. Next to me was a young man. He looked like a college student. He hadn't said a word to me when he got on the bus in D.C. Just played games on his phone for half an hour before slipping it into his pocket and crashing. He'd been asleep ever since.

The bus slowed down, and I opened my eyes. Ahead of us traffic was moving slowly. I couldn't see why. Maybe an accident.

But I couldn't afford to make assumptions. I kept looking ahead.

Five minutes later, I saw flashing lights on the highway ahead. We were four hundred yards away, moving at crawling pace.

Most likely an accident, I repeated to myself.

But as we got closer, my stomach flipped. Two squad cars were parked horizontally across the highway. A gap the width of a truck was between them. That was the only way to get through. Other cop cars were stationary behind the makeshift roadblock. And in the gap, two officers were allowing vehicles to slowly go through. Each time, they lifted a spike strip. Once the car was through, they replaced the strip and checked the next vehicle in the queue. I bet the cops had another spike strip farther down, in case a car tried to rush the gap behind another car.

On the Amtrak, I'd had room to move. But in here I was trapped. The roadblock had to be for me. The police would pay particular close attention to public transportation. We'd be thoroughly checked.

My heart was beating fast, and I could feel perspiration on my back.

What to do?

I could force the driver to let me off.

But he'd call the cops. There could be dozens of them at the roadblock. The detectives who'd earlier pursued me had used clever discretion and caution. They wanted to catch me without escalating matters and endangering lives. But the guys ahead of me might not be so patient. With the number of vehicles around me, this could turn into a chaotic shootout.

A thought occurred to me. The cops ahead would know about me holding up a car outside of Philly. Maybe they were expecting me to have done the same to get here. I looked at the guy next to me. He was still sleeping. Most people in the bus were oblivious to what was going on outside. Very slowly I started easing the guy's cell out from his pocket.

He moved.

I froze.

But he was just adjusting his position while still sleeping.

I got the phone out.

His eyes were shut. He didn't move.

I entered the bathroom. The place stank and would have been a dreadful sight for anyone needing to use it. I didn't care. What I needed urgently was privacy.

I called 911.

A woman answered. "Operator."

In a Virginian accent I spoke in fast, hushed tones. "I'm in my blue Porsche. An Englishman's held a gun at me. Think he's the guy on the news. We're on route 81. Traffic's not moving because there's a police roadblock ahead. He's out of the car, freaking out. Oh, shit, he's coming back!"

I hung up and turned off the cell in case the operator tried to call back. I turned on the sink tap, removed the battery, and held it under the running water. Replacing the dripping wet battery into the phone, I was sure the device was now completely inoperable. If its owner were to wake up, turn it on, and get a call or SMS from the police, he'd take one look at me and work out what was going on.

I went back to my seat and slid the phone back into the passenger's pocket.

God knew if the cops were going to fall for this. I chose a blue Porsche because I thought it would be unusual. And I hoped the police at the road-block would be desperate to get me close enough to them so they could gun me down.

For one minute the methodical checks contin-ued. Then everything changed. The guys in the gap remained in place. But two other officers were ahead of them, waving traffic through. The spike-strip cops were no longer lifting and setting the trap back down with each car that passed.

They were getting traffic moving.

And hoping the mythical Porsche driver would feel comfortable to proceed. Once he was close to the roadblock, the cops would fling the spike strip back in place and draw weapons.

At least, that's how I hoped they were thinking.

We were very close now. Thank goodness there were no real blue Porsches in front of us.

The cops were pointing at vehicles and instruct-ing them to pass.

I held my breath.

Three vehicles were in front of us. Vehicles one and two were told to proceed. Ditto vehicle three.

Come on, come on, I thought to myself.

The bus engine rumbled as we picked up speed and passed the police.

Now I saw two more squad cars positioned in exactly the same way as the first, plus two officers with another spike strip.

But the strip wasn't in place. We were let through.

I exhaled as the bus changed lanes and continued its journey.

It was 7 P.M. as the bus pulled in to Roanoke. I disembarked, with only fifty-three dollars in my pocket.

I went to the station's men's room and changed into my newly acquired clothes—a Windbreaker jacket, jeans, and hiking boots. I looked at my face in a mirror. I looked like shit: face drawn and heavily stubbled, eyes hollow and red with dark bags underneath, and lips that were cracked in places. The good thing, though, was that from a distance I would look nothing like the guy in the newspapers. But close up I was sure I'd be recognized.

Still, the beard would grow. And every day of being on the run, I'd get thinner.

I was used to being alone. Parents killed. Sister keeping her distance from me because she knew that lots of people wanted me dead. My work as an operative mostly done without support.

But God, this was different. What I'd give to see just one friendly face.

Anyone who could look me in the eyes and tell me they knew I wasn't guilty of murder.

That encouragement would mean more than a hundred hot dinners, a bed, and a full night's sleep.

Time to focus.

On foot, I made my way out of Roanoke.

One hour later, I was in the outskirts of the city. I found a quiet street and stopped under a streetlamp. Most of the street was in darkness and there were few houses in this area. I ate the last of the food I'd bought in the Baltimore convenience store, my stomach rumbling as I did so.

That's when they stepped out of the shadows and came at me from different directions.

Three men.

With knives.

Muggers.

They were wearing hoodies. Two of them white, one black. All of them in their early twenties. They surrounded me.

I held up my hands and said in my fake American accent, "I got no money. That's why I'm on the streets. Got no place to stay."

They were circling.

The black guy said, "What's in the pack?"

"Just old clothes. You *definitely* won't want them."

"How come you don't look scared?"

"This ain't the first time this has happened. Comes with the territory."

The gang leader said, "Give us the pack."

No way was that going to happen. I definitely needed my gun and the encyclopedia.

Casually, I said, "You've got the wrong guy. Unless you're looking for a pair of muddy pants and a sweater that smells like crap. I can show you."

All three took a step closer.

"Just throw it here."

"Come on, guys. I need my bag."

The leader came right up to me and put the tip of his knife against my gut. He didn't say anything. Didn't need to.

"You'd seriously stick a knife in me, just for what I got?"

The leader nodded.

I wished he'd said something different. This was the last thing I needed right now.

"Okay, okay," I said with resignation, unslinging my pack.

I dropped it and swooped my leg against the man's heel, causing him to completely lose balance and topple away from me. His head smacked the pavement. He was out of it. I ran at one of the other men. He lunged with his knife. I dodged, elbowed him in one eye, grabbed his head, and hurled him at his pal. His colleague moved his knife, but not quickly enough. It sliced into his friend's arm as they connected. The wounded man fell to his knees, his face screwed up as he clutched his arm. The one still standing rushed me. His knife was aimed at my stomach. I twisted, locked my hands on his wrist, kicked him in the balls, and kneed him in the face. Still gripping his wrist, I slammed my other knee into his elbow. I wrenched back on his arm, hearing bones snap. He screamed and dropped the knife. I kicked it away. The man with the slashed arm was trying to get to his feet. I walked up to him and punched his face so hard that his body lifted off the ground as he flipped sideways.

I checked his colleagues. They were moaning, starting to regain consciousness. "Don't get up," I said to the mugger with the broken arm. I pulled off his hood and patted his head. "It's in all of our interests that no one hears a thing about what just happened. Agreed?"

The mugger nodded while gasping.

"Good." I smiled. "I did warn you that you'd got the wrong guy."

I walked on, needing to cover twenty miles before I reached Robert and Celia Grange's house.

FIFTEEN

Thyme Painter was giving a briefing to a room of forty-six uniformed and plainclothes Charlottesville cops, midway in the 277 miles between Baltimore and Roanoke. Her cell phone rang, and it was a call she had to take—Detective Inspector Toby Rice from the London Metropolitan Police. "Excuse me for one moment." She listened to the call, glanced with a look of excitement at Kopański, and said to Rice, "Excellent work, Detective."

When she ended the call, all eyes in the room were on her.

She said, "Ladies and gentlemen, by chance, we've had a breakthrough. A man in Scotland called the British police because he was concerned about the whereabouts of his English wife. In tandem, NYPD forensics reached out to the UK with details of the Waldorf victim's DNA. London's Met Police compared the DNA of our victim with the

DNA of the missing wife." She smiled. "We have a match." Her smile vanished. "But this takes the situation to a whole new level. The victim is Sarah Goldsmith. In the next hour, I will be revealing her details to the media and asking members of the public to come forward if they have any information about her that might relate to her death. It appears she was lured to New York on the false pretext that she was being interviewed for a job. That fraud may or not be related to her death. We will be investigating it. More important, her identity, the fact that she was murdered in Cochrane's room, and the fact that he fled mean we're damn sure Cochrane is guilty of her murder."

Everyone else in the room was silent.

"Sarah Goldsmith is Will Cochrane's sister."

The diner in Roanoke was one of the twins' favorite places to eat out because it served burgers as big as their heads and offered second helpings of fries and soft drinks for free. This evening, Billy was alone with his aunt Faye, too nervous to eat because he knew they were about to have a grown-up discussion. He thought it would make his tummy churn again. And he knew that the conversation would be about Uncle Will.

Faye watched him stab at his fries but not lift them to his mouth. "Billy, Uncle Will's done something very bad."

"Killed someone," muttered Billy.

"Yes. Well, maybe not. We don't know, but we do know the police are trying to catch him so they can ask him what happened."

"Why doesn't he just go to the police and tell them he didn't do it?"

Faye's eyes moistened. "Maybe because if he does that, they'll arrest him and put him in prison for a very long time."

"Not if he's innocent."

"And if he's guilty?" Faye hated saying the words, though she knew that right now Robert and Celia would be having the exact same conversation with Tom. They'd agreed that in order to give the twins certainty about their immediate future, they had to use unambiguous language and not supply false hope. But talking this way still made Faye feel terrible. "When people run away from a dead body and don't contact the police, it usually means they're guilty of killing the person."

Billy dropped his fork, tears running down his face. "He could be scared. That's why he ran."

"A man like Uncle Will doesn't get scared easily."

The ten-year-old blurted, "I wasn't scared on the valley swing we made. Then one day I was and couldn't go on it. I don't know why. Uncle Will just got . . . just got suddenly scared."

Faye placed her hand on his. "It's possible, but the police think he murdered a woman. They want to arrest him. He can't be your father if he's a wanted man."

"Wanted?"

"If the police want to catch him and put him in prison."

"But . . . but . . . he bought us a new home, close to our school. He got a job in the school so he could always be close to us. Tom and me were going to teach him how to open a Microsoft account so he could . . . could . . ." His face turned red as his sobbing intensified. "Who's going to look after us?"

Faye rubbed his hand. "That's what I wanted to talk to you about this evening. Uncle Robert and Aunt Celia and I have spoken about this. We will continue to look after you, though I will be your parent. Even if it's just temporary because it turns out Uncle Will is innocent."

"But you couldn't look after us before. You kept crying."

"I'm better now. At least . . ." She paused to be sure of what she was about to say. "The most important thing is that you and Tom know that life will continue as normal. You'll keep going to school, have your own rooms, play in the garden, life as normal. And I'll stay in the house until . . . until we know what's happening with Uncle Will."

Viktor Zhukov, six other men, and one woman were standing by three vehicles on the side of a dark, deserted Virginia country road.

The males in the team comprised ex-military and technical experts, the female a doctor who'd had her license revoked. Zhukov didn't know any of them, but that didn't matter because Edward Carley did. All that mattered to the Russian was that the others did what they'd been told to do this evening, with clockwork precision. If any of them deviated from that task, he wouldn't hesitate to kill them.

Zhukov and his team had covertly watched the house for two days. However, the plan of action was not his. After Zhukov had relayed surveillance updates to him, Edward Carley had told him exactly what to do.

"Two of the family are away this evening. That doesn't matter. But if they return while I'm there, I will deal with them. First I need to take care of the car." Zhukov looked at each person in turn. "Give me five minutes. Once that's done, I will call. Move very fast then. And make no mistakes."

He left his vehicle and walked alongside the road, away from the group.

Tom had been sent to bed, emotionally and mentally exhausted, pulling the drawstring on the back of his teddy so that the hidden device inside could activate its ten-minute sound recording operation. But he had no words to record, and just let the thing listen to empty air.

At the downstairs kitchen table, Robert and Celia were grasping undrunk mugs of coffee. Robert wanted to be angry about the situation. He wanted to be able to channel that anger into energy and leadership, but all that remained in him was a feeling that they had somehow let the twins down, giving them false hope by agreeing that Will could adopt them. He wished he could turn the clock back and say to Will, "No. You can't father the boys. You're not suitable because one day you're going to murder a woman."

Celia could sense her husband's mood, though her thoughts were different. She recalled the way Will had spoken to them about his plans for the twins' future. She'd sensed no malice in him.

Nothing but a genuine desire to give the boys a stable, healthy, and loving future. He'd seemed like a good man; one who was carrying demons, for sure, but not someone who could do something as catastrophic as this. Perhaps her judgment was becoming more flawed with age; perhaps Will Cochrane had hidden his dark side from her.

"Can Faye find the strength?" she asked her husband in a voice that sounded as unreal as the thoughts in her head.

"With us by her side, I think she can." Robert wasn't looking at her or anything in particular. The normally in-control man now felt like a fish out of water.

Celia went to him and put her arms around him. "None of this is our fault. We have and will continue to look after the boys. And when we were real parents, we raised two fine daughters."

"We were younger then and knew what we were doing. Things change."

"You're being too hard on us."

Robert looked at his wife. "Faye *has* to be strong enough. I can't have the boys going into foster care."

"It will never come to that. Our daughters would step in if—"

"They're up to their necks in their own kids, and mortgages, and every other responsibility under the sun. Their hearts would be in the right place, but no way do they have the resources to take on more responsibilities."

Robert was right. Short of Will being miraculously found innocent, Faye and the Granges were the twins' only hope.

Robert glanced at his watch. "Faye and Billy will be home any time now."

The detective who was taking the night shift entered the room. "My colleague's going to bed, though he'll be up in a second if there's need. I don't want to disturb you folks, so is there a room I can use tonight?"

Celia answered, "You can use the living room. In fact, most downstairs rooms. Robert and I will just be using this room until bedtime."

"Okay, ma'am. I'll leave you alone in here. I might also be taking some walks around the property, checking perimeters. And I'll have constant lines of communication with the squad car at the bottom of your lane. If Will Cochrane is out there, we will find him."

SIXTEEN

I'd been in some of the most arduous situations and harshest environments in the world. The physical side of things can become excruciating. There comes a point when you feel like you're wearing lead boots. Your back wants to give out. Not one part of you feels good. Adrenaline comes and goes. But it's not enough without sufficient food and water. Keeping moving can be a relentless nightmare. Throw into the mix people who want to kill you, and it becomes a whole new ball game. I've seen men in these situations reach a breaking point. Some of them just sit down and wait for death. Doesn't mean they're weak. Everyone has a point where they can't go on. None of us knows when that will happen.

I desperately wanted to rest.

But I couldn't.

I walked through the rural countryside beyond Roanoke.

The main road leading to the Granges' lane was one hundred yards to my left. I'd only driven up it once before. Back then, everything was different. New life ahead of me. Parenting. A challenge, for sure, but for once not one that required me to put my neck on the line. Two months earlier, the idea of adopting Billy and Tom hit me. It just made perfect sense.

The difference between my last visit to their home and now was vast.

I had a further ten miles to cover on foot. I quickened my pace.

Zhukov approached the police squad car parked at the bottom of a long lane that headed up to the rise above the valley. He was calm and didn't give a damn about personal danger. All that mattered was that things went according to plan. He knocked on the driver's window and stepped back, raising his hands to show he meant no harm.

Two uniformed cops were inside. The one on the driver's side partially lowered his window. "Yeah?"

Zhukov pointed back up the road and said in his lisping tone, "I've just hit a deer. It's smashed up the front of my pickup. I'm about a mile back."

The cop's eyes narrowed. "How did you know we were here?"

Zhukov shrugged. "I didn't. I waited for a while for some cars to pass by and help, but I didn't see one vehicle in twenty minutes. So I decided to walk until I could find a house where I could call for help."

"Why didn't you call from your cell phone?"

"I don't have one. I don't permit them in my family, ever since my daughter got stalked on Instagram."

"You got someone back there with you?"

"My wife and daughter. They're in the vehicle, but scared. The engine won't turn over, so they've got no heat."

The cop on the passenger side got out of the vehicle but stayed close to it. "Your accent—you a foreigner?"

Zhukov shook his head. "Not anymore. I'm from Romania, but have all the necessary paperwork to be here. It's in my pickup."

"You got vehicle insurance?"

"Of course."

The cop in the driver's seat said, "We can't drive far from here, but if you're only a mile away that should be fine." He got onto his radio and spoke to someone. "We're leaving post for a few minutes because we've got a family in distress to deal with. Nothing suspicious. Road traffic accident. But we'll be mobile and minutes away if needed." He turned to Zhukov. "We're just going to need to check you're not carrying anything dangerous before we allow you in the car. You got a problem with that?"

Zhukov shook his head. "Not at all."

The driver got out of the car. He glanced at his colleague standing on the other side of the vehicle. "I got this." He looked at Zhukov. "Okay. Don't be concerned. Just put your arms out straight and to the side. I'm going to search you just like the guys do at airports."

Zhukov put on a fake look of fear. "I've just remembered I've got a steel wrench in my pocket. I was using it to try to lever open the pickup hood."

To Zhukov's joy, the officer replied, "That's okay. Toss it on the ground, then put your arms out. Slowly though." Both officers had a hand on their holsters.

The Russian reached into his pocket, grabbed the metal object, said, "I'm so glad I found you here," and with lightning speed and accuracy pulled out his sound-suppressed pistol and shot both officers in the head.

I had five miles left to the Granges' home.

I guessed the twins would be in bed by now, possibly asleep. What mattered was that Robert and Celia were awake. But I had to approach with great care. I assumed the police knew about my missed appointment with the attorney in New York and the purposes of that meeting. Plus, I'd been sighted heading south from Philadelphia. Pair those two facts, and they'd know I was heading to the Granges' place.

Cops would be monitoring their home. Though how was unclear.

Covertly observing the property from close proximity would be intensive and a diversion of valuable resources away from capturing me in open ground. More likely, they'd position a fast-response squad car close by and plant at least two detectives in the house.

I'd need to get past whichever one of them was on night duty.

Faye had hated nighttime driving ever since she'd started to wear glasses. Intensified and distorted by her lenses, it was the glare from the headlights of oncoming vehicles that scared her, forcing her to urgently reduce speed. Three miles outside of Roanoke and with seventeen to go, thankfully, traffic was almost nonexistent. Still, she was driving at a snail's pace.

"We'll be home soon, Billy. It's way past your bedtime, young man."

In the back, Billy yawned. "Will Tom be in bed now?"

"Yes, he will. You're lucky to be the one allowed up this late." Faye bet Billy felt anything but lucky right now. But she was making light of their circumstances, and bizarrely, it was having a positive effect on her mood. Maybe this was the return to the get-on-with-it attitude that she had once shared with Celia. And if that was the case, she needed to keep being like this, even if it started as a charade. "I bet Tom didn't get a burger the size of the one you had tonight."

"Probably not."

"Hey, I've got a special recipe for burgers. It uses fresh ground steak, eggs, crushed biscuit crackers, and herbs. Actually, in my recipe I add paprika, but we might hold back on that until you're older.

Want me to cook you and Tom my secret-recipe burgers sometime?"

"Sure."

"And I cook really fabulous homemade fries." She knew she was babbling but didn't want there to be silence in the car. "I cut them chunky and double-fry them. Ten minutes on a low simmer, then drain them off and let them cool down. Then five minutes before eating, I refry them on a high heat to get them crispy. Sound yummy?"

"Why didn't you cook the burgers and fries when we lived with you?"

The question gave Faye pause for thought. "Things were different then. I'm better now."

"*Things* aren't better now, though, are they?"

Faye glanced in her rearview mirror and saw a young boy who was scared, confused, angry, and sad. Quietly, she answered, "Not everything, no."

Zhukov had dragged the two dead cops off the road onto rough ground between trees.

The bodies would be easy to spot during daylight hours, but by then it wouldn't matter. In any case, Zhukov wanted them to be found. It would further add to Cochrane's misery. He walked over soft ground around the squad car, to make absolutely certain his footprints would be found. They were very special prints in boots that had been expertly modified. The soles' size and markings exactly matched the bootprints found in Cochrane's Waldorf room.

Fifteen minutes later his team and all three of their vehicles were around him, next to the road and five hundred yards away from the squad car that was still in position facing up the lane. Two of the former military men were wearing Roanoke city cop uniforms and insignia, along with the dead officers' boots.

Zhukov changed clothes and said, "Showtime. And remember: only I use a gun." He looked at the two fake cops. Their military expertise and demeanor made them perfect, because they not only looked like cops but could do what was necessary.

On foot, Zhukov and the two men walked to the police car. The uniformed men got in the front of the vehicle; Zhukov got in the rear and lowered his body so he couldn't be seen through the windows. They drove up the lane, headlights off, engine noise minimal due to their slow speed. Around them, the valley was still and in near pitch darkness, the men relying on moonlight to navigate the narrow and increasingly steep track. It was only when they got to the rise of the valley that they put their headlights on.

"Okay, here we go," said the driver. He parked the car outside the front of the Granges' home.

Both fake cops got out of the car and waited alongside it, the engine still running.

Within seconds one of the detectives watching over the Granges exited the front door and sauntered over. "Everything okay?"

"Yeah," replied one of Zhukov's men. "We've just taken over the night shift. Our colleagues had to return to the station. One of them had an urgent family crisis. We thought we'd come up here and take a peep. Nothing going on down the lane. Quiet as the grave."

"You want coffee? I could do with some. We've got a long night ahead."

The fake cops glanced at each other and shrugged their shoulders. One of them answered, "Can't see why not. We're just as much use up here. More so."

"The Granges are getting ready for bed, so I've got access to the kitchen now. Come in."

He turned and headed back to the house. Zhukov sprang out of the car, walked right up to the detective, and shot him twice in the head with his silenced handgun. He said nothing to his men. They knew exactly what they had to do. They got in the squad car and waited.

All was silent in the house as Zhukov rapidly entered and moved through the dwelling, his gun expertly held at eye level. He worked angles as he went from one room to another. He knew the precise layout of the house, having studied it with long-range day- and night-vision equipment. And he knew the exact ground-floor back bedroom where the second detective would be resting. Carefully, he turned the bedroom's handle and eased the door open. The detective was by his bed, his back to Zhukov, shirtless and loosening his belt. One bullet smashed through his skull and sent blood and fragments of brain and bone onto the bedsheets. Zhukov shot him again.

He moved fast along stairs and entered the upstairs hallway. At the far end was Robert Grange, wearing pajamas. Behind him was the bathroom.

Adjacent was an open bedroom doorway. Lights were on inside. Robert stood stock-still, terrified when he saw the man at the end of the hall, who was wearing an all-in-one white paper boiler suit, dentist's mask, and green Wellington boots with strange thick soles that extended beyond the cut of the boot.

"Celia! Danger!" They were Robert's last-ever words. The old man slumped to the ground with a thud after one bullet hit him in the eye and a second went through his heart.

From inside the bedroom, Celia screamed and jumped out of bed as quickly as her arthritic limbs would allow. Directly opposite her room was the boys' room. She didn't know how quickly she could cross the six-foot-wide hallway without getting knocked off her feet. She hadn't run in decades. But she had to try to get there. Tom was all that mattered right now.

With no time to waste, she hurled herself across the room, her eyes focused on the door handle to the twins' room. She grabbed it and turned, just as a bullet tore through her frail arm. A second bullet raced toward her, but she piled into the bedroom and shut and locked the door. She looked urgently at Tom. He was wearing his favorite Star Wars pajamas, sitting up bleary eyed in his bed. Every nerve in Celia's body was in utter pain.

What to do? She didn't think the door and its flimsy lock would stop a firm kick. She looked at a nearby chest of drawers and grabbed it while whispering, "Tom, hide! Get under your bed! Don't make a sound no matter what, you hear me?"

She tried to move the heavy piece of furniture, but it was no good. Her body at the best of times would have struggled. Now her shot arm was limp by her side, blood pouring out of the wound, the pain so excruciating that she couldn't help loudly crying. Tom too was crying, his eyes fixed on her horrible wound.

"Under the bed! Quick!"

Tom dived out of bed and wriggled under it.

"You must be silent," Celia implored. She knew it was an impossible request. A killer was out there and he was now taking his time. She had to do everything she could to protect Tom. She put her body weight against the door. Most likely it was a pointless thing to do. But logic didn't feature. All she felt was an instinct to protect.

It was probably her last maternal act. But she was damned if it wasn't going to be her bravest.

The kick to the door slammed it off its hinges. Celia was lifted off her feet and sent crashing to the carpeted floor, landing on her injured arm. The pain made her eyes feel like they were going to pop out. She was losing consciousness, her mind punch-drunk. But she still retained enough focus to see the white-clad killer standing in the doorway, his sickening clinical appearance making him all the more terrifying.

"I . . . came in here to hide. No one else here. Children are away." The room clearly belonged to kids. "Please, it's true."

Zhukov stood over her bloody body.

On her back, Celia stared up at him. She knew what was coming.

And she just knew in her bones that this was proof that Will Cochrane was innocent.

The man in the room wasn't here for money.

He was here to kill.

No chance this was random.

It had to be connected to Will.

He'd been framed in New York, and now he was being framed in her home.

She wished he were here.

Will would protect Tom.

And he'd kill the scum standing over her.

Zhukov was laughing as he pumped bullets into her body.

Underneath the bed, Tom screwed up his eyes and rolled back his lips in an attempt to seal his mouth completely shut. He felt like his head was going to explode. He grabbed the teddy bear Will had bought him.

An adult's legs were visible and getting closer.

The man sniggered. "I know you're under the bed. It's going to hurt if I have to drag you out."

Tom was shaking uncontrollably, threw his teddy to the space underneath the head of his bed, and placed his hands over his mouth.

Unable to control his bladder any longer, he wet himself.

Zhukov grabbed Tom's ankle and wrenched him out from under the bed.

I was in the forested valley, one mile from the Granges' home.

I could see the lane leading up to their house, and also the main road it joined at its base. I froze.

Five hundred yards away were three vehicles, headlights on and engines running. I pulled out a pair of binoculars from my backpack and studied the group.

Four men and a woman were standing adjacent to the cars, two of them smoking. Three of them looked like they could be detectives, the others less so, though that meant nothing—one of the requirements for being a detective was to avoid looking obvious. On Waldorf Astoria stationery, I wrote down the vehicles' license plates and a description of their appearances. No doubt now I'd have to be extremely careful entering the Granges' property.

Part of me wondered whether it was worth the risk. But I just had to look the Granges in the eye, ensure they were capable of looking after the twins, and tell them that whatever they heard in the media, I was an innocent man.

Keeping the lane to the Granges' home in sight, I began my ascent up from the valley.

Faye and Billy were five miles away, the boy half asleep in the back of the car and willing them to be home so that he could tuck into his warm bed. Many times he'd wished he could stay up this late. But now he felt woozy with fatigue and wished Aunt Faye would drive faster than thirty miles an hour. Her car seemed to be crawling.

"When are we going to get home?" His voice sounded slurred.

"We're nearly there." Faye tried to hide her irritation with his repetitive questions. She wasn't irritated with the boy. Rather, she was angry with herself for being such a lousy and panicky driver. "I could make you a hot chocolate when we get home, if you'd like."

"Just wanna go to bed."

"That's okay. It's been a long evening."

Her thoughts turned to tomorrow. She was due to conduct a Web-based seminar on mathematics for some of her university students. That would take ninety minutes, though she'd need that much time beforehand to prepare for the session. Robert and Celia would have to keep an eye on the boys while she worked. Thank goodness they were here to help, and thank goodness she didn't need to physically be back at work for ten days. By then everything might have worked out.

Who was she kidding? Will Cochrane was in a hopeless situation.

Tom was screaming and fruitlessly writhing as Zhukov held him in an iron grip and carried him down the stairs. He placed a hand over Tom's mouth and muttered, "Time to be quiet, or I'll snap your neck. You choose."

Tom immediately complied.

Zhukov added, "You'll stay quiet until I tell you not to be. Understood?"

Tom was still.

"Understood?"

The ten-year-old nodded emphatically.

"I might not hurt you if you're a good boy. No promises, but at least it's a start." He swiveled the twin around so that he could see Zhukov's face and white cloth mask. "I'm going to take you outside and put you in a car. You'll see a dead man on the ground. Might scare you. But that will be nothing compared to what I'll do to you if you make a sound. Got it?"

Tom nodded, his eyes wide with terror.

"All right. Let's go." After Zhukov removed his mask, he carried Tom to the squad car, dumped him into the rear passenger area, forced his body and head low, and lay on top of him. The fake cops in the front said nothing as the driver engaged gears and drove at a steady pace down the valley track.

I threw myself to the ground as I saw a police squad car drive away from the Granges' home. It was driving carefully, navigating the twisty route with precision. Burying my face into grass, my fingers gripped soil.

The cruiser drew nearer, its engine noise suggesting it was only in second gear to compensate for the gradient of the lane. I waited, motionless, anticipating what I'd do if the car stopped close to me and doors opened. I'd fire warning shots from the pistol I took from the hotel, and run. There was nothing else that could be done, short of murdering the cops. And I wasn't going to do that, or injure them.

The vehicle drew nearer as I desperately prayed for it to keep moving down the valley. I didn't give a fuck about anything else. Nothing else registered. Not the smell of the wet grass around me, my aching limbs, or the sound of a woodpecker drilling into a tree. All that mattered was the damn cop car and whether it spotted me.

Don't stop.

Just. Keep. Fucking. Moving.

The squad car was as close as it could be to me. I glanced up. I couldn't see the cops' faces clearly. But the interior light was on and I could see a man in the back. Black hair, pale face, not in uniform. He was moving about. Maybe putting stuff in a bag.

The car kept moving.

My relief was overwhelming.

I estimated it was now at least a hundred yards farther down the valley. I risked a glance. Yes, its taillights were still visible but growing more distant. I waited until the cops were at the base of the lane. They stopped; one minute later the three-car convoy I'd seen earlier drove up to the car. All headlights were extinguished. I looked through my binos, could discern human movement around the car, but the light was too bad to ascertain exactly what was happening. Five minutes later, the three unmarked cars drove off, leaving the cop car to maintain its vigil at the base of the valley.

I got to my feet and jogged toward the house.

Then stopped dead.

In front of the Granges' home was a male, wearing a shirt and slacks, prone on the ground. Oh, no. I pulled out my gun as I urgently looked around and listened for any signs of movement. All was quiet.

I ran up to the man; he'd been shot dead. Heart

beating fast, I entered the house and dropped my backpack to the floor. It took me twenty seconds to check the ground floor and to find the second dead detective. Now my heart was sinking as I raised my gun and climbed the stairs.

My mind was doing overtime.

Fake cops had killed real ones in the valley, I was sure.

They or someone with them had entered the house.

Then, two possibilities.

Everyone slaughtered.

Or, most people murdered apart from someone they wanted kept alive.

And the fake cops had gotten in their car and driven back down the valley.

Me watching them join their colleagues at the base of the lane.

Willing them to leave.

Delighted when they did.

Oh my God.

Reaching the top of the stairs, I saw Robert Grange's shot-up body at the far end of the hall. No way was he alive with those wounds. I didn't go to him right away. First, I checked the nearby rooms—a laundry room, two studies, three spare bedrooms, all empty.

Standing over Robert, I listened for any sounds, but there were none. Crouching low, I rapidly glanced into the master bedroom. The room looked empty. I entered to be sure.

Sheets on the bed were ruffled. Celia must have been in there, though she was nowhere to be seen.

I'd expected that. There was blood on the opposite door, leading into the twins' room. She'd dashed there, been injured in the process, but almost certainly managed to get in the room. That gave me zero comfort; the door was off its hinges and the room was completely insecure.

The twins' room was the last to check in the house. If the twins were dead, my life was over.

I wiped sweat off my hands, gripped the gun, moved across the hallway, and got ready.

Faye spotted the police squad car at the bottom of the lane that led up the valley. She was relieved because her eyes were getting tired and much more driving would have been hazardous. Her headlights picked up the squad vehicle while she turned onto the lane, and she could see that the car was empty. Probably they were on foot, checking their surroundings. She was relieved the cops were nowhere to be seen. If they had been, she'd feel obliged to stop and engage in small talk with them. Fatigued at this late hour, she was crying out for her bed as much as Billy was. Thank God she'd driven up the lane so many times that she could do it with her eyes closed. Five more minutes and they'd be home.

I kicked the door back and rushed into the twins' bedroom. Celia was on the ground. Whoever had shot her had done so either with amusement or anger. As well as the bullet entry wound in her forehead, she'd been shot six times in the chest and stomach. I imagined the killer standing over her, her dead body flinching as he pumped more rounds into her frail torso. Bastard.

The twins were nowhere to be seen, yet one of the two single beds had been slept in. It was Tom's bed. I sat on his bed and murmured, "Dear Lord, no."

What the hell was happening? Had they been kidnapped? Murdered and their bodies removed? That would make no sense. The only blood in the room was that surrounding Celia's dead body. The poor woman had come in here for a reason. And it was to protect. One of the twins had been in here; the other was most likely out with Faye. Unless Faye and the other twin were dead somewhere on the property.

I had to get my thinking straight and search for anything in the room that might help me understand what had happened. So many times I'd searched rooms—partly in the way that police forensics teams do, but also looking for things that only spies know may be relevant. Though time wasn't on my side to conduct a thorough search. My thinking accelerated in the way it always did when I was under extreme pressure.

Only Tom was in here. Celia comes in. Locks the door. Knows it won't hold. Courageously puts herself between the killer and the boy. She tells the boy to hide. Where would he go?

I rolled under Tom's bed. The teddy bear that I'd bought him was there. Why would he discard the favorite toy, when in a situation of abject terror he would have clung on to it for dear life? If it had been grabbed off him, it would be lying on the floor away from the bed. I picked it up, got out from under the bed, and pulled back the drawstring to activate its voice recorder. What I heard chewed me up.

An eastern European man's voice. Most likely Russian.

Lisping.

His words: "I know you're under the bed. It's going to hurt if I have to drag you out."

Tom had recorded the man's voice, knowing it was his only chance to be rescued.

I had no idea who the man was.

I tensed as I heard a car approaching.

Pulling back the window curtain slightly, I could see a car's headlights. It was drawing closer. But I had no way of identifying who it was in this darkness.

I muttered, "Shit," ran downstairs, and shoved Tom's teddy in my backpack. After grabbing the detective's SIG Sauer P229 pistol and four spare magazines, I put my backpack on. I left the house and picked up the other murdered detective's pistol.

Just as a car reached the rise of the valley, fifty yards away.

One of the house's external security lights came on as it detected the movement of the approaching vehicle. I could clearly see that the driver was Faye and that in the back was Billy. She screeched to a halt when she saw me standing stock-still in her headlights, a gun in my hand and a dead body close to my feet.

I shouted, "Faye, Faye!"

Faye's mouth was wide open in shock and terror. She put her car into reverse and drove fast away from me.

I sprinted toward her, desperate that she should know what I'd found and that things were not as they appeared.

Faye stopped the car at the head of the lane, tried to put it into first gear, and fumbled the action.

Billy was shouting something.

I was twenty yards away, still calling to Faye.

Faye finally engaged gears and put her foot to the floor.

I lunged at the driver's door, but missed the handle by inches as Faye sped down the lane.

She was always a dreadful driver. Not now, though. She was too fast for me to pursue her on foot and try to persuade her to stop and listen.

I dropped to my knees, my head to the sky.

I heard sirens in the distance. Many of them. But I stayed still, tears rolling down my cheeks, wanting the world to swallow me up. Just let them take you, I told myself. The cops can end the pain. Or shoot at them and allow them to gun you down. Anything is better than this.

Tom had been kidnapped.

I'd be blamed for it, but that outcome didn't even feature in my thinking. I imagined the poor boy in the back of one of the cars I'd spotted on the main road at the bottom of the valley.

I had to get him back.

No. I just couldn't let this end here.

I had a boy to save.

And a bastard to catch.

I got off my knees and vanished.

Zhukov looked at the boy by his side.

Next to him was the female member of his team, the doctor. She rolled up Tom's pajama sleeve, momentarily rammed his head down as cop cars raced by in the opposite direction, and injected him with drugs. Tom yelped. Within ten seconds he was comatose.

Zhukov called Edward Carley. "Sir—it's done. We have the package and are heading to the location."

That location was outside Washington, D.C.

Carley replied, "Good. Supervise proceedings at the location. Then I want you to head back to Roanoke and await my further instructions."

Carley hung up. Everything had gone according to plan.

Things were bad enough for Will Cochrane. Now they were about to become infinitely worse.

SEVENTEEN

The Scottish police car wound its way along the country lane outside Edinburgh, rugged hills on either side. Sheep that had been sheltering from the blustery weather bleated and scattered.

The lane was a dead end, only one house at its end.

The police car stopped outside the house. One male and one female exited the vehicle and knocked on the door.

Inside, James was rubbing flea powder into the fur of his beagle, Tess. She seemed to love the attention. James, however, was going through the motions. He was in a daze, thinking only about Sarah.

He kept telling himself not to panic. Sarah wasn't dead. She was in some kind of trouble, probably. Or she was being unfaithful. Funny how the thought that she might be screwing another guy was one he hoped turned out to be true. No, not funny. Nothing was funny.

If she was dead, his world would collapse.

He knew the knock on the door was the police. Few people came here. Those that did were usually Amazon deliverymen. But that only happened when Sarah was around and in full online shopping flow. And he'd been waiting day and night for the police to show up.

He went to the door, his hands clammy and still holding the flea powder. "It's to do with my wife," he told the female uniformed police officer who was standing in front of him.

She nodded.

It was 6:20 A.M. when detectives Painter and Kopański arrived at the base of the drive leading up to the Granges' home.

Just off the main road, the squad car belonging to the murdered cops was still in situ. Tape cordoned off the area and forensics experts were poring over the scene. A cluster of uniformed and plainclothes officers were standing outside the cordon, just watching.

The NYPD detectives walked over to a man they knew—Detective Andrew Haine, Richmond PD.

"Quite a mess, Andrew." Painter looked at the car and the bloody area of scrubland twenty yards away. The cops' bodies were no longer there. All the murder victims had been taken away hours before. "I've got the headlines, but tell us in more detail what happened?"

Haine barely glanced at Painter. "We're still collating results."

"Yeah, but what happened?"

The Richmond detective resented the presence of the NYPD on his patch. They had no jurisdiction here. "We have three scenes. This one; the one outside the house; and the one in the house. What happened here is that Cochrane approached the vehicle, probably got talking to them, they got out of their car, he shot them. Then he dumped their bodies where you can now see their blood. Last night you wouldn't have been able to see them unless you were looking with a flashlight."

Kopański said, "You know it's Cochrane because of bootprints?"

"Among other things, correct. The prints match the ones you supplied us from his room in the Waldorf Astoria. They're everywhere—around the car, around the bodies."

Painter said, "Remember, Cochrane is still only a *suspect*. There's a possibility he's innocent."

Detective Haine laughed. "Would you bet your house on that?"

Painter didn't reply.

Her acid-scarred colleague stated, "Motive was to get the cops out of the way before he approached the house. You think he did that on foot?"

Haine nodded. "We've got his tracks going up the side of the lane to the kill zone. There's also evidence of the squad driving up there last night, but that would have been a routine check on the Granges and their guards before the officers came back down here and got murdered." Haine pulled out a stick of gum, tore it in half, and popped it into his mouth. "Got murdered," he repeated. "I've drafted in everyone I can from state and county. We've put a net over the area. Still, it's a vast zone to cover."

"The boy will slow him down."

"That's what I'm hoping."

"But then again, Cochrane's evaded capture so far," Painter said. "Where are Faye and Billy?"

"We've put them in a safe house in Roanoke. Billy's going to be homeschooled for the time being. Faye's got an emergency leave of absence from her work. And they'll have twenty-four-seven protection until Cochrane's caught."

"We need to go up to the Granges' house," Kopański said.

Haine looked him in the eye. "This is my investigation."

Kopański shrugged. "No, it's not."

"What did you say?"

"I said it's not. In fact, all things to do with Cochrane are our business." He showed Haine the attorney general's letter authorizing Painter and Kopański to have primacy on the case and ordering all other officers to assist them in every way possible.

"You've got to be kidding me."

Painter stepped in and played diplomat. "Joe and I don't want the glory. We just want to catch the son of a bitch. Whether we arrest him or kill him, everyone involved will get the credit, you included." She added something that was true. "In fact, Joe and I would prefer not to get any publicity.

That kind of stuff doesn't flick our switches." She knew Haine was the opposite. "*Please*. Take us to the house."

Haine hesitated before saying, "Okay, then. But I'm coming with you." He drove them up the lane to the house, stopping his car at the rise. "This is as far as we can go by car. The rest is on foot. Here." He handed them plastic shoe covers. "And don't touch anything."

They walked to another cordon that surrounded the spot outside the house where the first Roanoke detective had been gunned down.

"Any new updates?" Haine asked one of the three forensics officers working the scene.

The expert replied that nothing had changed. The police squad car had come up here at some point in the evening. After it was gone, Cochrane had arrived—his bootprints were everywhere. The murdered detective was either already out doing a perfunctory check of the perimeter, or more likely he'd heard something and came to check. Probably Cochrane had deliberately lured him out, based on the fact the detective wasn't wrapped up warm. He'd come out here quickly, thought there was nothing to see, turned to go back in, and that's when Cochrane attacked him.

"Attacked?" asked Painter of the forensics officer.

"Walked up to him and shot him twice in the back of the head."

"Come with me," said Haine to the NYPD detectives.

They followed him into the Granges' home.

The place was abuzz with Virginia state and

county officers and forensics experts. Police tape
was everywhere, cameras were flashing, videos
being recorded, and everyone was going about
their business while barely uttering a word. Haine,
Painter, and Kopański walked along a white paper
path that had been laid down by the forensics team
and designated the only place that other officers
were allowed to walk. The tape around the path
had various signs at stages in the house, including
STOP, ONLY FORENSICS PAST THIS POINT, AREA NOT
ANALYZED, and DEAD VICTIM.

DEAD VICTIM was the sign that greeted them
at the entrance to the only downstairs bedroom.
Inside were two forensics officers, head to toe in
white coveralls, masks on their faces, and rubber-
gloved hands taking swabs from the bedsheets
belonging to the second murdered detective.

"Anything deviate from what you last told me?"
Haine asked one of them.

The forensics officer shook her head.

The Richmond detective led them up the stairs.
"This is why Cochrane came here." He pointed at
the pool of blood belonging to Robert Grange at
the end of the hall. "Mr. Grange came out of the
bathroom, intending to enter the master bedroom.
He stopped when he saw Cochrane standing close
to where we are. Cochrane immediately shot him."
He walked along the strip of white paper laid over
the cream carpet. "This is the master bedroom.
Celia Grange was in bed here, door was open, she
saw her husband gunned down. Her immediate
instinct was to protect the boy." He led them into
the twins' room. "She rushed in here, got shot in

the process but not badly enough to stop her locking the door. Tom Koenig was in here. She stood in front of the door—a human shield—knowing that someone as strong as Cochrane would easily be able to kick it in. It was incredibly brave. She got knocked onto her back. Was then shot. The boy was grabbed."

Painter surveyed the room, though most of it was off limits to them. "Keep an open mind, Andrew. It may well be Cochrane walked into this. He wasn't the killer and kidnapper."

Haine pointed at the forensics officer. "These days, investigators can move very fast. Ain't technology a wonderful thing? All of the bullet shells around the bodies and all of the bullets *in* the bodies have been examined. We've compared the results to the ballistics analysis you released from the Waldorf murder. One hundred percent match."

Half a mile away from where the two uniformed police officers had been shot, Simon Tap watched the numerous officers working the scene through high-powered binoculars, while listening to the intercept device Knox had given him.

Painter and Kopański came into view. It was the first time the former Delta Force operative had seen them in person, having come here based on an earlier intercepted call. But there was no doubting it was them because they matched the photos Knox had given him. Painter was walking awkwardly because of her artificial limb and one side of Kopański's face was an unmistakable mess.

They entered their vehicle.

Tap didn't follow them. Cochrane was somewhere in the area. All that mattered was that if he was spotted, Painter would be immediately notified.

With Cochrane cornered, the cops' duty was to first try to negotiate him down. Whether that worked or not didn't matter to Tap.

What did was that he'd have a window of opportunity to get into position. From a distance. With a rifle.

And end this—once and for all.

EIGHTEEN

After the Scottish police car departed, James Goldsmith was sitting in the kitchen with his head in his hands.

Grief hadn't yet taken hold. Instead, he was in shock, his mind and body filled with pain and dread.

Every brain cell in his head had wanted the police to say there was a perfectly good explanation for his inability to locate Sarah.

Instead, they'd looked him in the eye and said, "Mr. Goldsmith—brace yourself." And they then told him what they knew.

When they left, Tess was curled up on his feet. Whether she sensed something was wrong or not, she seemed to want to keep him warm.

James smoothed her while crying. "What are we going to do?" he said, looking at nothing. His nostrils were burning, head giddy and throbbing. Nothing seemed of this world.

Will Cochrane and his sister Sarah had barely spoken during the last few years. For a long time, she hadn't known he was a spy and had assumed that he was a criminal because of his furtive attitude and frequent absences. When he told her the truth in an attempt to win his sibling back, the declaration backfired because Sarah realized it put her and James in significant danger. They'd had to be protected by Will's allies from a man who wanted to kill Sarah just to make a point to Will. One of the protectors, a retired woman called Betty who was like a mother to Will, had been killed. Sarah had never forgiven Will for putting her in such danger. Even though none of it had been his fault.

Some good did come out of that. The event was a catalyst for James and Sarah to reappraise their increasingly bourgeois London lifestyle. Suddenly, their surroundings and ambitions seemed shallow and unsustainable. With no kids to rein them in and ground them, it had felt like they were approaching an age where they were acting like grown-up children at a party full of people half their age. It was time to get out.

All was now lost—the house, the money, the new beginnings, any sense of normality or hope. Most of all, James had lost the woman he'd been with since university.

His lovely Sarah, tall, with long blond hair— though the police said she'd cut her hair and dyed it brunette before she was killed. That was a strange thing to do. Mind you, she'd been increasingly prone to whimsy. He liked that about her. No longer the highly strung metropolitan lawyer; instead, a woman who didn't take life so seriously. Until recently, that is.

This would be his greatest test. His beloved was no longer there to be the strong one in a wretched set of circumstances. He had to be that person. He had to dig deep and summon the courage to sort out his affairs, somehow focus his thinking and do the right things. Grief had to wait, he told himself over and over. If he sprang into action, then he could grieve properly without his mind being befuddled by worries about the future.

He got to his feet, unsteadily at first, grasping the back of the chair until he felt ready to move. Taking Tess out was the first thing he needed to do. He clipped on her lead and said, "Come on, girl. Bit of rain outside, but not enough to bother us, eh?"

Wellington boots and raincoat on, he walked as fast as his asthmatic lungs would allow him, Tess pulling hard on the lead as they moved over the hills surrounding their home. Ordinarily, the fine rain and windless air would have made the trek a pleasure for James, who adored this type of weather. Now it didn't register, his brain screaming at him to turn back, shut the door to his home, and just wait for all the pain to go. But he had Tess to think about. She needed this, and step one was that he wasn't going to let her down.

Four miles later, they reached the nearest dwelling to their home—a thatched cottage belonging to a blunt-talking but nice farmer and his family.

No doubt the farmer was away working in the fields somewhere, but his wife was usually to be found at home.

Smoke was coming out of the chimney, lights were on inside. James knocked on the door, rainwater dripping off his coat's hood onto his face. "Mrs. McTavish. Good morning. I have a favor to ask."

The stout middle-aged woman, apron covering her blouse and ankle-length skirt, looked suspicious. "Good morning to you, Mr. Goldsmith. I don't have much time today for favors."

"It's just that . . . I've got a lot to do. I may need to go to London. Certainly I'm going to be stuck in Edinburgh for a few days. There's a lot of paperwork. Things I need to sort out. But I can't leave Tess on her own." He held out her lead. "Will you look after her while I'm gone? It may only be a few days. She's no bother and will eat anything." He tried to smile. "In fact, she'll try to eat too much of anything. I have to watch her on that."

The Scottish woman rubbed her hands on her apron, not touching the lead. "Can't you put her in a kennel? It's a madhouse here, and one more mouth to feed and set of legs to walk isn't going to make my life any easier."

"I'd pay you, same rate as kennels."

"I wouldn't accept your money."

"I know . . . I . . . Everything is all so last minute. I don't know what else to do."

"Not sure my husband would be happy when he gets home and finds your Tess staying with us."

James couldn't stop his grief. "Sarah's . . . Sarah's . . . Mrs. McTavish—the police have just visited. My wife's been murdered in America."

The woman's demeanor instantly changed. "Oh, you poor, poor man." She grabbed the dog lead. "You must come in. I'll make you a cup of tea."

"No, no. Thank . . . You'll look after Tess?"

Sympathy was all over Mrs. McTavish's face, together with shock. "For as long as it takes, my dear. You need people around you right now. You can't be on your own."

James nodded. "That's why I need to get busy now."

"Come on in, Tess," she said while pulling gently on the lead. Tess's tail wagged as she picked up the scent of baking inside the cottage. To James, she said, "I genuinely don't know what to say. Sarah seemed like a lovely lady. I'm so, so, very, very sorry. You have got to focus on helping the police find the killer."

"It won't bring her back, though, will it? And she's so far away right now." He walked away, rubbing tears from his eyes, stumbling a bit.

One hour later, he reached his home. Knowing his mind was weak, he told himself to just go through the motions and get ready. Performing tasks might distract him and strengthen his mind. He showered and shaved, put on the suit he always wore when he had the most important business to attend to in Edinburgh, picked up a pen and paper, and laughed as more tears ran down his face. For the briefest moment, out of habit, he'd been about to write Sarah a note saying that he was leaving. How absurd.

He opened his attaché case, checked its contents, and ensured the back door was bolted on the inside. All was nearly ready for him to depart. But there was one more thing to be done. He collected a length of rope from the workshop, knotted and arranged it so that it was hanging from a large meat hook that was screwed into an oak beam in the kitchen ceiling, stood on a chair beneath the beam, placed the noose over his head, and said, "I'm coming to get you, Sarah my love."

He kicked the chair away and dropped.

One minute later, he was dead.

"I don't need to get on that bloody contraption, I'm perfectly capable of walking by myself." Dickie Mountjoy was infuriated that his momentary ill health on the flight had been flagged to JFK airport staff. They were trying to insist that he be shuttled to baggage claim and immigration on a motorized cart.

No doubt used to dealing with such difficult passengers in these types of situations, the American ground crew woman in front of him kept a fixed grin on her face. "Sir, look at it this way. Everyone else has to walk. We're giving you VIP treatment."

"No, you're not. You're treating me like some damn invalid!"

"The captain of your flight was worried about you."

"He should have been more worried about flying

the plane. It was just a bit of heartburn. I get it all the time. All this fuss and bother is likely to give me even more indigestion if you keep this up."

"Mr. Mountjoy—I . . ."

"I'm not getting on that thing! Have I made myself clear enough?"

The woman knew she wasn't going to win the argument. "Okay, sir. But if you need anything, you just approach a member of our staff. Deal?"

"What?"

"Will you do that for me?"

"Yes, yes, whatever."

He straightened his back, ignored the pain in his legs from the cramped flight and old age, and marched toward the baggage claim area.

Forty-five minutes later, he was standing by the airport's taxi rank, ready to be taken to the apartment he'd secured for two days near Times Square.

In Dickie's London home, Phoebe was watering the major's plants and adjusting the settings of his radiators due to colder weather hitting the city. David was with his girlfriend, watching her putter about the place while he sat on the sofa drinking a mug of tea.

"Sure there's nothing I can do to help?" the mortician asked Phoebe.

"No. I'm nearly finished. I'll come back tomorrow, just to make sure everything's fine before he returns the day after."

"He should never have traveled that far at his age. And what on earth does he hope to achieve, anyway?" David blew over the lip of his mug. "Cochrane's nowhere to be found, despite the fact it looks like half of America is searching for him. What's Dickie going to do? Just turn up in New York and find him?"

Phoebe turned to face David. "I've no idea. But you know what the major's like when he gets an idea in his head."

"Yeah, he becomes a raving liability."

Phoebe laughed, though the sound wasn't quite right. She patted a duster against a radiator, her expression now quizzical and her voice distant. "Will can't have done what they say he's done. That's not him. It's just not him."

David agreed. "Heard on the news this morning that today American police are going to reveal the identity of the victim. Maybe that'll help Will. Somehow prove he's innocent."

"How would that work?"

David shrugged. "Dunno, really. Perhaps if she's some criminal or something, police might realize another criminal killed her. Wanted her dead."

"You're not making any sense."

David knew he wasn't, but like Phoebe he was trying to come up with any reason why Will hadn't gone insane. "What do you fancy for dinner tonight?" was all he could think to ask.

Phoebe collected her watering can and other items. "Maybe a Chinese takeaway?"

"I've got a better idea. How about I cook our favorite Szechuan chicken?"

"Perfect. That sounds . . ." She felt herself

getting teary. "Will never told us why he was going to New York."

"He said he'd tell us when he got back, remember? That he was making plans. He's always been a bit secretive like that."

"Not with us." She smoothed a finger against David's face. "You know one of the things I love about you? You don't do things like running around being a spy and then murdering people."

David could sense Phoebe's emotions were high. "I'm not *that* normal. I'm a mortician." He smiled, hoping his dark humor would lift Phoebe's spirits. "Sometimes I have to cut up dead bodies to make them look pretty again."

"When you put it like that . . ." Her thoughts became distracted again. "I feel cross with Will. Why didn't he hand himself in to the police and tell them he was innocent?"

David stood and put his arms around her. "Either because he knew they wouldn't believe him, or he's guilty as sin."

"Don't say that."

"What?"

Phoebe's face was flushed, her head shaking, tears now visible. "The guilty thing. He can't be guilty. Can't!"

Marty Fleet entered the U.S. Attorney General's oak-paneled office, as ever wondering how it would feel to sit in the man's chair. That possibility was at least a decade away, probably longer. By then one or two other AGs would have come and gone. Fleet didn't begrudge that. He deeply admired his boss, a man who'd served his time in the trenches as a prosecuting and defense lawyer, as well as being a visiting professor of law at Harvard.

Behind the hawkish-looking and bespectacled sixty-three-year-old AG were bookcases crammed with leather-bound volumes about U.S. law. On his huge oak desk was only one piece of paper. That was typical of the AG. He was the most uncluttered and unflustered man Fleet knew. Compared to Fleet's desk in his adjacent office, which typically was strewn with piles of case files, the AG would meticulously deal with one matter at a time, and to do so he had the uncanny ability to summarize huge amounts of information onto a single bullet-pointed sheet of paper.

Fleet sat opposite him. "You heard what happened at the Granges' place?"

The AG looked at him over the top of his glasses. "Yes, I've heard."

"It escalates matters."

The AG knew his employee was angling for something. "Beyond authorizing technical interception, which we did earlier, it doesn't escalate to my department."

"Even considering Will Cochrane's background?"

"His background has no relevance to what is a straightforward criminal matter, beyond informing certain law enforcement officials of the nature of the man they seek. It's a manhunt conducted by police officers. Let them deal with it."

Fleet could see that he was wearing the AG's patience down. "I have a thought that may be pertinent to our office."

The AG waited.

"The U.S. government is constitutionally blameless for Cochrane's crimes."

The AG laughed. "Of course it is. Cochrane's the one who pulled the trigger. He will be caught, tried, and if, as seems certain, he's found guilty, he will be severely punished. At the least, life imprisonment. More likely it will be capital punishment, since Virginia has the death penalty. He's a cop killer now. If he's convicted, I'm not going to ask for clemency."

"I'm not suggesting you do."

"Then what *are* you suggesting, Marty?"

Fleet placed his fingertips together. "The first duty of government is to protect its citizens."

"Get on with it."

"But that doesn't mean we have to protect everyone all the time, does it? Sometimes we tell our citizens to do things that will put them in danger."

The AG glanced at his watch. "You know full well the answer to that. There is nothing in the Constitution on this subject, though the precedents and assumptions have over time been accepted as sacrosanct. A soldier is sent to war by us, and we know he might be killed. A fireman is deployed into an inferno. A police officer is told to stop an armed robbery. And on and on it goes. But the accepted and correct presumption in all such cases is that those individuals know the risks and are directed to take action that will save numerous lives. Thus, the government's first duty is upheld accordingly."

"But we're missing something." Fleet smiled. "Will Cochrane has made me think about this."

"What do you mean?"

Fleet answered, "I think Will Cochrane's case requires us to make an amendment to the United States Constitution."

NINETEEN

Lieutenant Pat Brody of the Office of the Deputy Commissioner, Public Information, faced cameras and journalists with recording devices in the Waldorf Astoria's ground-floor Empire Room. He gripped the sides of the lectern hard enough for his knuckles to whiten, and read out verbatim the script supplied to him by Kopański over the telephone.

"Ladies and gentlemen. At the rear of the room are information packets containing more details on what I'm about to tell you, including precise locations, identities of most of the personalities involved, timings, and various other data, all of which you are at liberty to reveal to the public.

"Yesterday evening there was a major incident approximately twenty miles outside of Roanoke, Virginia. Two uniformed police officers and two detectives from Roanoke were shot dead while protecting a rural home belonging to the married retired academics Robert and Celia Grange. Alongside their niece, the Granges were looking after their grandnephews—twin ten-year-old boys.

"The identities of the twins and their aunt are *not* in the information packets, nor will I reveal their identities. If any of you ascertain their identities by other means and reveal their names, that will be deemed by the NYPD as a criminal offense, and charges *will* be brought against you.

"After shooting the police officers, the killer went to the second floor and shot Robert Grange. When this happened, one of the twins was in Roanoke, dining with his aunt. But the other twin was sleeping in his room. In an attempt to protect the boy, Celia Grange put herself between him and the killer. She was murdered as a result."

The room was silent as Brody took a sip of water.

"The boy was taken by the killer. There are no indications that he was injured enough to cause blood loss. The boy and the killer then vanished. There is a manhunt underway for both throughout the state of Virginia."

A journalist called out, "Why can't you reveal the kidnapped boy's name? If we release it, witnesses might come forward."

Brody answered, "The kidnapped boy's twin brother is in protective custody. His identity must remain a secret. You guys might not deliberately do it, but if you print any details that give the kidnapper a hint of his whereabouts, we will have a major situation."

He continued his briefing.

"Our prime suspect for the killings is a man who was attempting to legally adopt the boys. During the last few days, his circumstances changed drastically. The adoption became impossible, and he became desperate. He went to the house to snatch both, found only one of them there, but by then it was too late. He had already killed six people. He decided to take the boy who was there.

"Forensic tests remain ongoing, but here's what I can tell you. The murder weapon used to kill the above-mentioned victims was the same murder weapon used to kill the woman in the Waldorf earlier this week. I can now reveal the Waldorf victim's identity. Her name was Sarah Goldsmith. Her family has been notified of her death."

The journalists frantically wrote in shorthand.

"The boots worn by the murderer in Virginia are the same boots that were worn by the man who occupied room 1944 on the night of Mrs. Goldsmith's murder.

"That man was sighted by the aunt and nephew upon their return home to the Granges' property.

"Will Cochrane is the man we seek. Sarah Goldsmith was his sister."

Questions were fired at him.

Brody held up his hand. "I can't add anything further at this stage beyond encouraging you to advise your readers and viewers to exercise absolute caution if they spot someone resembling Cochrane. He's already proven that he is highly dangerous. Almost certainly, he's mentally unstable. There are other reasons to do with his background, which we cannot go into, but please make it clear that nobody—repeat, nobody—must approach him. If anyone sees him, they should immediately inform the police. We'll then send in a SWAT team to take him down." Brody looked around and saw that the journalists were hanging on his every word. "Make no mistake—right now Will Cochrane is the most dangerous fugitive on U.S. soil."

Michael Stein drove his rental car along a glistening Virginia lake, the vista to his right undulating and steep with forests and outcrops of rock. In the distance he could see an isolated wooden house that sat partially on stilts above the shore, along with outhouses and what appeared to be a wire coop, possibly for livestock.

He'd never been here before. A year ago, Will Cochrane had told him about the Russian man who lived here and the teenage daughter he cared for alone.

Back then, Will's instruction had been clear. "He's a last resort if anything bad happens to me. If you're able to, talk to him." Aside from supplying him with details about the man, Will had said nothing more to Michael on the subject, no matter how hard the Mossad operative tried to pry out of him what he meant.

He parked by the front door of the house, got out, and pulled a chain attached to an old-fashioned bell, having already decided that if the man wasn't in he'd wait for him to show up.

But the door opened. A man in his sixties with graying blond hair stood before him, wearing oil-skin waders and a hemp sweater that made him look like a nineteenth-century whaler. His eyes gleamed with intelligence, though one of them drooped, and his smooth face had clearly been subject to reconstructive surgery.

The Russian looked him over. "I suggest you might be Michael Stein, formerly of Israeli Intelligence."

"How did you know that?"

"Because a year ago William Cochrane told me that one day you might visit me. He described you. You match that appearance. Plus, I can smell an intelligence officer a mile away."

"But you were right that I'm a *former* intelligence officer."

"The stink never leaves us."

"A year ago I was still in service. He told you subsequently that I'd left?"

"No."

"Then . . . ?"

"You have a look of contentment. It's not an expression ever shared by serving operatives."

Michael had been warned by Cochrane to be very careful with the man who used to carry the code name Antaeus. Once he had been an opponent of Will Cochrane's, a brilliant puppeteer spy and the most powerful intelligence officer in Russia's foreign spy agency, SVR. Cochrane had tried to kill him by placing a bomb in the car Antaeus always drove in alone. Due to last-minute unforeseen circumstances, Antaeus had picked up his wife and daughter. He survived the explosion. They didn't. Will was tormented by their deaths. Years later, when they had their last head-to-head confrontation and Will had outsmarted Antaeus, Will was able to offer the Russian spy some small recompense. Will had discovered that Antaeus had a daughter he didn't know about from a pre-marriage fling with an American diplomat. When the mother accidentally killed her husband and ended up in life imprisonment for treason, Will had orchestrated events so that Antaeus could step in and act as father to his daughter, Crystal, providing he defected to America. The enticement had been sufficient to bring him here.

Antaeus was no longer a participant in the secret world. Alongside parenthood and the peaceful existence he had in America, he flexed his vast intellect by producing groundbreaking theses on archaeological sites on the East Coast. The discipline suited him, because he was a man from another age, and not just in appearance. A gentleman who'd eschewed the crudeness of murder while fighting the West, he favored a calculated guile that would have made a chess master blush with envy.

And that's what made him so dangerous. He was always ten steps ahead of most people with comparable cognitive power to his own.

"May I come in?" Michael asked.

Antaeus glanced over his shoulder. The sound of a piano came from inside. "My daughter is practicing for her music exams. She cannot be disturbed by the sight of a strange Israeli man entering our home." He withdrew a World War II tobacco tin from his wader pocket and placed a cheroot in his mouth. "In any case, I have a job to do outside. Join me if you wish; go back to where you came from, if you don't."

He grabbed a walking stick as tall as him, on its head a curly ram's horn.

Michael watched Antaeus for a moment, noticing the limp in his right leg. That too would have been Cochrane's doing. Even though he'd united the Russian with his daughter, Michael wondered how much resentment Antaeus retained toward the former British operative.

He caught up with Antaeus as he walked inches from the lake's gently lapping edge.

The Russian didn't look at him as he said, "The last time I saw Cochrane, we walked this exact same path. Like you, he came here for my help."

"It must have taken courage to do that."

Antaeus lit his cheroot. "It did, but it didn't diminish the desire I had to club him over the head and toss his body into the water. Possibly the only reason I didn't was because I fly-fish in these waters and wouldn't want to dine on a trout that had fed on his carcass."

"Perhaps that would have been appropriate?"

"Not to a man of my tastes." He stopped, staring out to his beloved lake. "You've come to talk to me about Mr. Cochrane's predicament."

"Of course."

"Do you know why he told you to come to me if ever he was in trouble?"

"No."

"Factually, nor do I—he never told me—though I believe there is one strong probability."

Normally repulsed by the scent of tobacco, for some reason Michael was enjoying the aromatic smell emanating from the Russian's cigar. "He respects your intellect."

"I've never been susceptible to flattery, Mr. Stein." Awkwardly, Antaeus bent over by a large tree stump that was partially excavated. He seemed to be doing something to the stump, though Michael couldn't see what because he had his back to him. He returned to Michael by the lakeside, uncoiling a length of wire between him and the tree stump twenty yards away. "I believe it's more to do with trust. He trusts that I of all people would know what it feels like to be out of the secret world and alone. If he's in trouble, that means his former masters no longer support him. Ergo he is alone, and ergo he tells you to visit me because I will, as our dear Americans say, *get it*."

"You know what happened in New York?"

"Yes."

"The train out of Philly?"

"Everything, including what happened last night near Roanoke."

"Is he guilty of those crimes?"

"No."

"How can you be sure?"

Antaeus dusted mud off a flat stone, then stopped and looked at Michael. "Will Cochrane *is* a murderer. He may not have meant to destroy my family, but he most certainly intended to end my life. And it would take me hours to recount to you the numerous other killings he's conducted, those that

I know about, in any case. I suspect you too may know he's quite capable of pulling a trigger."

"I saved his life. He did the same for me."

"And in the course of his saving you, others died."

Michael nodded.

A rainbow trout jumped nearby, prompting Antaeus to smile and wonder if he should take his boat out this afternoon and try his luck with a nymph and two wet fly droppers. Crystal adored his baked trout and bacon recipe. "Will Cochrane is a lonely man. Other people are not like him. He knows that, and to a large extent has been able to live with that reality because he adores people and finds them fascinating. In that respect, he is like a human-looking creature who has fallen to earth and been told to make sense of it all. And, crucially, to protect those who live here. That's his purpose. For him to go on a rampage would be tantamount to him putting a gun to his own head. He'd be destroying himself."

"Maybe that's the point. He wants to destroy the kinds of people he once secretly protected. This is his suicide pill."

Antaeus wagged a finger. "He's not that man. And if there were any chance his mind could snap, that would have happened years ago, given what he was put through. No, no. He'd made plans to adopt twins. That would have been his focus."

"So what's happening? None of this makes sense."

"It makes perfect sense."

Michael said nothing.

"This is calculated revenge. He's been set up. Some person or persons wish to take away the one thing he cherishes the most."

"His purpose to serve the West?"

"No. He was prepared to give that up for a new kind of purpose. What's being expertly and systematically taken away from him is his dignity. Everything he's done, every sacrifice, act of heroism, rescue, result: none of it matters now. He'll be remembered as the man who killed his sister, American cops, and a family, and kidnapped a boy. If he manages to stay on the run, I fear it will keep getting worse for him."

"How has he been set up so convincingly?"

"I'm only armed with the same media facts as you. And there'll be facts missing from the media reports. I don't know for sure how this has been constructed."

Michael wasn't going to accept that answer. "How would *you* have done this?"

Antaeus weighed his response. "Whoever is orchestrating this revenge is extremely clever. He or she has trained experts on the payroll. But they do what they're told. There is a master hand at play, though it's hidden from me. In answer to your question, I probably would have been able to get Cochrane to this stage, though where I'd go from here, I've no idea. There are several possibilities about what happened in the New York hotel room. I think all of them are plausible and ingenious. The setup at the Granges' was also elaborate. The mastermind predicted Cochrane would go there, though he had no way of knowing, nor did he care, that he might be there on the evening of the massacre. That was a bonus but unnecessary. The damage to Cochrane had already been done."

"Do you think Cochrane will come to you in person for help?"

"For three reasons, no. First, he knows that police and Secret Service occasionally check up on me to make sure my former Russian peers aren't trying to serve me a cup of polonium in return for my betrayal. Second, he won't want to inadvertently draw cops to my home, risk a shootout, and potentially compromise the safety of Crystal. Third, he knows that if he comes here, part of me will be amused at the sight of his wretched condition. He wouldn't like that."

"I doubt his self-respect and ego are at the top of his agenda right now."

Antaeus shook his head. "It would be out of respect for me that he wouldn't want me to see him like that."

There was so much to Antaeus that remained hidden from Michael. He gave off an impression of shrewd intelligence and insight. Michael had worked with some of the sharpest minds in Mossad, but had never encountered anyone like this. "Is there anything that can be done to help him? That's why I'm here—to seek your guidance."

"And why would I help him?"

"Why not?"

"I expected a better response from you." Antaeus attached a small device to the end of the wire. "The correct answer is that I'll help him because if I don't, I fail myself. I could easily have been Will Cochrane." He gestured toward the tree stump. "That damn thing has been bothering me for months. I can't dig it out because the roots are too big. Thankfully, I have a license to purchase and safely utilize equipment that may help." He pulled Michael a couple of yards farther away from the tree stump. "You can be in Washington, D.C., in three hours. I need you there no later than that. You have a busy evening ahead of you. The chances of my idea working are approximately three percent. Even then, it won't help Cochrane stay alive much more than a few more days." He detonated the device, and an explosion wrenched the tree trunk out of the ground.

Antaeus examined the damage. "The problem has been uprooted." He turned to Stein. "That's what's happened to Cochrane."

Because of the late hour, all the offices in the attorney general's department were empty save Marty Fleet's.

He regretted having to work so late, though at least he had the reassurance that his sister's daycare nurse was willing to wait at his home for however long it would take. And he had no choice but to work for at least another couple of hours. His meeting with the attorney general and the country's top judges was set for 3 P.M. tomorrow. Before then he had to complete his research into U.S. constitutional law, state laws, medical codes of practice, mental health acts, and other regulations.

He took a gulp of his black coffee and continued reading the legal journals piled on his desk.

He doubted what he was doing would make one bit of difference to Cochrane. But he felt he had to do this to help others like him. Brave American heroes. Soldiers. Men who'd served their country with distinction. People who should have been decorated, but instead were hung out to dry by the government.

Men like Cochrane deserved so much better from the people who sent them to their deaths.

TWENTY

Tom Koenig had been awake for a long time, though he had no way of knowing whether it was night or day.

Some time ago, he'd awoken in the room and screamed, unable to see anything because a black hood was over his head, and unable to remove it because his hands were tied behind his back. He remembered last night being put in a police car, transferred to another car at the bottom of his granduncle and -aunt's lane, and being driven off. Then the woman in the backseat next to him injected his arm.

He didn't remember anything after that.

There were voices around him in the room. One of them belonged to the bad man who'd grabbed him from under the bed. His accent was weird, a bit like the pastry chef in the Roanoke bakery. And he could tell the woman was here. He'd never forget what she said to him last night in the car, before jabbing him with her syringe.

"Keep still, you little shit."

And there was a third person in here. A man. The sound of his voice made Tom rock back and forth while blubbing his young heart out.

In the chambers of the Supreme Court of the United States, Marty Fleet and the attorney general were sitting at a boardroom table facing the chief justice of the United States and eight associate justices.

The AG had told Fleet that he'd done a superb job and that he was to stay silent in today's meeting. Fleet's day would come when he could take the lead in such senior-level assemblies. But the judges—five women, including the chief justice, and four men—were extremely powerful individuals. The AG was nearing the end of his career. It didn't matter if he pissed off anyone. But he wasn't prepared to risk Fleet doing so while his career was still developing. So, Fleet was to keep his mouth shut and observe.

The AG commenced proceedings. "Your Honors, the purpose of this meeting is to ascertain whether legal resources should be devoted to exploring the possibility that we should petition for an amendment to our Constitution."

The judges were silent.

"The issue has been raised in my department"—the AG made no reference to Fleet—"based on the atrocities committed by wanted murderer Will Cochrane."

The chief justice interjected, "This isn't another attempt to interfere with states' decisions on whether to have the death penalty or not, is it? Or gun control? You know we've fought and lost those battles in the past."

"No. If Cochrane is caught, I'm certain he'll receive capital punishment. We can't and shouldn't interfere with the judicial process of the state he's tried in. But his case is a curious one, though not unprecedented."

"Damn right it's not unprecedented." The chief justice had too much respect for the AG to get impatient, though she was wondering where this was leading. "There've been plenty of other murders on our watch."

"And some of them have been conducted by men trained by our government." The AG produced his single sheet of notes, summarizing the vast amount of research Fleet had conducted. "Soldiers who run amok after they return home, cops who crack after visiting one crime scene too many—these are men and women we trained to shoot to kill. And we sent them into situations that would be psychologically intolerable for the average citizen."

"That's their job."

"It is, but the issue is what happens when that job is done? How can we ensure they don't put a gun to their head; or worse, point it at American people?"

"We can't guarantee they won't, and you know that."

The AG shook his head. "A traumatized officer, whether military or law enforcement, is currently subject to three forms of intervention. The first is the welfare from his or her unit. If they spot cracks beginning to appear, they can help rehabilitate the officer and keep an eye on him while he adjusts back into society. Sometimes that works. Other times warning signs are missed. Often, there simply isn't any welfare. The second is for the officer to voluntarily submit himself to the provisions under our mental health laws, or for those provisions to be forced onto him. That's essential, but again, mistakes can be made, or sometimes action is taken too late. The third is the law. If we suspect a former operative is about to go crazy and go on a mass shooting, or we catch the guy after the event, we apply the law."

The chief justice said, "I can't see how any of this relates to the Constitution."

"The fact that it *doesn't* currently relate to our Constitution is why we're in this room today." The AG knew that Fleet's heart would be in his mouth. He'd worked so hard on this. If it paid off, the AG would ensure Fleet received all praise. If it didn't, no one would know that this was Fleet's idea. "Will Cochrane is a former intelligence officer."

"A *British* Intelligence officer. Wherever you're heading with this, he can't be used as an example to change U.S. law."

"Actually, he's half British and half American. His father served in the CIA. And Cochrane served our country just as much as he served Britain. In any case, he's one of many examples of former American operatives falling foul of the law after they've been discharged." The AG eyed the judges.

"The issue is culpability. In Cochrane's case, who is to blame for his actions?"

One of the associate justices replied, "Cochrane, of course."

"Yes, Cochrane must be held to account for his crimes and pay the ultimate price. But who else is culpable?"

Nobody said anything.

"His former employers MI6 and CIA? The people who trained him to kill? The controllers who ordered him to go on missions? The ones who knew that the intolerable pressures they were placing him under would one day break even the strongest man? And ultimately we should ask ourselves"— this was the moment the AG had been leading up to—"whether the United States of America should be held to account if it doesn't prevent massacres such as those conducted by Cochrane."

An associate justice slapped his hand on the table. "You've got to be kidding, right? Why should we take the blame for the actions of a madman?"

"Because we made him mad." This came from the chief justice.

The AG added, "I'm not suggesting we take all the blame. But I do pose the question of whether we should consider absorbing *some* of the blame. My department has spent hours researching this. On the issue of state culpability for the criminal actions of a man it used to employ there is currently absolutely nothing in law that says America should take some responsibility."

"So what are you proposing?"

"I'm suggesting that our Constitution should be

amended to clearly state that if we train someone to be a killer and that person uses skills we taught him to commit murder without us doing everything in our power to care for the man and prevent his crimes, that the state should be tried alongside the perpetrator."

"Now hold on." The chief justice had a withering expression on her face. "Do you realize what you're asking?"

The AG held her gaze. "At this stage, I'm merely introducing a motion that we devote energies to further research my proposition."

The justices started talking fast and over each other.

The chief justice called for quiet and returned her attention to the AG. "You'd be opening a Pandora's box. Crime's on the increase, ergo more cops are likely to get traumatized in the line of duty. The war on terror has become an unpredictable mess, so we're going to have to deploy more soldiers who are likely to see and do stuff that gives them nightmares. Things are getting worse. It's almost certain we're going to see more men like Cochrane going crazy. By amending the Constitution in the way you're suggesting, if we don't stop our former officers from going on a rampage, we'd be in breach of the law. People would lose their jobs. For some of us the ramifications could be worse. And that's before we even get onto the subject of how much money we'd have to pay out to victims."

These were precisely the points the AG had earlier made to Fleet. Verbatim, the AG told the chief justice what Fleet had said. "The point of our

Constitution is to set in stone the duty of government and the expectations our citizens should have of our government. Our first duty is to protect America and its citizens."

"And in the context of people like Cochrane, we do that by applying the law."

"But in doing so, we wash our hands of any guilt we may have." The AG placed his sheet of paper in his jacket pocket. "The issue is one of prevention. If the amendment was made, imagine the lengths we'd go to in order to prevent men like Cochrane having access to firearms. We'd force him to have medical treatment. He'd get welfare support—not just when transitioning into civilian life but also for an extended period thereafter. We'd monitor him. He'd have regular psychological assessments. We wouldn't let someone like Cochrane slip through the net, because he'd be profiled as precisely the type of man who'd one day crack, kill seven people, and kidnap a child." For Fleet's sake, he dearly hoped that what he was about to ask the justices to do would produce the right result. "Perhaps we could recess for thirty minutes and return so that you can take a vote on whether we should explore my proposition. My colleague and I would not participate in the vote."

The justices left the room, leaving Fleet and the AG to remain at the table, deep in thought.

Fleet said, "Sir, I want to thank you for this."

"I've laid it out, Marty. But I've no idea which way this'll go." He smiled sympathetically. "There are a lot of self-interests at stake. You realize that?"

"Yeah."

"So, why did you want to take this on?"

Fleet sighed. "Because Philip Knox of the CIA said that Cochrane was a dog whose masters didn't love him anymore and kicked him out of their backyard to fend for himself. If Knox thinks that way, so do others. It occurred to me that mentality is very wrong."

The justices came back into the room earlier than expected.

The chief justice asked those in favor of the AG's proposal to raise their hands.

Only one associate justice did so.

Edward Carley's luxury cruiser was gently rocking in the harbor at the Montauk Yacht Club, in an erratic wind that caused the numerous vessels berthed there to sway, their fittings clanging.

Dark skies and sleet had sent most of the boats' owners scurrying back into the holds of their vessels or onto dry land to lunch in five-star restaurants. Carley had no desire to eat. He'd ordered his crew to leave him in peace as he sat in his boat's office and cut out segments of the *Washington Post*.

What had happened at the Granges' place had been front-page news; the subsequent NYPD briefing had been too late to make today's papers, though Carley had watched it on his laptop. If Cochrane was able today to get hold of a copy of the newspaper, it would be interesting to see how he reacted. If successful, it would be the end of matters for Cochrane or would keep him on the run in a world of pain.

The former battlefield surgeon wondered how

Cochrane was feeling—no doubt mentally and physically exhausted, utterly alone, and driven to help Tom. The latter was important. His yearning kept Cochrane moving. Without it, he'd hand himself in or kill himself. That could still happen, but Carley was hoping that the kidnapping would keep him on the run and in agony.

That was the objective. Prison and death would be too easy a way out. A life on the run would be a life of misery.

He called Viktor Zhukov. "The latest classified ad is now in print. We must anticipate the possibility that this will break him and he will call the police. I hope that proves not to be the case. It's essential his voice is heard and equipment is then removed."

He ended the call and smiled.

Dickie Mountjoy unpacked his belongings in the apartment near Times Square. Outside, the brash and constant noises of the city would have irritated some visitors, but Dickie was a Londoner; he knew city life all too well, and the din of New York barely registered in his ears and brain.

The apartment was adequate for his needs and not dissimilar in size to his own home, though this one only contained one bedroom. He'd already examined the kitchen and decided the oven was man enough for the job of cooking his favorite beef and ale pie, a dish his wife always used to cook him on Saturday evenings.

When she had died three years ago, Dickie had no idea how to cook the dish. But his wife had a handwritten book of recipes that her mother had given her when she and Dickie tied the knot. It had taken him dozens of attempts to cook her pie before he was satisfied he'd gotten it right.

Later today, he'd take a stroll through the city to find the ingredients. He had no idea where to look. But, though Dickie was a man of rigid discipline and routine, he had no fear of the unknown. One can't be in the army, he'd often declared, if one's afraid of what might be over the horizon.

He pulled out the gilt-framed photograph of his wife, taken in the year of her death, and placed it on the bedside table. Whoever had prepared the apartment before he'd arrived had placed fresh chrysanthemums in a vase on the mantelpiece. He took two of the red flowers out of the vase and put one next to the photo and the other on the opposite bedside table.

Smiling, he said to the photo, "My Edna—me in New York City, eh? Who'd have thought, petal?"

He felt his bottom lip tremble as he recalled holding his wife's hand in hospital as she died from cancer.

Enough of that now, he told himself. You've been there already, and you got it out of your system. Edna doesn't want you getting all poncey again. She'd give you a right slap round the chops and tell you to pull yourself together. And she'd be damn right.

The suitcase on the bed was still half full and Dickie decided to move it closer to the closet so he could hang the remainder of his clothes. Lifting the case, the old man suddenly felt giddy, his knees buckled, and he and the case crashed to the floor. He shook his head, his teeth gritted. Four minutes later, his head cleared and he managed to get back to his feet while muttering, "Trying to do this at your age. Stupid."

More cautiously, he continued unpacking, before taking a bath and dressing in his suit and overcoat. Standing at attention, he picked up the telephone—available for local calls only, its adjacent sign declared—and called the New York Police Department. "My name is Major Dickie Mountjoy, retired. I have traveled to the United States of America to meet the officer in charge of capturing William Cochrane. I'm assuming that officer is based in New York City. I'm here as well. I need you to tell me which police station I need to visit. I have some urgent information about Mr. Cochrane that I must impart to the officer."

Painter's cell phone rang and its screen declared it was a call from her NYPD precinct. "Detective Painter."

The precinct captain told her that an old Englishman was in the station waiting area and was refusing to leave until he'd spoken to the detective in charge of capturing Cochrane. "He says he knows Cochrane very well and has information pertinent to the case."

"Is he credible?"

"No idea. He says he wants to tell you something you don't know. Something that might change your mind about the man you're hunting. But he'll only talk to the detective in charge in person. No

one else. So that'll be Kopański or you. I can't tell
you what to do, but it's a hell of a call to come back
and hear what some old guy has to say."

While still on the call, Painter relayed this to
Kopański.

Back on the call, she said, "Okay. I'll get a flight
back from Virginia. But, jeez, it's going to take me
hours to get to NYC. Tell him to come back to
the station at"—she glanced at her watch—"seven
P.M." She hung up and said to Kopański, "It's a risk,
but I need to hear what this guy has to say."

"No problems. I'll hold the fort down here."

It was midafternoon as I entered the city of
Lynchburg, Virginia, fifty-six miles northeast of
Roanoke.

I'd walked twenty-nine miles all night, my
intention to be anywhere but Roanoke or its surroundings. Crossing countryside and staying away
from roads, I'd used stars to navigate my way to
the city. Lynchburg had no particular meaning to
me beyond that it had a population of seventy-five
thousand and would be a place where I could work
out what the fuck I was going to do.

My legs were in agony, as were my shoulders,
despite only supporting my small backpack. My
stomach felt like it was eating itself because I was
so hungry. I had to get food inside me, rest, and get
a copy of today's *Washington Post*. The chances of
me getting caught in the process were significant.
Nothing I'd ever done in the past had required
such a monumental effort as what I'd had to do to
get this far. But I couldn't go on like this.

I knew I was at a breaking point.

My state of mind was dreamlike, and my body felt like it was walking into a force 10 hurricane, when in truth it was consuming the precious reserves left in my torso. Marathon runners call it hitting the wall. I'd hit that wall long ago.

What kept me moving was my overwhelming concern for Tom. That, and the fact I had his kidnapper's voice on tape and the license plate numbers of the cars I'd seen in the valley.

I purchased a copy of the *Washington Post* from a store, rubbing my face as I did so. Nearby was a diner. I could smell fried onions, burgers, and bacon. My stomach wrenched, imploring me to go in there and eat. Under normal circumstances, I'd never have taken that risk. But these weren't normal circumstances. I was slowly dying. All clarity of thought and honed expertise were evaporating fast in favor of one final instinct—to sit down, clasp a mug of hot black coffee, and gorge myself from the menu. That would leave me penniless. Right now, I didn't care.

I entered the diner and took a seat at the rear table.

"What can I get you?" asked the waitress.

I placed my order, using my fake Virginian accent. "I might also ask for seconds. Been working part of the night and all morning. Timber plantations. Builds up quite the appetite. Keep the coffee coming."

"Sure thing." The waitress frowned. "Think I've seen you in here before. You look kinda familiar."

I smiled. "Last time I was in here was about a

month ago. I've been out west on another detail. Am back now. Always love eating here."

Three mugs of coffee and two plates of bacon, eggs, hash browns, beans, fries, and steaks inside me, I was indeed now penniless but fully satiated. A condemned man's last supper, I thought. But it felt simply awesome to sit in the warmth and feel energy returning to my limbs.

I opened the newspaper to the classifieds and saw another coded message. Using the old encyclopedia, it took me ten minutes to crack the code.

MY LAST MESSAGE TO YOU. IT'S BEEN FUN. I'M SURE WHAT HAPPENED LAST NIGHT HURTS YOU. AND WHY DID THE EVENT HAPPEN? TO KEEP YOU FREE AND ON THE MOVE. I WANT YOU TO HAVE HOPE THAT YOU CAN RETRIEVE THE PACKAGE. SO, I'M GOING TO GIVE YOU A BIT OF HELP. THE PACKAGE IS IN WASHINGTON D.C. PROVIDING YOU STAY ON THE STREETS ALIVE, THE PACKAGE WILL REMAIN INTACT. DOES THAT MAKE SENSE? DO WE HAVE A DEAL?

Tom would remain alive if I stayed on the run. That was the deal.

It was one I had to comply with.

There were two possible reasons why my tormentor was telling me Tom was in D.C. The first was that it was complete bullshit. Tom wasn't there and his kidnapper wanted to throw me off the scent. The more likely scenario was he wanted to lure me there. As soon as I was spotted, he'd kill Tom and dump his body in the city. Having us in the same city would remove any doubt as to whether I'd kidnapped him.

But aside from that, the kidnapper just knew I had to go to D.C.

I quickly scanned the front-page headline about the massacre at Robert and Celia Grange's home. The article cited a police briefing this morning wherein crucial new information would be revealed about the crime. The paper said it would publish full details in tomorrow's edition of what emerged from the briefing. I decided I had to get tomorrow's paper to read that article.

All night I'd considered calling the police and giving them the three license plates I'd seen at the Granges'. The problem was, cops probably wouldn't take the information seriously. But they'd still make a routine check on the vehicle owners. That would spook the shit out of them. The risk to Tom's life would be severe. I had to find another way to trace the plates.

I gathered up my things, left the remainder of my cash on the table, stood to leave, and froze.

The waitress and her manager were at the far end of the diner, standing together behind the counter. Both were looking at me, the waitress with her hand to her mouth, the manager talking fast to her with a look of total concern. The manager stopped talking when he saw me looking at them.

He raised his hands, eyes wide, and called out,

"We're not going to stop you walking out of here. We mean you no trouble."

Other diners in the establishment stopped eating and stared at me. Some started screaming, others shouted.

"Dear God, that's him!"

"That man on the news."

"The murderer!"

"Don't do anything stupid."

"Let him walk!"

I moved through the diner slowly, looking at everyone I passed, seeing the terror in their faces as mothers clutched their children and sweethearts hugged each other. A huge trucker was staring at me, no fear in his expression. He had hostility on his face as he pressed his hands against the table as if he was about to launch himself to his feet. No doubt what he was thinking.

I shook my head and said, "Don't."

I maintained eye contact with the man as I moved past him toward the exit. The momentary sound of exertion behind me was followed a split second later by me spinning around, blocking the trucker's punch, stepping into the man, placing a foot behind his heel, using the flat of my hand to smash the man's nose, and punching him in the jaw with sufficient force to lift the three-hundred-pound beast off his feet and force him to crash on the table behind him.

The man moaned as he clasped his face. And he couldn't get up.

Making no attempt to hide my English accent, I shouted to everyone, "I'm going to walk out of here. You don't touch me, I don't touch you. And you don't touch your phones until I'm gone."

I turned, walked out of the diner, and sprinted down the street past a row of stores. One minute later I heard sirens.

The NBC News helicopter was preparing for takeoff, its rotors moving slowly as the pilot made last-minute checks in the cockpit. A cameraman and audio specialist were making sure their equipment was securely fastened to the sides of the hold and doing dummy tests of their transmitter to be certain that anything caught on camera would be relayed to anyone tuning in to the network.

The only person missing before takeoff was Patty Schmidt, and she was walking fast to the craft, cell phone fixed to her ear as she spoke to her editor. "No doubt it's him. Virginia's putting in more cops. Lynchburg's where this will end. Question is whether he's going down with a fight."

It is always difficult for a woman to enter a high-sided chopper when she's wearing a skirt suit and heels, but Patty had done this so many times she could clamber on board with the same panache as the numerous times she'd walked onstage to collect journalism prizes garnered during her two decades working for CBS, Fox, CNN, and NBC. And her blond hair, lacquered to the point that it was as solid as rock, was not going to budge despite the downdraft from the aircraft's blades. Microphone in hand, she looked every inch the consummate pro that she was.

She gripped a handrail as the craft ascended,

shouting to her film crew, "We've got the airspace scoop on this. Cops have only allowed NBC in the air above Lynchburg. So let's not fuck this up. And we may only have one shot. Every possibility that Virginia PD helos tell us to get out of their way."

The two men gave her the thumbs-up. Both of them were also seasoned veterans, and between them they'd reported from the sky more than three hundred times.

The chopper was now moving at speed, its nose tilted down. But this didn't prompt Patty to sit down and buckle up. Instead, she poked her head into the cockpit. "ETA?"

The pilot told her forty-five minutes to an hour.

Her cell phone rang. When the call ended she shouted at the pilot above the craft's noise, "Gunshots have just been heard in Lynchburg. You better make it no more than thirty minutes!"

She sat down and nodded at the cameraman. "Let's get an en route report out."

After checking his equipment, the cameraman put three fingers up, two, one, then his thumb.

"This is Patty Schmidt reporting live from NBC. I'm heading to Lynchburg, Virginia, where I've just received reports that wanted fugitive Will Cochrane has been sighted by multiple witnesses. He's assaulted a man and is now being pursued by police. There are unconfirmed reports of gunfire, though we don't know whether the weapons fired belong to Cochrane, the police, or a combination. In thirty minutes we're going to give you a view of the city and the pursuit of Cochrane. Other networks might be on the ground. But only NBC will be your eye in the sky."

Edward Carley watched his laptop showing the NBC report as he called Viktor Zhukov. "He's in Lynchburg. I'm assuming you can be there very quickly. Listen very carefully to what I'm about to tell you."

I sprinted around a corner into a street in Lynchburg's inner suburbs. Placing my hands on my knees, I sucked in air before racing up the street. The sirens were drawing closer. There was a bullet hole in my jacket—the result of a cop who'd fired two warning shots at the ground near me, one of the bullets ricocheting off the pavement and penetrating my jacket but missing my flesh.

As I raced onward, darting down a side street before turning onto a larger suburban road, I desperately hoped I'd lost the cops. Just then a police car tore around a corner and came hurtling toward me. I pulled out one of the Roanoke detectives' handguns, stepped forward, and fired three rounds into the car's engine block and front tires, causing it to swerve and judder to a halt.

The cops leapt out of their vehicle, using their doors as shields as they prepared to return fire. From one hundred yards away, I fired again, smashing the windshield and putting warning shots into the doors, inches from their bodies. I kept my handgun at eye level and trained on the cops as I walked backward. It was my silent warning to them that if they broke cover and tried to gun me down, they'd lose.

Behind the cover of their vehicle, veteran officers Ken Chen and Simon Carter were focused. The man down the street was walking slowly backward but seemed calm as he kept his pistol pointing at them. In his second volley, he hadn't hit them, but his first volley had been precise and had made their vehicle obsolete. He knew exactly what he was doing and was prepared to let the officers live. For now.

Chen got on his radio and relayed updates. "We have him in our sights. Where the hell's our backup?"

The police controller replied, "Just hold that end of the street. Multiple mobiles and on-foot units are flanking the road. Get closer if you can."

The man was now too far away to risk a shot that could miss and enter one of the homes that lined the suburban street. Chen and Carter glanced at each other, gripped their guns, and ran after Cochrane down the center of the street.

Doors of the houses I passed were opening and closing fast—people glancing out to see what was going on. They saw me sprinting down the street, leaping over a picket fence, and running down the alley between two houses.

Gun in hand, I didn't slow as I bolted through a backyard with a swing set and other children's paraphernalia, leapt onto a stack of firewood, and jumped over the rear hedge into another backyard.

I repeated the same process three times, my pack and the guns inside banging against my back. Breathing fast, I ran along a small arterial road, desperate to get out of Lynchburg.

Officers Chen and Carter had to slow to a jog so that Carter could speak on his radio.

"We've lost visual. Last seen on Rivermont Avenue, heading west. Please advise."

The controller immediately responded. "Stay on him. We need your eyes. All units, all units—I need a perimeter around Rivermont."

Chen led the way through the alley between two houses, shouting at a woman who opened her window, "Get back inside!"

They entered the yard containing the swings, moving carefully in case he was hiding here.

Neither of them were wearing adequate gear to protect them from a handgun powerful enough to stop their car dead.

The pilot of the NBC helicopter called out, "Okay, here we go."

The outskirts of Lynchburg were visible.

Patty Schmidt was on her cell to NBC's office. "What do you mean they fucking lost him? What's the last location?" She hung up and desperately scoured a map of Lynchburg on her lap. To the pilot, she said, "Got it. Rivermont Avenue. Runs northwest in the city. He's got to be around there somewhere."

The pilot adjusted course, his craft now moving fast over Lynchburg's outer sprawl.

* * *

The success of escape and evasion depends on four factors: the skill of the pursued operative, the amount of lead time, chance, and mistakes made by the pursuers. Even with all four factors in place, it is still an awful undertaking. On multiple occasions, I'd needed to extract myself from hostile locations, including Russia and Iran, and each time I'd finally reached safety I'd felt mentally and physically debilitated.

This was infinitely worse.

Lynchburg PD was a professional force, and I was running out of places to run to. There was nothing but danger wherever I went.

But I kept moving, just trying to put as much ground as possible between me and the cops. Partly it was professional pride in my skills that made me do this. Mostly, though, I just had to find Tom.

As I zigzagged along different streets and yards, my gun in hand, I saw a helicopter in the distance. Cops, I instantly thought as I clambered over a fence. No, news crew, I decided, as the shape of the craft became more distinct. But behind the news helo was a Lynchburg police chopper. Matters had just gotten terrible.

"Stop! Police!"

The voice was behind me.

I glanced over my shoulder and saw the two cops I'd earlier shot at heading toward me from the street.

Shit.

Alongside a police helo, the NBC helicopter was over Rivermont Avenue, one of the cameras pointing down at the city, the other capturing Patty Schmidt.

She began her broadcast. "We're here live from Lynchburg, Virginia. Below us is Rivermont Avenue and its surroundings. Somewhere down there is Will Cochrane." She glanced at the monitor showing the city in real time. "I'm going to tell you what you're seeing right now." Viewers of NBC would be watching a split screen of Patty and what was happening at ground level. "The police are putting up a perimeter. I'd say about a mile, maybe a mile and a half wide. Must be about thirty squad cars down there. Looks like they're erecting barricades on the north of Rivermont. I can see two, no, three ambulances. Got more police cruisers moving across the city. Probably a combination of city, state, and county. Officers on foot. And we've got . . . Now, I can't confirm this, but south on Rivermont, looks like we've got a fifteen-man SWAT team moving along the road. These guys don't look like regular cops." Like all good broadcasters in live situations, Patty was telling her story as she saw it. She turned to her cameraman. "Eddie—can you zoom in on these guys?" A moment later the unit was in plain view, the initials SWAT emblazoned on their black paramilitary outfits and Kevlar. "So there you have it. In light of recent terrorist threats, SWAT and other elite firearms units have changed tactics. Faced with a situation like this where civilians are at severe risk, officers are now tasked to always step toward the threat. Gone are the days of standing back. Instead they close in for the kill, and ignore any injured or dying in their path. These guys will be heading straight for Cochrane."

The cameraman gestured to her as he saw something else on his screen.

Patty instantly recognized its significance. "Okay, what you're seeing now are two regular cops." She glanced at her map, not caring that viewers momentarily didn't have her eye contact. "I'm putting this as Hollins Mill Road. Residential street. Houses, all of them detached, on both sides of the street. They're entering the backyard of one of the houses and . . . oh my goodness!"

The Asian American cop came into view in the yard, holding his gun in both hands.

From my position against the back wall of the house, I grabbed his collar, threw him to the ground, and stamped on his jaw and gut. All his partner would have seen was the cop suddenly move left. I heard his fast footsteps. The moment he appeared in the yard, I struck his gun-carrying hands to one side, wrapped one arm around his arms, twisted them up, and punched the officer so hard he just crumpled to the ground.

I didn't like doing that one bit.

I clambered over the hedge at the back of the property.

The whole of Lynchburg was a blanket of wailing police sirens.

"Any police commanders watching this broadcast— you've got two officers down on Hollins Mill Road! And we've got a visual of Cochrane. He's heading west. Off the road on open ground between Hollins Mill and Elmwood Avenue." Patty made no attempt to hide the intensity in her expression. "He's running at full speed, but erratically. I guess he's looking for a different route. He's . . . Where's he gone? Eddie—get that camera closer. *We* need to get closer!"

The pilot, however, elevated the craft by a further two hundred yards, shouting "Police orders!"

Though she was utterly pissed off, she adopted a composed expression as she addressed the camera. "Ladies and gentlemen, quite rightly, we've been instructed to move aside and make airspace for the police helicopter. Cochrane's got to come back into view any second, and the police need to be all over him when that happens. But we're still here and are keeping our cameras rolling on everything that's happening down there."

I opened the back door of a house on Norfolk Avenue. The house was random. I had nowhere left to run; a net had been tossed over the city and the nearby police chopper combined with the news helo meant I didn't have a chance of escape until it got dark. And that wasn't for another two hours. Even then, the city would be swamped with searchlights.

I entered the house, silently closing and bolting the door behind me. It wasn't large—a family home with a downstairs kitchen and living room and three upstairs bedrooms. I could tell the place belonged to a married couple with no kids. Everything was too tidy: no cute children's drawings stuck to the refrigerator, no piles of dirty gym clothes, no drying dishes from breakfast, no signs of sugary cereal, no toys, nothing. I wished the occupants had been away at work.

But the back door had been unlocked.

And the living room TV was on, broadcasting a news network.

I moved slowly forward through the kitchen, my gun in both hands.

In the living room was a thirty-something woman watching the news, her face partly visible, though she had her back to me. She was engrossed in the live broadcast coming from the helicopter hovering over her neighborhood.

I strode up to her, put my hand over her mouth, and held her head firm. Her body jolted.

I whispered, "I won't hurt you if you do exactly what I say." My gun was against her head. "I want to stay here for an hour or two. Nod if there's anyone else in the house."

Wide eyed, the woman shook her head.

"I only said nod! Stay still if there's no one else here."

She was motionless, but I could feel her trembling.

"Turn off the TV. Carefully."

She grabbed the remote and complied.

"Once again, only nod if someone is due home in the next two hours. Kids? Husband? Anyone?"

She didn't move.

"I'm going to remove my hand. If you scream or shout or do anything stupid, I'll shoot you in the back of the skull. You happy with that trade-off?"

She nodded fast.

I removed my hand. "Is your front door locked?"

"No."

"Speak quieter. You're going to lock the door, then turn off all downstairs lights. I'll be right behind you the whole time. Then we're going upstairs."

It took her thirty seconds to complete the tasks. She whimpered, "Please don't hurt me!"

"I can't promise that." It was a lie, but she didn't need to know that.

When we were in the upstairs bedroom that faced Norfolk Avenue, I told her to close the curtains. All upstairs lights were now off. The room was in half-light.

"Sit on the edge of the bed."

She did as she was told.

I sat in a chair opposite her, my gun still pointing at her head. Outside, the city was bedlam, with emergency services racing in different directions. But in the room, all was calm, even though the woman had tears running down her face and was shaking.

"What's your name?"

The woman frowned, as if this question was absurd under the circumstances. "Ni . . . Ni . . . Nicola."

"Okay, Nicola. We're going to sit together until it gets dark. Within that time frame, there're three possibilities. The first is we get on swell, and I walk out of your life once all the fuss out there has calmed down. The second is cops storm your house and things get messy. The third is you freak out, try to get help, and I have to kill you just to shut you up. Two of those options are within your control." I didn't mean a word about killing her, but Nicola had to believe I was capable of such a thing. If I showed the slightest doubt, she might risk summoning help, thereby jeopardizing her safety.

"I . . . I get it. I'll be quiet."

"Good." I smiled. "My name is Will Cochrane. I've been framed for murders I didn't commit. But just so we're clear about things, that doesn't mean I haven't killed lots of people before. And I'll kill you if I have to."

TWENTY-ONE

Viktor Zhukov parked his car half a mile north of the police barricade on Rivermont Avenue and walked, wearing an earpiece attached to the cell phone in his hand. He was listening to the audio feed from NBC, receiving updates on police movements.

Patty Schmidt was on air. "Police are building their perimeter. The barricade on north Rivermont remains in place. They've got a smaller one in the south. Plus they've got extra security around Randolph College. Guess they don't want Cochrane going in there. Looks like SWAT teams and other law enforcement are doing house-to-house searches. It's a large area to cover, that job's going to take them well into the evening. Hold on—just getting some updates. Ah, look, guys, I'm sorry to do this, but we've just been told there has to be a news blackout on police movements. But we're still permitted to report as things unfold. Stay tuned. Anything happens, you'll hear it from us first."

Zhukov slipped his cell into his jacket pocket, alongside his gun.

The last time Simon Tap had killed a man from long range was when he was in Delta Force in Afghanistan. Back then, he'd been a clinical operator who had no views on whether his country's military policy was right or wrong. Rather, it was a case of doing the job to the best of his ability. But when the job was done he did have feelings. When he and six of his colleagues protected a village from a Taliban assault that would have entailed all Afghan men of military age being executed, and all women and children given a worse fate, Tap had immense pride that he'd achieved something tangible and good. The trouble was, when his unit left, the Taliban returned the next day and slaughtered everyone in the village.

He supposed it started then—the ebbing away of emotion. More tours with Delta and the paramilitary work he did with the CIA evolved him into a man whose well of compassion was now dry.

Still, it made him good at what he did. Tap didn't know any other former American operative who'd be prepared to do what he was doing on U.S. soil.

He'd put the backseats down in his car so that he could lie prone and watch the police barricade at the north of Rivermont Avenue through a zoom camera from a distance of half a mile. The Lynchburg police had more pressing issues right now, but if anyone challenged him he would say he was a freelance photographer and was hoping to get a scoop on Cochrane being caught and led handcuffed to squad cars. The city was now awash with media. He wouldn't look odd. And no law enforcement official would have the time or inclination to search the belongings next to him, including the long metal object wrapped in blankets.

But if they did, he'd kill them.

The silenced sniper rifle was how he was going to kill Cochrane.

Next to him he had his phone intercept device. Painter was talking to Kopański. Having heard the news about what was happening, Kopański was heading toward Lynchburg. Painter was about to board a flight to JFK.

Tap looked around. This far north, there were few houses to observe him on the street, though in case, he'd put up interior black curtains on the side windows. They were for purposes of camera lighting, he'd tell an inquiring busybody citizen or cop. He unrolled the blankets, extended the rifle's tripod, and aimed the barrel through the rear window at the barricade. If Cochrane was arrested, Tap was 90 percent sure he'd be taken there. It had a massive concentration of police units, plus fire engines, ambulances, and a large black police van that was either a critical response unit or a prison vehicle.

Knox's instruction to Tap had been clear: Cochrane must not be allowed to be taken into custody.

If he got him in his sights, Tap would take his head off.

He draped the blankets over the weapon, knowing it was zeroed in and ready to fire at a moment's notice.

Four cops and two detectives were helping officers Chen and Carter recover from the assault on their bodies and pride. The injured men were told to get to the southern barricade on Rivermont and grab a coffee. They'd tried to object, but the sergeant in charge could see how badly shaken they were. No matter how desperate the situation was becoming, he couldn't afford to have officers in the team whose decision-making skills might be impaired through hurt, fear, or anger.

Reluctantly, Chen and Carter agreed to comply, their fellow officers patting them on their shoulders and telling them they'd get commendations for their bravery.

They headed on foot to the southern barricade.

"Very carefully, Nicola, I want you to go to the curtains, open them an inch, and tell me what you see." I was no longer pointing my gun at my hostage's head, but I was still gripping it in my lap. "If you deviate from that, I'll shoot you in the ankle. Then I'll put a pillow to your head and blow your brains out."

I watched her carefully for any signs that my violent imagery might inadvertently invoke shock or far worse symptoms. I had to maintain the façade of brutal murderer to ensure she didn't do anything that would risk her life from trigger-happy cops. But words can also be destructive. She looked fit and healthy, and was at an age where fear was unlikely to induce fatal symptoms, but I had to be sure.

"What do you do for a living?" I asked as she stood.

"I . . ." Nicola was staring at the curtains. "I'm a nurse. This week I'm on nights at the hospital."

"A noble profession." I kept my eyes locked on her. "No doubt you've seen your fair share of awful things."

She glanced at me with an expression of bemusement. That was good; she was getting some fight in her. "Nothing on this scale!"

I waved my hand dismissively. "Scale doesn't come into it. Impact on persons involved is all that matters. Now—open the curtains a fraction and tell me what you see."

Nicola looked at the street. "Police are everywhere."

"Descriptions?"

"What?"

"You know this city. Are they all local cops?"

"Not all of them, no. They've got some guys from the sheriff's department. They're all just standing around. Nobody seems to be doing anything."

"They're controlling ground, waiting for the specialists to do their job. Do you see SWAT?"

"No."

"Then they're probably still on Rivermont, doing house-to-house before moving to another street. They *will* come here."

"And what will you do to them if they come here?"

I didn't answer. "Sit back on the bed."

Once again facing me, Nicola asked, "Is that the gun you used to kill the woman in New York?"

"No. I took this weapon from a dead detective."

"For a man who thinks he's been framed for murder, you seem to be in the wrong place a lot."

"I agree."

"You seem too calm to be innocent."

"I didn't say I was innocent. My conscience plagues me every day. I said I was innocent of this particular crime."

"You're going to be dead very soon. You should be terrified."

I nodded. "Not terrified for me." That was true. I'd been expecting a sudden death for years. "Terrified for someone better than me. A boy in danger." I paused, then continued.

"Listen. Whether I'm arrested, dead, or somehow get out of here, I want you to do something for me. Tell the cops that I said I didn't kidnap the boy. Tell them I'm scared about his safety. I don't know who took him, but know it's linked to a vendetta against me. I think the boy is in Washington, D.C."

Ninety minutes later, Patty Schmidt felt that she'd exhausted all descriptions to her viewers of what she could see and all conjecture about what was taking place. The police were being patient and methodical. Their perimeter around Rivermont and its surrounding streets was fully in place. Newly arrived SWAT reinforcements were joining in with the house-to-house searches. The police helicopter was moving over the area, its searchlight on because light was fading fast. And dog handlers were now in situ.

She'd filled in time by cutting to interviews with a former SWAT commander, a hostage negotiator, and the governor of Virginia. But the airtime waffle was in danger of losing viewers who were hoping for a gun battle or spectacular arrest. As day turned to night, the image of illuminated Lynchburg made for a more engaging shot—the sense that in the darkness lurked a highly dangerous man. But Patty knew that soon NBC viewers would be switching channels or attending to other business. She prayed that something would happen soon.

Officers Carter and Chen were by the southern barricade on Rivermont, drinking coffee and trying not to think about the way they had been walloped to the ground.

There was a paramedic nearby, plus two other uniformed cops. It was wholly unlike the northern barricade a mile away, the place designated as the on-the-ground command post. Carter and Chen had been relegated to the most insignificant post in the Lynchburg perimeter. Everyone knew Cochrane was trying to escape the city by heading north. This post was a token one, designed more for show.

Still, they were grateful to be on the ground. And the sweet coffee was good. When Cochrane was killed or captured, the officers were looking forward to getting home to their families and taking a long soak in their baths to relieve the bruising they'd suffered.

The cops around them had been initially supportive, saying they'd been extremely brave for pursuing Cochrane alone, and it wasn't their fault he'd gotten the drop on them. It was nice of them to say that, though Chen and Carter saw it as no compensation for the fact that they'd lost their man. Now the two other cops and the medic were ignoring them. They'd probably run out of things to say and were embarrassed.

Joe Kopański reached the northern barricade on foot, showed his ID, and approached Captain Richards of the Lynchburg PD.

Richards was in charge of the manhunt in his city, and Kopański wasn't going to interfere with that. Richards knew his patch and was trained to manage serious critical incidents like this; Kopański's skill set was wholly different. Their paths had crossed before when a bank robber from New York had holed himself up in a Lynchburg gas station, was surrounded by cops, and blew his head off with a shotgun.

"House-to-house?" Kopański watched the hive of activity on Rivermont, police everywhere and SWAT systematically checking houses.

Richards nodded. "Going to take time. I've locked down the area."

"You need me for anything?"

Richards knew the tough New York detective would love nothing more than pulling out his gun and searching for Cochrane alone. "Can't say there is, Joe. But when we get him, we'll hand him over to you."

On Patty Schmidt's instruction, the NBC helicopter pilot cruised around the perimeter. Patty was desperate to spot anything she could report on—new police arrivals, different streets being searched, anything.

They arrived over the southern barricade, one of the cameras in the craft picking up what could be seen on the street. Five people were there—a paramedic and four cops. Two of the cops had their hats off and were drinking out of paper mugs. To all intents and purposes they looked off duty.

"Hey, Eddie—are they the two cops who got attacked earlier?" asked Patty.

The cameraman zoomed in on their faces. "Can't be sure. Possibly." He spent several minutes backtracking through earlier captured video footage before looking at the officers again through his camera. "Yeah. Their tunic ID numbers match."

This was good. Patty could waste a few minutes doing a feature. She addressed the second camera. "Ladies and gentlemen, we're over Rivermont, at the southern barricade. It's clear police don't think Cochrane's heading this way, as it would take him into the heart of the city. The two officers we're showing you are the same officers who courageously pursued Cochrane and got attacked. I guess they've been told to stay out of the action now. They deserve that after everything they went through. And thanks to NBC, the community of

Lynchburg and everyone else watching our network saw their bravery in action. I'm sure they're going to get a warm welcome when they get home tonight."

Viktor Zhukov observed the police southern barricade on Rivermont. He'd walked around most of the police perimeter and decided that this was the best place to watch. There were no news teams here—most of them were gathered at the northern barricade—and no civilians. Everyone anticipated that the action would take place somewhere around a mile north. Here it was quiet, and he'd spotted no cops farther south. He waited in the darkness of a closed shop doorway. He just needed a few more minutes until the city was completely black.

I asked Nicola to glance out the curtains again.

"The place is crawling with police."

"Is it dark now?"

"Yes."

"Good. Then it's time for me to think about leaving you."

Nicola hesitated before saying, "I don't believe you."

"That I'm innocent?"

"That you'd have shot me." She sat opposite me. "I've treated criminals in hospitals, some of them violent. You can always tell what they're capable of. I suppose it's a look. I don't doubt you've killed people. You have *that* look. But there's something about you that tells me you couldn't shoot an unarmed woman." She gestured to the curtains.

"You'll be gunned down in minutes if you go out there."

"I'll be gunned down if I stay in here. But with the city in darkness, I stand a better chance on the street."

"Why take the risk? You could hide out here. There's attic space."

"Why would you suggest that?"

She didn't answer.

I placed my gun in my backpack. "They'll be searching houses top to bottom in case I've coerced someone into hiding me. If I stay here, they'll find me. Plus, you might get caught in the crossfire."

My comment seemed to surprise Nicola. "You'd go out there, knowing you'll be shot instantly, rather than risk me getting hurt?"

"Yes." I meant every word. "Also, I want you to relay to the police what I said about the kidnapped boy being in D.C. You can't do that if you've got police bullets in you."

Nicola blurted, "I hope they don't shoot you."

I stood, ready to leave. "Truly, I'm sorry if I scared you. I'd never have hurt you." I paused. "I'd like to ask you a favor. You must call the police after I'm gone. But could you wait for, say, ten minutes before doing so?"

Uncertainty was obvious in Nicola's expression.

"*Please.* A boy's life's in severe danger. I don't know why he's been kidnapped, but it's most certainly somehow linked to me. I need to find the boy."

"Are you a good man?"

It was a smart question. "It depends on your

perspective. But I don't kidnap children and I didn't kill the people they say I did. I used to be in government service. I killed people then, but always as part of my job. The man in the newspapers is not the man in this room."

She seemed to be weighing her response. Finally, she answered, "I'll give you fifteen minutes before I call the cops."

Zhukov could see the NBC helicopter hovering four hundred feet above his position. If its cameras were trained on the southern barricade, that would be a bonus, though not essential. In any case, no one could see him. He was fifty yards away, in shadow, with ample time to vanish after what he was about to do.

It was time to enact Edward Carley's instructions and give Cochrane a chance to escape the city and stay on the run. And in doing so, further make Cochrane Public Enemy Number One and his life hell.

He raised the pistol that he'd used in the Waldorf Astoria and at the Granges' homestead. He fired the silenced weapon twice, his bullets striking the backs of the heads of police officers Chen and Carter.

He dropped the gun, turned, and disappeared.

"Oh my God!" Patty Schmidt had her hand to her mouth, one camera on her, the other zooming in on the southern barricade. "Two police officers in southern Rivermont have just been shot. From *outside* the perimeter. Dear Lord. This is awful.

Awful!" Though she'd wanted some action for her viewers, this wasn't what she wanted, no matter how much NBC's viewership would soar. "Somehow Cochrane's gotten outside of the perimeter. He's heading south. Oh, those poor men."

The helicopter rose higher so it could capture a larger image of the Lynchburg police zone. All seemed chaotic—emergency lights flashing, squad cars and ambulances racing south, SWAT officers sprinting on foot toward the southern barricade, the police chopper swooping low with its searchlight scouring the ground around the murdered officers, and the entire perimeter being dismantled as law enforcement officials diverted all efforts toward the new crime scene.

None of them had any intention of arresting Cochrane. He'd just killed their brothers.

And he'd made a big mistake in heading toward the center of the city.

He'd be more exposed there.

And that's where they'd get their payback.

Simon Tap cursed as he watched all officers at the northern barricade abandon their post and speed away.

Cochrane must have been sighted elsewhere. But everything was now fluid. Tap had no way of knowing at short notice where Cochrane was likely to be escorted after arrest. And in all likelihood Tap wouldn't be able to drive his car to a location that would afford him a shot at Cochrane's head.

That was okay. By intercepting Painter's phone, he'd find out where Cochrane was taken after arrest. And maybe he wouldn't be arrested; instead he'd be killed by the police. That too was a perfectly adequate result.

All that mattered was that Cochrane ended up dead.

He waited, as he heard Kopański tell his colleague that he'd just heard Cochrane had killed two Lynchburg officers and that all officers were heading to the scene with a direct shoot-to-kill policy in place.

Tap smiled, deciding that he would stay where he was until the matter was resolved.

Kopański rushed to the southern perimeter, his gun in his hand. Officers were all around him, shouting and dashing south to find Cochrane. He barely glanced at Chen and Carter; his priority was to locate their killer. All law enforcement were moving to the zone and beyond, mounting a frenzied assault to strike while Cochrane was nearby.

Kopański looked back up Rivermont and called Captain Richards. "Something doesn't feel right about this. Why's Cochrane heading to the center of the city?"

"Because he can't go north, for Christ's sake." Richards sounded like he was running.

"You should keep at least twenty of your officers in the north, in case Cochrane's doubled back."

"Doubled back to what? Two hundred uniforms running toward him? I need everybody to be on his heels." He hung up.

Kopański looked south, in the direction everyone thought Cochrane had fled. It was the logical thing to follow them. He looked north along the street that was soon to be empty of cops.

That's where he went.

Outside the back of the house, I saw the last police officer leave the area. They must have had a false lead about my location elsewhere, though it made no sense that everyone had abandoned their posts purely based on a sighting. But I had no time to dwell on the unusual police redeployment. This was my one window to get out of here by heading north.

Making use of the large swathes of shadow between streetlights, I ran up the empty road. Many lights were on inside the houses, though I suspected the city was now in lockdown and people had been told to stay inside. Or they were too petrified to leave their homes.

I had no plan of what to do other than get out of the city and somehow get to Washington. But I had no money. Everyone knew what I looked like. I was labeled a child kidnapper and murderer of three citizens and four cops. And the distance between Lynchburg and D.C. was approximately 180 miles.

How far would I go to do what was necessary? Rob a liquor store or bank to get cash? Break into another person's home and steal essential items and a car? Kill a civilian if he got in my way? A few days ago these questions wouldn't have occurred to me. And even when I'd been in desperate situations while in the service, I'd always retained a strong sense of right and wrong. Because I operated in a morally ambiguous zone, that wasn't always easy.

Nevertheless, there was a line I wouldn't cross. Now, I wasn't so sure. I was in survival mode, and Tom Koenig was in severe danger.

I entered the northern tip of Rivermont Avenue. The police sirens were now distant. Why on earth they'd moved position still confused me, but I kept moving.

In the back of his vehicle, Simon Tap trained his camera lens on a solitary figure who was wearing a jacket, jeans, boots, and a backpack.

The man was tall and was running along Rivermont toward him, his hood up. He couldn't yet see his face, because the man was avoiding streetlamps. But what he was doing was all wrong—if he were a journalist, he'd be running toward the action, not away from it; his attire was not that of a jogger; and Tap couldn't imagine there was anything remotely urgent to rush to in this sleepy northern part of the city. He kept his camera trained on the man.

For one second, his face came into view when he couldn't avoid a small area bathed in artificial light.

It was Cochrane.

Urgently, Tap grabbed his sniper rifle.

Kopański ran up Rivermont. The place was now deserted, all cops having repositioned to the zone one mile behind him. He moved into side streets, his handgun in both hands, not knowing where to look, but every sense telling him that Cochrane had tricked the police into thinking he'd fled south.

* * *

Just get out of Lynchburg, I kept telling myself. Focus on that and don't even think now about what needs to happen next, because in all probability there'll be no *next*.

I stopped running and bent over to catch my breath, and as I did so a high-velocity silenced round tore a chunk out of a tree right behind me.

I dived to the ground just before a second round raced through the air where my head had been a split second earlier. Rolling to one side, I leopard-crawled to the cover of a low stone wall.

What was happening? The police rarely used suppressed weapons and would have no need for them to take me down in Lynchburg. They were brazenly using a sledgehammer approach and wanted to be visible to flush me out.

The marksman was ahead of me somewhere, but I couldn't risk looking. The shooter was an expert shot, and it was only by chance that I wasn't dead. And he'd been going for head shots—no attempts to wound and incapacitate me. Everything suggested the gunman wasn't a cop.

I crawled alongside the wall for one hundred yards until I was off Rivermont and in a deserted side street.

Certain that I was out of the sniper's line of fire, I got to my feet and bolted.

Tap leapt into the driver's seat, started the engine, turned the car around, and sped toward the place where he'd last seen Cochrane. By his side, he had a handgun, ready to point through the windshield and take out the Englishman. After that, he'd get out of the car, put two more shots into his head, and drive off.

He drove to the end of the side street where Cochrane had run, urgently looking left and right. Reaching a T-junction, he glanced in one direction, saw nothing, and looked in the other direction.

Cochrane was there, standing next to a small copse, looking right at him before running between the trees.

Tap put his foot to the floor, his tires screeching as they tried to get traction, his car hurtling to the spot where Cochrane had vanished. He squealed to a stop, threw open the door, and raced into the woods, his handgun held high, ignoring Knox's advice not to get close to Cochrane, because he was ex-Delta and this was precisely the thing men like him were trained to do.

The blow to the back of Tap's head made him double over but not fall. He spun around, staying low and ready to shoot. The punches and knees to his face, throat, groin, and ribs were delivered so fast that Tap could do nothing but simply crumple to the ground. Cochrane's heel smashed onto his breastbone so hard that Tap thought his heart was going to explode. All he could do was lie there, desperately trying to breathe, his handgun discarded during the assault.

I dropped to the ground and wrapped both arms around his throat, positioning my body so that he couldn't move his arms.

"Who are you?" I asked.

He didn't answer

"Are you part of this? Part of the setup to frame me?" I squeezed tight.

The man tried to kick his legs and move his arms, but he wasn't going anywhere.

"Who sent you?"

"Fuck . . . fuck you!"

"Wrong thing to say." My face was inches from his. "Talk, or you know how this will end. Was it you who framed me for murder?"

He tried to shake his head, but the action caused him to choke. "Not . . . not talking."

"Where's the boy?"

"No idea. I've had nothing to do with any of that."

"Liar!"

"You can . . . torture me all you like. Kill me. But I can't tell you something I don't know."

"I'll let you live if you tell me who you're working for."

Silence.

"You'd die for your employer?"

He looked hesitant.

"Fair enough. Let's get this over with."

"Wait! Wait."

"I'm listening."

"Philip . . . Philip Knox. CIA."

I frowned. "The CIA framed me for murder?"

"No. It just wants your mouth permanently shut. Doesn't want you arrested and revealing any embarrassing secrets you know, in exchange for a plea bargain."

"The Agency wouldn't authorize my death on U.S. soil."

"This was Knox's idea. No one else knows about my work for him. That's everything, I swear."

I'd met Knox twice while working for the Agency. He was a piece of shit. What I was hearing now was precisely the type of thing Knox was capable of.

"That's everything," the man said. "You can take my gun. My car, even. I'm not going to come after you."

"I *will* take your gun and car. And no, you most certainly *won't* be coming after me again."

A moment ago this man wanted me dead. Well, good things come to those who wait. I clutched his throat and squeezed hard until his legs stopped thrashing.

Kopański was walking, feeling stupid for following his hunch to search the northern area of the perimeter and beyond. Captain Richards was right—Cochrane was so desperate that he'd gone in the only direction available to him. He'd be caught or killed very shortly, and Kopański would have no satisfaction in that because he'd gone off on a wild goose chase in the wrong direction. He reached a T-junction on a quiet side street in a residential suburb. All was quiet, streetlamps the only source of light in an otherwise black night.

Three hundred yards to his left, he saw a car's reverse lights and heard the sound of its engine being gunned. The reverse lights turned off. It was impossible to make out the license plate or the car model, but as it sped off, he knew in his heart that it was Cochrane.

Two hours later I was by the side of a pond in the center of Monongahela National Forest. Everywhere around me was deserted. I took off the dead assassin's clothes and set to work. It wasn't pleasant. Removing the dental work, eyes, and fingerprints never is. And getting the air and buoyancy out of a corpse requires a strong stomach to inflict massive puncture wounds. The hunting knife I'd found in the car enabled me to cut open the chest, throat, and gut. I hated doing so. My only solace was that he'd have done the same to me. I placed rocks in his chest cavity, mouth, and stomach. After stripping, I swam, towing the corpse, to the center of the pond. I let it sink, then returned to the shore.

It wasn't a perfect removal of a body. That would have involved a furnace or hungry pigs. But I doubted he'd be found for days. By then, I would be in Washington.

I was certain that was where everything was going to end.

PART III
THE JUSTICE

TWENTY-TWO

Thyme Painter was on her cell, receiving updates from Kopański. She ended the call with "I'll be leaving here in about an hour. Meet you in D.C."

She walked into one of the central Manhattan precinct's interview rooms. The room was warm, but the man was wearing a Royal Navy woolen overcoat over his immaculate suit. She sat opposite him and apologized for being late.

"Apologies are for quitters. Are you a quitter, missy?" the man said in his precise but gruff English voice.

"No, and I'm not a *missy*."

"Missus, then."

"I'm not one of those, either, Mr. Mountjoy—you can call me *Detective* Painter."

"And you can call me *major*. What you limping for?"

"People don't usually come straight out with that question."

Dickie shrugged. "Life's too short to pussyfoot around."

Painter resisted a smile. "I got blown up in Afghanistan. I have an artificial leg as a result."

"You were out there being some charity do-gooder?"

"No, I was in the army on active combat service."

Dickie huffed. "Women in the army. What is the world coming to?" Though secretly, he now had respect for Painter. "What unit were you in?"

"I flew helicopters."

"Heaven forbid—one of *those* types."

"Yes, and I also held the rank of major." She placed a pen and paper in front of her. "You said you had important evidence relating to my manhunt for Will Cochrane. It's taken me hours to get here just to hear what comes out of your mouth. I'm hoping I haven't wasted my time."

"And I flew all the way from London just to be here." He straightened his tie. "While I was waiting, your colleagues told me something was happening in Lynchburg. Have you arrested him?"

"He hid until it was dark in a woman's house while holding her at gunpoint. She said she'd called us right after he left her house, but we know she's lying. She waited several minutes, probably longer, before making the call."

"How do you know she was lying?"

"Because by the time she called, he was a mile south of her house and had killed two police officers."

"Killed?" Dickie was shocked. "You're sure?"

Painter nodded. "He left the murder weapon at the scene. Probably it was of no further use to him because it was out of ammunition. As we speak, more tests are being done on it, but we already know for a fact it's the same gun he used in New York and in the massacre outside Roanoke. He'll get the death sentence."

"You've got him, then?"

"No. He escaped."

"And what are you doing about it?"

"Every inch of Lynchburg is being searched. We had a solid perimeter around the area where he was spotted, and we can't figure out how he got out. But we'll find him."

"And if you don't?"

Painter didn't tell the old man what Cochrane's hostage had said about Tom Koenig probably being in Washington D.C. "Tell me about the information you have."

Dickie cleared his throat and averted his gaze. "Probably it might all sound a bit daft."

"What do you mean?"

"Well, look—I can't *prove* to you Cochrane didn't kill all these people. I can't say he was in a different place at the time. In fact, I've got no evidence that he's innocent."

Painter rolled her eyes. "My time is valuable. I've come all this way just—"

"Steady, missy." He raised a hand and said in a soothing tone, "It's all right. I'm not wasting your time."

She was silent.

"Mr. Cochrane lives three floors above me in London. He moved in four years ago and I've known him ever since. For a while, I didn't know what he did for a living. But then there were events that brought that information to light." His eyes narrowed. "I've seen no mention of it in the press, but do you know his background?"

"Yes. I'm keeping his profile out of the media. He was a covert operative, joint with the UK and U.S."

"Correct, but do you know much about what he did?"

"Actually, no."

"You know nothing about the time he prevented three thousand child musicians and the wives of premiers from the States, Europe, and the Middle East from being blown up at a New York concert?"

Painter shook her head.

"How he averted war between Russia and America? Stopped the U.S. from unwittingly conducting a biological attack on China and killing millions of civilians? Prevented the assassination of the Russian foreign minister that would have been blamed on your president? And solved a mystery that enabled the United Nations Security Council to persuade Israel not to invade Lebanon to obliterate Hamas? You know none of that?"

"I don't." The detective wasn't writing any of this down, but she was listening attentively. "How do you know this?"

"Rest assured he didn't come to me and brag about it all. He's not that type. Quiet man. Private. Modest. No, I know about it because three years ago his reputation was wrongly challenged because an operation he was involved in went wrong. Mind you, that was nothing compared to the shit he's in now. In a closed court, I had to provide a character testimonial of him. Beforehand, they made me sign all sorts of documents saying I wouldn't reveal anything I heard about him in court. The missions I just mentioned were revealed by senior members of MI6. Suppose I shouldn't be telling you all this, but I got to thinking I had nothing to lose."

Painter felt sorry for the old man as she said, "Mr. Mountjoy—none of this changes anything. Actually, it reinforces in my mind that Will Cochrane was pushed to the breaking point. We think trauma has driven him over the edge. From what you've just told me, I'm amazed he didn't snap a long time ago."

"But . . . but he always does the right thing."

"Not anymore, and you must accept that, sir."

"We both hold the rank of major. It's inappropriate for you to call me 'sir.'" Dickie was trying to use humor to offset the rising emotion inside him.

"Cochrane served the West with distinction. But none of that exonerates him for what he's done. Nor does it cast any doubt on his guilt."

"That's not why I came here." Dickie's eyes were getting watery.

"Then why?" asked Painter in a sympathetic tone.

"Because . . . because." Dickie's thoughts were a mess. He tried to hold himself together. "He's a right decent gentleman. I know him. He's got his hard side; men like us always do. But he always does the right stuff. Helps me out. Helps Phoebe and David out."

"Who . . . ?"

But Dickie was blurting and unstoppable. "Makes me dinner when my club's shut. Plays chess with me just to keep me company. Sorted out some DIY in my home that my old bones weren't up to. Got me a VIP ticket to watch the Trooping of the Color. Every Christmas buys me a bottle of Bailey's because"—he laughed, though tears were evident—"he knows I hate the stuff and it annoys the bejesus out of me. And"—he bowed his head—"he takes me for walks in Green Park and talks to me just to keep me distracted."

"Distracted?"

"I miss my wife."

"Oh."

There were times when Painter truly loathed aspects of her work. The worst was when she had to present hard facts to people suffering grief. Now was one of those moments. "Major Mountjoy—the character of the man you've described belongs to a loyal friend. Hold on to that thought. That is the Will Cochrane you know. He should always be that person to you. The Will Cochrane I'm after is not that man. Separate the two."

"It can't be like that, though. He wouldn't do these things. Just wouldn't."

"Mr. Mountjoy . . ."

The major placed a hand over Painter's. The lack of formality surprised her, and under other circumstances she would have removed his hand. Now, she let it rest over hers.

He said, "I know him. That's what I wanted you to hear. My statement on his character. He's a good man. I wanted to look you in the eye and have you hear this from me. And I've no reason to lie to you."

"I don't doubt that."

"And it's the last thing I can do to say thank you to him for everything he's done for me, Phoebe, and David. You see"—he patted her hand gently—"I've got a heart condition. Too old for a bypass operation. I suppose I shouldn't have flown, but had to take the risk. I'm dying, Detective Painter. Don't exactly know when it will happen, but I've been warned it'll be any day. So what I've just given you is a dying man's statement."

TWENTY-THREE

Though he had a backlog of work that had piled up while he'd been conducting his research for the Supreme Court meeting, Marty Fleet wasn't in the mood to stay a moment longer in his office.

His fast-track career had had significant successes, but, like everyone else in the AG's office, he'd also had his share of failures. They came with the territory, and he'd always had the ability to shrug them off and move on to the next project. But the outcome of the Supreme Court meeting hit him hard. Unable to shake the disappointment, he decided that he'd take tonight and tomorrow off and spend a little quality time with his sister.

He entered his luxury apartment in Chevy Chase and saw that his health aide was spoon-feeding Penny.

"I'll take over. You take the rest of the evening off," he said to the aide. When she was gone, he kissed

Penny on the cheek and gave her more pureed food. "Not my best day at work. The chief justice and her justices didn't buy my constitutional angle."

Penny murmured something.

"I know. What makes it so damn hard is that these operatives' minds are being broken all the time; and when we're done with them, they're just left in the gutter. I feel I've let them down."

Penny murmured something else that Marty partially understood.

He brushed his hand against her cheek. "That's kind of you, sis. Yeah, at least I never let you down. I got that right."

The knock on the door of the Dupont Circle hotel room came at precisely the time Michael Stein had been expecting two visitors. He opened the door and ushered in the investigative journalists from the *Washington Post*. One of them was the interviewer, the other a photographer. With the door closed and locked, Michael pointed to an area of the room containing two armchairs and a straight-backed office chair.

Michael sat in the latter and said, "Thank you for coming at such short notice."

"You calling me and saying Will Cochrane was a spy got me interested." The interviewer smiled. "The fact that you said you'd worked with him and would go on record got me sniffing a scoop."

"I'm not going to give you my real name." Stein glanced at the photographer. "And my face will have to be blacked out or in shadow. After this is done, I need to get out of America without being stopped at the airport." And the airport he departed from and his route to Israel would be unusual, in case American authorities decided to stop any Israeli man heading home from a major airport who might look like a former Mossad combatant.

The interviewer weighed up options. "I've got no problem hiding your face. If anything, it'll add to the intrigue." Before he started the interview, there was one key thing the journalist had to ascertain. "Credibility of sources is paramount in our business. How can we be sure you're ex-Mossad and not some Walter Mitty character?"

Michael knew that was the first question he'd be asked. "Intelligence officers don't carry badges or licenses to kill or any other documentation saying who we are. And even if we did, I'd have been forced to hand those documents back when leaving the service."

"We get that. Look—I've interviewed guys from the CIA, NSA, and others. I've hung around with enough of them to know if they're the real deal. Maybe start by telling us a bit more about yourself."

Michael spoke for fifteen minutes about his time in Israeli special forces and Mossad, sanitizing sensitive details, but supplying sufficient information and using vocabulary that only a real spy would know.

He asked, "Satisfied?"

The interviewer grinned. "Absolutely. Okay, we're going to get the tape rolling. While you and I are talking, Brian will be moving around you, taking shots. Don't worry—he'll be editing the photos. If he accidentally captures your face, that shot will be deleted."

"It had better be." The way Michael said that momentarily unsettled the journalists. "When will you be going to print?"

"This'll be in tomorrow's edition, and I'm hoping it gets front-page mention as well as a two-page spread." He activated his recorder. "Ready?"

Michael nodded.

"Okay. Let's start with you giving us an introduction about your background—exactly the way you gave it earlier. Then we'll go into the meat of the interview about your work with Cochrane a year ago."

Two hours later the interview was complete.

The interviewer said, "That's everything I need, unless you've got anything to add."

Michael did, and it was the entire reason why he'd requested the interview. But first, he asked, "I suppose you might have to cut out bits of what I've said."

The interviewer replied, "I'm hoping not too much, but there will be a word count limit in the feature. Rest assured, all the good stuff will stay in."

"And you guarantee this will be in tomorrow's edition?"

The journalist beamed. "You kidding? This is gold dust. My editor's going to grab this by the balls."

This was superb. Michael said, "There's one more thing I'd like to say, but I have to be certain you will assure me it will make the print article."

The interviewer frowned. "I can't guarantee . . ."

"You have to assure me!"

The interviewer felt clammy as he looked at the tall assassin. "If it's brief, I guarantee you it will make the final edit."

Michael spoke for thirty seconds, clasped his hands and said, "And that's everything I have to say."

Though he was tired, when Dickie returned to his apartment near Times Square, he was determined to make his wife's steak and ale pie. It would mean he wouldn't be eating the dish for a couple of hours, but that didn't matter. What did was that he imagined his dear Edna here with him, both of them chuckling at the absurdity of such old-fashioned English types being ensconced in the neon glow of Manhattan. She was a carefully spoken and prim lady, but Dickie knew that if she were here with him she'd have become entranced with the dynamism of the city. Edna would have broken out of her proper ways and become like a giggling girl who'd been told she could buy what she wanted in the world's greatest toy store. He would have loved to have seen that transformation.

In the kitchenette, he sweated finely chopped onion, added herbs, and braised cubes of beef and kidneys. He added a pinch of nutmeg and cinnamon to the mix, then poured in a can of stout and a tin of tomatoes. After it had simmered for an hour, he prepared pastry in the way he'd seen his wife make it so many times, poured the meat and sauce into a casserole dish, and fitted the pastry on top as a lid.

Thirty to forty-five minutes in the oven would be long enough. When ready, he'd open a window so he could hear the sounds of New York City. He'd sit at the table while still wearing his suit, and imagine his wife eating with him.

He cracked open a second can of stout and poured it into a glass. "To us, my love. Our last adventure." He raised the glass to his lips and took a swig. "Getting a few more aches and pains these days. Bloody old age."

He sat in a chair and smiled. For some reason, he liked being here. Maybe it had gotten him out of his comfort zone. It was his last trip overseas, for sure, and Manhattan had unwittingly put a smile on the face of the grumpy bastard. For that, he was thankful.

Edna couldn't have children. It didn't diminish the love he had for her. And in recent years, Will Cochrane had become a sort of adult son he'd never had. It was nice for Dickie. Though nearly three decades older than Cochrane, they had a bond. And they got each other's way of thinking.

It broke his heart to think of Cochrane now, so alone and in such awful circumstances. He wished he were younger and could have done more to help—maybe try to find Cochrane, tell him to lay low while he bullshitted the cops, anything. It was now all a fantasy, but he'd have done that back in the day.

The smell of his cooking wafted through the apartment and gave him the greatest pleasure.

Tomorrow he'd be flying back to London. He was looking forward to seeing Phoebe and David.

He hated the idea of being alone in his London apartment.

Twenty more minutes until the pie was ready.

"Sod it, me dear. I'm putting me slippers on," he declared with a smile on his face. He walked across the open-plan apartment to the bedroom area, and that's when his heart gave out. He knew what was happening as he collapsed to the floor and crawled with all his might toward the bed. The pain was excruciating and increasing by the second. His breath was short. His mind was dizzy from lack of oxygen. But he kept his eyes on the photo of Edna by his bed. She was looking back at him, a gentle smile on her face.

He pulled himself onto the bed, a gargantuan effort and one he'd never be able to repeat. He couldn't get to the phone. Even if he could call 911, he doubted it would make a difference.

He grabbed the flower on the bedside table and the photo of his wife, and drew his last breath.

TWENTY-FOUR

Dinner with Billy Koenig was a somber affair, and Faye Glass was pleased that the female officer in the Roanoke safe house kitchen wasn't leaving them in peace. It gave her the opportunity to make small talk with the cop, rather than be alone with Billy and say something dumb like, "I hope Tom is okay."

But she was in utter shock.

And that's why the cop, a forty-year-old mother of two named Katherine, was staying with them in the room.

Billy didn't touch his food. His eyes were glazed, and his legs swung back and forth under the table.

"Ma'am—perhaps Billy needs to go to bed?" said Katherine.

"Yes." Faye felt she was in a dream as she tucked him into bed. She thought about telling him a story, or just talking to him. But she could see in his eyes that he wasn't interested. There was absolutely nothing that could be done to offset the agonizing situation.

Faye made to leave, but Billy grabbed her wrist and blurted, "Why did Uncle Will kill Uncle Robert and Aunt Celia and steal Tom?"

Faye pulled his head to her chest and held him as she replied, "We don't know. We just don't know."

Billy was shaking as he asked, "Is Tom going to be hurt?"

Faye rubbed his hair. "Uncle Will wouldn't do that." She didn't know if she was right.

"Why did he take Tom and not me?"

That was a typical sibling question, thought Faye. Even in a situation as dreadful as this, the brother wonders why the other was more special. She told the truth. "He would have taken both of you if he could. It was only by luck that you and I were in Roanoke that evening." She tried to control her emotions as she added, "I love you, Billy."

In the kitchen, Katherine made her a coffee. "He needs you."

The statement irritated Faye. "Of course he does."

"More than you need yourself."

"What the hell do you mean?"

The cop handed her the mug. "I know about what happened to your sister—the boys' mother—a year ago. I also know from speaking to the twins' school that you've been struggling."

"That's none of your damn business."

"Struggling to look after them. So you handed the twins to your uncle and aunt." Katherine knew her words would provoke anger. That was why she was here. As a qualified counselor and family liaison officer, her remit was to ascertain whether Faye was tough enough to look after herself and her dependents. The two other cops in the house were the protection detail. "Despite their age, they did a mighty fine job until they were killed."

"I moved in with them to help them out."

"You told me that was only because they asked you to."

Faye bit off a sliver of nail. "I'm still grieving the loss of my sister."

Katherine walked to her. "And it's time for you to get over that and focus on the boys. Even if we get Tom back, I can't recommend they stay somewhere they may be vulnerable because you're a mess. Do you want them to go into foster care? Moved around from one family to the next? Changing schools every year? Is that what you want?"

Billy ran into the kitchen and hugged Faye with all his might, clinging on to her as if he'd fall to his death if he let go. "*Please*, Aunt Faye. Look after me. Don't send me away!" His face was flushed, his sobbing uncontrollable.

As Faye held him while looking at Katherine, the moment seemed frozen in clarity. Something changed inside her. Grief for her sister faded. Everything in the here and now was urgent. What mattered was Tom and Billy. She realized that nothing else was as important.

And she finally felt in the bottom of her heart that she was ready to do this.

She held Billy close. "We're going to stay here

until they get your brother back. Then we're going to move back into my home. I'm never letting you go. I'll be strong for you all the time." She kissed him on the forehead. "That okay with you?"

Billy looked at her imploring, "Yes, yes. Just get my brother home safe."

Viktor Zhukov's exit out of Lynchburg and drive north had been without incident. He entered the basement of the isolated farmhouse twenty-nine miles north of D.C.'s outer limits. The Russian nodded at the man and woman in the room before crouching in front of the hooded boy. Tom Koenig was sitting on a chair in the center of the room, a bare lightbulb hanging above his head. Zhukov lifted the black hood up a few inches so that his mouth was exposed. "How are you this evening, Tom?"

Tom peed his pants as he smelled garlic on the lisping lips of the man who'd grabbed him from under his bed.

"Are my friends giving you enough food and water?"

Tom shook. "Yes . . . please let me go."

"Soon, soon." Zhukov went to the other side of the room, where there was a table containing audio equipment. The digital recordings stored here had been very carefully crafted so that no background noise was present. In front of the equipment was a laminated sheet of paper containing typed notes of the recordings. He ran his finger down the list and found a sentence that suited his purpose.

He said in a clear voice, "Boss—we're going to

have to move the boy soon, and to do that we're going to drug him again. But there's always a risk with the drugs that he doesn't wake up. We don't know if he has any medical conditions or allergies. Are you happy to take the risk?" Zhukov silently activated the play function on one of the recorders.

A man's voice said, "I've got no problem with that, so just do what you need to."

The man and the woman next to Tom had to hold down the boy as he tried to leap to his feet and run.

Zhukov said to his colleagues, "Chain him to his bed." He went upstairs and made a call to Edward Carley. "Everything in Lynchburg happened as you said it would."

Carley replied, "I've been monitoring events. The police have had zero success. In two days, I want you to leave the assignment in a prominent place."

The assignment was Tom Koenig.

TWENTY-FIVE

In the Colonial Parking garage in Washington's Friendship Heights district, I made a thorough examination of the contents of the car.

The sniper rifle was a Heckler & Koch model, though expertly customized. It had a larger magazine and scope than standard. Its stock had extra cushioning. Lumps of metal were molded onto parts of the weapon to ensure that its alterations didn't change the weapon's perfect balance. The gun was military spec, and the person who'd adapted it knew exactly what he was doing. That would make sense. Philip Knox wouldn't use an amateur to kill me.

I'd earlier removed the dead man's wallet. Inside was a bank card in the name of Simon Tap and three hundred dollars. That cash was now in my pocket. There was a cell phone in the glove compartment, only one number listed in the contacts, under "PK." Philip Knox. And his number was the only one shown in sent and received calls and SMSs. I placed the phone and its charger in the jacket I'd stolen from the dead gunman. Though a different color, it was only a minor alteration to my appearance, but right now every little bit helped.

There was a camera on the passenger seat with a powerful zoom lens. Tap must have been using it to search for me. I guess he was going to kill me after arrest. Probably while I was being escorted to the police barricade in Lynchburg.

The last item that caught my attention was what looked like an oversized cell phone. It was plugged into the cigarette lighter in the dash. I examined it for several minutes. It was highly sophisticated equipment, the kind of thing that I'd used when I was a spy. The item intercepted the phone belonging to Detective Thyme Painter. This could only mean one thing. Painter was taking the lead in the manhunt to capture me, because interception of her phone would guarantee knowledge of the very latest police updates. Almost certainly, Knox had given the interceptor to his assassin.

The sniper rifle was of no use to me in an urban environment like D.C.—too cumbersome, impossible to conceal. In any case, I had more than enough firepower with the two detectives' handguns and the silenced murder weapon. But I kept it in the vehicle anyway, in case I'd need of it elsewhere.

I placed my head on the steering wheel, feeling wretched and exhausted. So many times in my adult life I'd been in danger. But I had purpose then. Now I was reduced to being viewed as scum. And that was the point of all that was happening—not to kill me or get me locked up. Instead, to strip away everything that mattered to me. Everything, including my ability to care for the twins. I thought about poor Tom, barely able to imagine where the ten-year-old was being kept and what state he was in.

Things couldn't be worse.

I lifted my head and stared at Washington, D.C. Tom had to be out there somewhere, I kept telling myself. Even though it was probable he was a thousand miles away from here. But if he was here, the odds of finding him were stacked against me. The city had a population of over 670,000; adding in commuters and tourists, the number was much higher.

The mental image of Tom stayed in my head. Feelings of self-pity vanished and were replaced by an energized focus and coldness.

Nothing was going to stop me from attempting to tear the city apart.

Edward Carley had no need to do anything further to the Englishman other than deal with Tom Koenig. He'd emptied Cochrane's bank account after obtaining his card details in the Waldorf, had framed him for the murder of three civilians and six police officers, and had added kidnapping to the list of felonies.

Whether Cochrane was in D.C. or not, Tom Koenig would be dealt with tomorrow night.

He walked on the deck of his yacht in Montauk.

In two weeks, he'd be sailing far away from America, his work complete. But he'd miss being in Long Island. It seemed such a civilized place.

Philip Knox would never ring Simon Tap to receive updates. The agreement they had in place was that only Tap could call, and that otherwise their communications had to be restricted to SMSs. From his office in Langley, the CIA officer weighed the phone in his hand. Cell phones were permitted in the building, but only if they were switched off and their batteries removed. Otherwise they could be hacked and used as a microphone receiver by hostile intelligence forces.

It wasn't unusual for Tap to go silent for long periods of time when working. But things were moving fast. Cochrane had somehow gotten out of Lynchburg, despite the city becoming an armed fortress. Tap would have been there, trying to sight him from a distance so he could remove his head. Now Tap would be waiting for Painter or Kopański to reveal further information if Cochrane was seen elsewhere. Knox was getting impatient. Cochrane had to be killed and Knox needed to know Tap was on the case. He exited the building, walked across the parking lot, got into his car, and sent Tap an SMS asking for an update.

I was at the base of the Friendship Heights parking garage when Simon Tap's phone beeped. A message from "PK" asking for updates. An idea came to me. It was possible the police wouldn't take seriously my sighting of the three vehicles at the Granges'. And there was no way I could trace the vehicles. Knox could. I sent him an SMS with details of the plates, telling him not to ask why they might be relevant to tracking Cochrane.

Across the street was a convenience store. There were things in there that I needed. But there'd also be security cameras, so I couldn't risk entering the place, even though I was wearing Tap's shades. I supposed I'd have to find a smaller store that didn't have CCTV. Even then, the risks were significant.

I spotted three teenagers loitering farther up the street. The kids eyed me suspiciously as I approached them. Perhaps they thought I was a pervert or undercover cop.

"Any of you want to earn some quick cash?" I asked in my Virginia accent.

They just glared at me

"It's nothing weird. I just want to get some stuff from the convenience store over there."

One of them asked, "Why don't you go in there yourself?"

"Because I got a court order ordering me to stay away from D.C. Part of the terms of my divorce. My ex lives here. She thinks I'm a threat to her. The police agreed. Can't have my face on camera if I enter the store. But I couldn't avoid being in the city today because I got a job interview with a construction firm that's headquartered here. The work is in another state. But to get it, I've got to be here. And there's some stuff I need to neaten myself up." I pulled out a wad of cash. "Here's the deal—if I give you cash for the stuff I need, and you don't run off with the cash, I'll give you double if you bring the stuff back to me."

The kids looked at each other.

The tallest of them said, "Okay, mister. Tell me what you need. But don't ask for any booze or cigarettes. That store owner is a complete bitch. She won't sell anything like that to someone my age."

I gave him the cash and told him what I needed.

Twenty minutes later I was back in Tap's vehicle. Cars were parked on either side of me, but both were empty. Out of the grocery bag, I withdrew a large bottle of water, a comb, and black hair dye. Soaking my head with water, I applied the dye, combing it through my beard and hair. I repeated the process three times. With the shades back in place, I looked different, though still recognizable to someone close up.

I would have loved to have done this makeover in the privacy and comfort of a hotel room. But even one paid for in cash would be high risk. If I were the detectives chasing me, I'd have told D.C. PD to contact every hotel and motel in the city and alert them to any man remotely matching my age and stature who paid for his room in cash.

I took bread, ham, and water from the bag and consumed it all, before taking out the last item I'd purchased.

On the front page of the *Washington Post* was the headline WANTED MURDERER WILL COCHRANE WAS A SPY—INTERVIEW WITH FORMER COLLEAGUE. There was a second headline about the latest police briefing on the case. I turned to the inner section containing a two-page spread of the interview. The paper declared that its meeting with a former Israeli Mossad officer had been initiated at his behest. The name used in the article was false, and the photo had his face in shadow. But within two minutes of reading the beginning of the article, I knew who the interviewee was.

Michael Stein.

A superb operative who'd once tried to kill me. Later, he'd allied with me to stop a major threat to the West.

I finished the article, confused. Stein had spoken glowingly about me, but his details of our work together were a complete fabrication. Maybe the reason why Stein had requested the interview was to say I was a good guy, the espionage activities being irrelevant. But Stein would have known that by now nobody would care if I'd been a saint in a previous existence. Too much death had taken place. I was now a mass murderer. I read the article again and stopped at the final section. The article read:

I asked the former Mossad officer if he had anything further he wanted to say about his work with Cochrane. What he said next was something he insisted I share with readers of our newspaper. He said, "I will never forget what happened to Cochrane and me in Vienna. I had to give him something. But we both suspected we were being watched by hostiles. The thing I had on me had to get close to Washington, D.C., and Will

Cochrane was the only person I could trust to take it there. I called him and said, 'Let's meet by the trains today at eleven.' We had the briefest of contacts. That day, Vienna was dangerous and we were too down the line."

This was another experience that had never happened. But there was something here that was vital.

I reread the last seven sentences. Words jumped out at me.

Vienna.

Give him something.

Watched by hostiles.

Close to Washington, D.C.

Meet by the trains.

Today at eleven.

We had the briefest of contacts.

Urgently, I pulled up the Web browser on Simon Tap's smartphone and searched for a map of the D.C. Metro system. I expanded the map and moved it in different directions, desperately looking at the names of each station in the city and its surroundings. I stopped moving the screen when I saw the name of one station on the Orange Line.

Vienna. In Fairfax County, Virginia.

It would be 11 A.M. in ninety-three minutes. And I had to navigate traffic and cover twenty miles to get there. I turned the key in the ignition and drove as fast as I could out of the parking garage.

Inside the headquarters of the Washington Metropolitan Police Department at 300 Indiana Avenue

NW, the large auditorium was full, with commanders and high-ranking detectives from all of the force's seven district divisions.

On the way over here, Kopański and Painter had bickered about who should give the briefing, neither wanting to take the stand.

Kopański had argued, "You know I'm not allowed to speak in public. I say the wrong thing, it goes in the press. Plus, half of my face scares people."

Painter had countered, "No press officers are going to be at the briefing. And half of your face is very handsome. Just turn sideways so they can only see that side."

Kopański didn't buy that argument. "You went to Stanford University. Your vocabulary is better than mine. You're articulate, eloquent, cogent, and even loquacious when the need arises."

"Your description of my vocabulary is proving that you're just as adept."

"I don't like being on a stage. It makes me grumpy."

"And I get stage fright, remember?"

"No, you don't. Being in front of that many people just reminds you how normal most folks are and what an oddball you are."

They'd continued bickering as they'd parked their vehicle, and barely paused for breath while they walked through the police headquarters. In the end, Kopański suggested flipping a coin. He lost the toss and warily took to the stage, notes in hand, a look on his face that suggested he'd pull out his gun and shoot anyone in the audience who ridiculed his performance. Painter took a seat in the wings, unfolding the *Washington Post* she'd picked up on the way over but had not yet read. Anger and intrigue seared through her as she saw the headline about Cochrane being a former spy. She read the interview.

Without any greetings or other pleasantries, Kopański growled into the microphone, "The only lead we have is that there's a possibility Cochrane's on his way here or is already in the city. He claims he's innocent of the kidnapping and has reason to believe Tom Koenig is being held captive in D.C. Even if there is only a one percent likelihood he's telling the truth, we have to follow that up."

"Detective Kopański," called out the commander of the third district, "he's thrown you a red herring to focus your energies here. *My* energies, for that matter."

"Probably, yes."

"I can't look you in the eye and tell you I'm going to dedicate four hundred of my officers to look for Cochrane and the boy. Cochrane will be holding the boy in a place as far away from here as possible."

Kopański knew he needed to tread carefully with such a senior officer. "Three possibilities: First, maybe Cochrane was just bullshitting his hostage in Lynchburg. Second, Cochrane's innocent of the kidnapping and genuinely does have good reason to believe the boy's been brought here. The third option is"—he paused and scanned the audience—"he kidnapped the boy, locked him up outside Lynchburg, brought him here after he escaped the city, and told us the boy was in your city because Cochrane wants this to end. He wants to be caught."

"Then why not get caught with the boy in Lynchburg?"

"I don't know. I didn't say it made sense. Very little of what Cochrane's doing makes sense."

"Well, is there anything that you *do* know, Detective?"

The sarcasm wasn't lost on Kopański. "I'm not standing on this fucking stage to be condescended to by you."

Only halfway through the article, Painter looked up, shaking her head and whispering, "Joe, Joe." She knew that when her colleague got like this, he'd rather walk through walls than suffer fools.

But Kopański couldn't hear her. "I'm going to ask you this: What if there is a possibility the boy is here? And third district sits on its fucking ass while the boy gets closer to death?"

The commander had never been spoken to this way.

Kopański breathed deeply. "Cochrane was in Lynchburg. We know that for a fact. Virginia police were absolutely correct to throw every resource at Cochrane. I'm not asking you to do the same based on a long shot. All I'm asking for is your cooperation."

He spoke to the assembled officers for a further thirty minutes before walking offstage.

"That could have gone better," said Painter.

"It could have gone worse. Head of third district's lucky I didn't strangle him."

As officers started filtering out of the auditorium,

Painter opened the Michael Stein interview fully and placed it on the chair she'd been sitting on. "The cat's out of the bag about Cochrane's background. Can't say I'm happy about that. Then again, maybe it doesn't matter now. There's something odd in the article. Look at the last few sentences."

Kopański scrutinized the final Stein quote.

"You thinking what I'm thinking?"

"A coded message."

Painter limped onto the stage toward the lectern and microphone.

The New Yorker spoke to the now half-empty auditorium. "Guys—before you go, does the name 'Vienna' mean anything in the context of Washington, D.C.?"

One of the nearby officers replied, "Not the city, but just outside there's a town called Vienna. It's in Fairfax County, about fifteen miles from here."

Painter glanced at Kopański before speaking to the D.C. cop again. "Does it have a train station?"

"It's the last stop on the Orange Line Metro."

"Who's the most senior person left in this room?"

The approximately one hundred officers left in the room looked around.

One of them raised his hand. "That'll be me. Commander of fourth district."

"At eleven o'clock, Cochrane's going to be at the Vienna Metro station. We can't scare him off. Can you mobilize an undercover task force right now? It needs to put surveillance on the place without being seen, ready to do a takedown when he's sighted."

The commander raced out of the room.

Painter walked fast to Kopański. "We've got thirty minutes max."

I drove off I-66 and onto a ramp that led me to the parking lot on the station's south side. I exited the vehicle, one of the detectives' stolen handguns in my jacket, and used an elevated walkway to access the station. Only three people were on my side of the barriers. Beyond the barriers, I could see five people standing on the platform. Nobody looked like an undercover cop. I had no idea whether I should wait where I was standing, or enter the platform. It didn't matter—the place was small enough for me to easily be seen.

My shades on, I purchased a return ticket to Ballston, with no intention of using the ticket, and passed through the barrier to the platform.

It was ten forty-five.

Kopański was loudly cursing the traffic. He had attached the flashing light to the roof of his unmarked car, and he raced through every opening on the highway.

Painter was on her cell to the chief of the Fairfax County Police Department. "If we've read this correctly, Cochrane's going to be at the Vienna Metro at eleven o'clock this morning. D.C. has deployed forty undercover firearms and surveillance specialists. They're ahead of us and should be there any minute."

The chief said, "I should have been consulted. They need authorization before they can operate in Fairfax."

Painter didn't have time for this. "I'm consulting you now. And if you have a problem with it, ring the attorney general and get his take on the chain of command in this situation."

The chief said nothing.

Painter continued, "But I need your help. Can you put squad cars in a perimeter five hundred yards away from the station? They've got to be out of sight. Their role is twofold: First, if Cochrane gets away on foot or driving, he runs into your guys. You've got to make that perimeter watertight. Second, if there's a gunfight in the station, they move in to assist."

The fact that his officers were going to be so crucial to the takedown fully placated the chief. "You got it. But what happens if he takes a train out of Vienna?"

"He can't. The last train into the station will arrive at eleven. We've arranged for it to terminate there, and trains for the next hour have been canceled." Painter hung up. "Can't you move any quicker?"

Grinding to a halt while beeping his horn to get two cars to move out of his way, Kopański replied, "I could if I had a missile launcher to clear a path."

To his relief, the traffic became much lighter. He put his foot to the floor and sped along route 66.

It was five minutes to eleven.

I watched a train pull in. Nobody got off; everyone on the platform except me got on the train. I walked along the platform, hands in my pockets, one of them gripping my pistol. The possibility that this was a trap hadn't escaped me, but I thought it was unlikely. Even if he thought I was guilty of the alleged crimes, no way would Michael Stein agree to set me up.

After our brief allegiance in the secret world, we'd shared a coffee together and spoke about our personal aspirations for the future. There'd been something about Stein that made me open up more than I ordinarily would. Most likely it was because Stein had said that the best spies are never loyal to the organizations they work for. Instead they're loyal to those who help them. He said that he would help me if ever I were in trouble. And he asked if there was anyone else I could trust. That's when I told him about Antaeus.

Stein's appearance in the newspaper had Antaeus's hand all over it.

I saw another train approaching.

Painter and Kopański were entering the town of Vienna.

Painter shut her cell after speaking to the head of the undercover task force. "Squad cars have their perimeter. If we want to, we can shut down every street and road in and out of the zone. They've got uniformed officers on foot too, in case Cochrane bolts without a vehicle. In the zone, the undercover unit is in place, watching the station. If he's in there, this won't be another Lynchburg fuck-up. There's no way out for him this time." She asked, "Do you want to be the one who goes in there? You owe Cochrane a visit after he put you on your ass on the Amtrak."

Kopański would dearly have loved to be the

officer who went into the station to get a visual on the Englishman. But he said, "No. I stand out too much."

As they drove past a stationary Fairfax County squad car that had been partially concealed between trees, he glanced at Painter and said, "I just want you to be very careful. No heroics. Promise me that?"

For a moment, she was unsure how to respond to the tough detective's genuine concern. Quietly she responded, "Sure, Joe. I'll be fine. Don't worry."

The train pulled into the station and three people alighted, one male, the others female. The male was over a hundred yards away from me.

I removed my shades and checked the time on my cell.

It was precisely 11 A.M.

Kopański parked his vehicle as close as he dared to the Metro station. "You sure the radio mic is working fine?"

Painter had fitted the device under her blouse in the car and had tested it several times. It had excellent connection to the radios of the D.C. undercover unit and the commander in charge of the Fairfax County troopers. "It's working."

She opened the car door, put one foot on the ground, and stopped as Kopański grabbed her arm.

"How close do you think you'll need to get to him to make a positive ID?"

She answered, "No idea. Depends what he's wearing."

With urgency, he said, "Just don't get too close."

"You care about my safety, Joe?" Her tone was jesting.

But Kopański wasn't seeing the funny side. "If he recognizes you, you'll be dead before you can do anything about it. Not too close."

Painter approached the station entrance. Earpiece in place, she spoke into her body mic. "This is Detective Painter. I'm approaching Vienna. Stand by. I'm now entering the station."

She hadn't felt this tense since her Night Stalker helicopter was shot down in Afghanistan.

I stood still as the solitary male passenger walked along the platform toward me.

All he was carrying was a satchel. He was tall, athletic, mid-thirties, wearing jeans and a jacket. He wasn't looking at me as he drew closer.

Painter stopped in the ticket hall of the small complex. A male and female in their twenties were buying tickets from a machine while laughing; the male was too short and the wrong age to be Cochrane. An elderly black woman was berating a staff member, telling him the subway prices were way too high. A father was bent over, wagging his finger at his naughty son. And a mother was negotiating her way through the ticket barrier, clutching shopping bags and pushing a pram.

Aside from getting on a train, the ticket hall was the only way out of here.

She purchased a ticket and walked toward the barriers.

* * *

The passenger was now fifteen yards away from me, his face easily visible. I stared at him. The man didn't make eye contact.

Other people in this situation would be desperate to look around to see if they were being observed by others. But that's not how this worked. The man coming toward me controlled the ground. He'd know if something was wrong. I had to put my complete faith in him. And if he walked past me and did nothing, that meant the shit was about to hit the fan.

Painter whispered, "Nothing in the ticket lobby. Going through the barriers."

In her earpiece she could hear the D.C. and Fairfax County commanders acknowledge her update and start issuing further orders to their men. The undercover unit was poised to storm the station on foot.

She placed her ticket in the barrier, it swung open, and she walked through.

The passenger was three feet in front of me, his satchel in his right hand. Still, he wasn't looking at me. Instead, he appeared to be staring at the ticket barriers forty yards behind me. There was a look of contentment on his face, as if he were looking forward to getting home.

Two feet.

One foot.

When he was directly alongside me, he quickly looked at my face. I glanced at him without moving my head. It was the man I'd worked with a year ago. Michael Stein. He gave me his satchel and continued walking.

I would have loved to have spoken to him.

But antisurveillance brush contacts don't allow for any kind of behavior that might show hostile observers that two agents know each other.

All Stein could do was keep walking.

I stayed still, my back to the barriers, waiting until I was confident that Stein had exited the complex.

"I've got one man on the platform. His back's to me. Approximately forty yards away."

"That's close enough," barked Kopański in Painter's earpiece.

She'd never heard him so concerned for her safety. Her handbag was in front of her, and she moved her hand inside it as if she were rummaging for a mislaid ticket. In truth she was gripping her sidearm.

The man turned.

She bowed her head, pretending to look in the bag.

Would all his expert training instantly tell him she was pretending to be something she wasn't?

She didn't dare speak into her radio mic. He was too close.

Her stomach flipping, hand ready to pull out her gun and fire, she looked up.

The man was not Will Cochrane.

A thought suddenly occurred to her as she recalled the last sentence in the *Washington Post* article. Not caring about maintaining her cover, she urgently said into her mic, "Whatever station is two stops away from here, we need to get there now."

I walked out of the West Falls Church Metro station and entered my vehicle. The parking lot was half empty and I couldn't see anyone else.

Everything had gone according to plan. Inserting the coded message inside the *Washington Post* interview had been a hell of a long shot, because the chances of my not reading the article were significant.

The final sentences of the article were a code telling me that Stein wanted to meet with me and give me something. But the meeting place wasn't the Vienna Metro. It was in a place denoted by the final sentence of the article.

That day, Vienna was dangerous and we were too down the line.

Two stops away from Vienna on the Orange Line was West Falls Church.

I knew cops were swooping on Vienna. I'd heard Detective Thyme Painter talking to the chief of the Fairfax County Police Department via the intercept device I'd found in Tap's car. Still, it had been a significant risk going to West Falls Church.

Were it not for my overwhelming fear for Tom Koenig's safety, I might have felt good about this moment. Just having the briefest of contacts with

Stein meant someone out there cared. Holding the satchel meant the world to me.

Rain started pelting the windshield of my car as I opened the bag and checked its contents. Inside were two packages and an envelope. One of the packages contained three hundred thousand dollars. The other was a bundle of dynamite.

I opened the envelope. Inside was a letter.

Have you considered that this might all be personal revenge from one individual? I'm sure you have. A powerful person is doing this to you. I don't know who that person is. But I do know that someone like that will have people watching over him. A blow is best dealt from distance. Consider that. I'm so very sorry to hear about your sister. —A.

A had to be Antaeus.

The former Russian spymaster had given me a lifeline. And a tactic.

But the sentence about my sister made no sense.

She was in Scotland, leading a quiet life, and would never cross Antaeus's radar. With a sense of impending dread, I grabbed the *Washington Post* and read the other article on the front page. It summarized a briefing to the press given by Lieutenant Pat Brody of the Office of the Deputy Commissioner, NYPD Public Information.

The first thing that jumped out was that the Waldorf murder weapon had been found in Lynchburg. In a part of the city where I'd never been. And ballistics analysis left no doubt that the same gun had been used to kill the woman in Manhattan. It had also been the pistol fired on the Granges, their cop protectors, and the two cops in Lynchburg.

The weapon I'd picked up in my hotel room was an identical model to the murder weapon, but not the same gun. I briefly wondered whether this was sufficient to absolve me of all crimes. No. My innocence couldn't be proven simply because I was carrying a weapon that didn't kill the people I was accused of murdering.

I carried on reading.

And stopped on the words *Sarah Goldsmith*.

My sister.

The victim.

In the Waldorf.

My head flopped to my chest. It might as well have been cut off.

I'd touched her fingers, because I wanted her to know someone cared. But I thought I didn't know her. How could I know? Her long blond hair had been cut short and dyed brown. Her face had been obliterated by bullets. There was no ID on her. But now I could feel my dead sister's fingers touching mine. It made the moment wholly different. And all I could think about was that I'd looked at a murder victim and hadn't known that she was the last remaining member of my family.

So much had been done to me. But for the world to now believe I was capable of shooting my sister was an unbearable agony. Worse was the utter loss. I'd intended to Skype her when the twins

and I were settled in our new home. I'd wanted
to build bridges with her, show her that I was living a peaceful life. I was sure that's all she wanted
to see—her brother no longer putting himself in
great danger. She'd have finally been happy that
she no longer had to worry about getting a call
saying I was dead.

I couldn't stop my tears as I continued reading
the article.

More details about Lynchburg.

Conjecture on my state of mind and motivation
for going on the rampage.

And then a line that made me drop the paper
and bang my fist against my forehead.

> The body of Sarah Goldsmith's husband,
> James Goldsmith, was found yesterday at the
> Goldsmiths' home in Scotland. Local police
> released a statement saying that the death
> was apparently a suicide and occurred shortly
> after Goldsmith learned of his wife's murder.

James—a nice man. Perfect foil for my high-
strung sister. He'd met her at university and was
besotted with her ever since. A guy who made
Sarah laugh.

And James went to his grave thinking I killed
his wife.

This was unbearable.

On Tap's intercept device, I heard Painter say that
I wasn't at Vienna but most likely was at West Falls
Church. I put my hands on the ignition key. Stay

here and let them capture me? The pain would end that way. Or drive out of here and try to find Tom?

What to do? I had to make a decision fast. But all I could think about was how much pain and death I'd brought to those around me.

In the basement of the isolated farmhouse twenty-nine miles north of D.C., Viktor Zhukov partially lifted the black hood up to reveal Tom Koenig's mouth. "How are you this evening?"

The rancid smell on the man's breath made Tom squirm. "Sc-scared. Please . . ."

"Hush now. This will all be over soon." He looked at the metal girder in the ceiling above Tom's chair. "You know who's done this to you, don't you?"

"Please . . . please . . ."

"Shut up!" Zhukov walked to the technical equipment on the side table. He moved his finger down the sheet containing the list of pre-recordings. Motioning for the colleagues in the room to be silent, he asked, "Sir, you still want to go ahead with this?"

He pressed play on one of the audio devices.

A man's voice said, "Of course. My mind's made up."

Zhukov smiled as he saw Tom fruitlessly try to get out of his shackles. He went upstairs and spoke to one of his colleagues. "Destroy and get rid of all the basement audio equipment. We've no need for it now. We'll finish the boy tomorrow evening."

TWENTY-SIX

Wracked by grief and shock, I was shaking as I drove my car onto the shoulder of a deserted country road north of D.C.

I turned off the ignition and sat in stunned silence in the blackness that surrounded me. Regret coursed through me. No doubt it would have taken time for Sarah to fully trust me in my new life, but I was convinced it would have happened. Now, memories—random, frenetic—cascaded.

Me crying when I was five and Sarah putting her arms around me and telling me Pa would come home soon. Even though she and Ma knew he stood little chance of anything other than death in his Iranian prison.

The time I was six and she was seven and I'd laughed as our mother walked us to school, Ma oblivious that Sarah's skirt had accidentally hitched in the lining of her panties.

Sarah telling me that she'd do my homework if I didn't tell Ma that I'd spotted her holding hands with a boy.

Age seventeen, me returning to my home in Virginia, so pleased to be able to tell Ma that I'd gotten school grades that would take me to England and Cambridge University. That's when my life turned. I'd walked in on four armed robbers killing my mother and about to do the same to Sarah.

The look of horror on Sarah's face when she saw me execute the men with the kitchen knife Ma used to carve our Sunday roasts.

Running off to the French Foreign Legion to escape punishment. CIA and MI6 friends of my father hushing up the incident. Five brutal years in the Legion. Returning to England and academia. And realizing that I was a fundamentally changed man.

Then fifteen years of near constant deployment by British Intelligence. I'd had little time to see my sister and zero ability to show her that underneath it all I was still the little boy who once had freckles and blond hair and used to laugh from his belly.

I got out of the vehicle and paced back and forth, like a caged lion that had grown demented in captivity. A pistol in my hand, I leaned against the car, the handgun resting on its roof and caressing my face.

It would be so easy.

Just pull the trigger.

End this.

Rain banged against the roof of the car and the nape of my neck.

A very different memory came to me. One where I was undergoing the brutal selection course to enter the Foreign Legion's special forces unit Groupement des Commandos Parachutistes. After five days of no sleep, the recruits had been forced to stand in an icy lake in the Pyrenees, water up to our necks, rain pounding our faces.

From the banks of the lake, an instructor had shouted at us, "If you don't like this, you'd better quit. How you feel now is how it's going to feel for every second of every day in GCP. If you embrace that, you'll survive with us."

And I recalled being pulled aside on the regular MI6 new entrant intelligence course. I was told that I'd been singled out for a classified twelve-month training course that in all probability would break my mind and body. I could only start the course after signing documents absolving the British government of any blame if I died in training.

In my whole life, I'd never quit.

For the first time, everything now felt different.

I was holding a gun.

And I was seriously thinking of turning it on myself.

My sister, her husband, Robert and Celia Grange, police officers—they'd all died as a consequence of me mightily pissing someone off. Tom and Billy had lost a surrogate father. Tom was kidnapped. Billy would be distraught with worry. So too his aunt Faye.

Why had Sarah been in New York? What had happened to me in the Waldorf? Why did James take his own life so quickly after he'd heard about his wife's murder? Who was doing this to me?

The questions prompted anger. I was deep in thought, imagining what I could have done to put me in this god-awful situation. The details of how this plot against me had been constructed hadn't mattered to me before. Understanding them wouldn't have changed a thing. Now, I needed to know.

Sarah had no business affairs in the States. Nor would she have been on holiday here without her husband. She was lured to New York on a false pretext. How? My mind raced. Money. The kidnapper had somehow put her and James into a desperate financial situation. Probably that had been done over weeks, more likely months. Once they were crippled with debt, a lifeline was offered, most likely a lucrative job offer. Sarah was in the States for an interview. But there was no job. It was bait to get her to New York. Once there, she was snatched. Her hair was cut and dyed. Rings and other identifying materials were removed. All that was left to identify her was her face. She was bound and gagged and placed into a large bag.

Men entered my hotel room, donned gas masks, and pumped sleeping gas into the bedroom. They injected me with a drug to completely knock me out. Windows were opened to let the gas drift out of the room, so there'd be no scent of it in the morning. My bank card was copied, and subsequently it was used to completely drain my account.

My bootprints were expertly copied, most likely using a mold to get their exact shape and dimensions. Those prints were used at the bottom of the Granges' lane.

Sarah was put in the bathtub and shot twice in the back of the head, obliterating her last identifiable feature. Her binds and gag were removed. Unconscious, I was hauled into the bathroom. My hands were dipped in my sister's blood and pressed onto the bathroom wall. One of Sarah's fingers was used to scratch my arm so that my DNA was under her nail. And the scratch was made over the puncture wound from the syringe. That way I had no reason to think the sting on my arm was anything other than a scratch. I was taken back to my bed. And the next morning when I woke up, I put my grogginess down to jet lag.

To have planned this and to know that I'd checked in to the Waldorf meant that I must have been under observation for some time. The kidnapper knew about the twins and my plans to adopt them. And he would have known that two months ago I'd planned my trip to the States. In making those plans, I'd triggered the move on Sarah. And after she was murdered, James had killed himself because it was the final straw.

I didn't know if my conjecture was correct. But it all made sense.

Still, even though I trawled my imagination, I had no clue as to who was behind all this. There were far too many candidates who hated my guts.

I withdrew Tom's bear from my bag and pulled the string on its back. I heard the lisping Russian man speaking to the boy. I pulled the string again, this time hearing Tom's voice from a recording he'd made before his kidnapping.

"Hello, Uncle Will. Billy and I are very sad. People are saying you did something wrong. Is it true? We don't understand because we thought you were happy and coming to look after us." Tom's voice was getting emotional. "Why haven't you come to collect us and take us to our new home?"

I couldn't turn my gun on myself. Tom's voice ensured that. I brushed the teddy bear against my face.

Someone's revenge had nearly finished me.

But I wasn't a quitter.

And now I was going to take my own revenge.

TWENTY-SEVEN

I was still in my car outside of D.C. as morning broke.

Simon Tap's cell bleeped. A message from Knox.

> THE THREE HIRE CARS WERE RENTED BY A GUY CALLED VIKTOR ZHUKOV. HE'S A SMALL TIME BUSINESSMAN IN D.C. OWNS A COMPANY CALLED LONGTRADE. CAN'T SEE HOW HE'D BE CONNECTED TO COCHRANE OR WOULD HELP YOU TRACK HIM DOWN.

I replied.

> OKAY. WAS JUST PURSUING A LEAD. PROBABLY UNCONNECTED. WE MAY NEED TO MEET SOON.

I spent an hour using the phone's Web browser. Viktor Zhukov's company was in a warehouse on New York Avenue NE. Primarily, it was a distributor of wholesale foods. There were no other directors in LongTrade. Public records and the manufacturer's Web site showed it was active and filing annual tax returns. I searched for any other companies, whether in D.C. or elsewhere, that might be linked to Zhukov but could find nothing. Surprisingly, there were no photographs of Zhukov. No pictures of him in marketing promotions. Nothing. It was clear he kept a very low profile.

But the company records listed him as a Russian with a work permit to be in the U.S.

Russian.

Was this the man in Tom's recording?

I waited two hours, until 9 A.M., and rang Long-Trade. Using an American accent, I said to the company receptionist, "This is FedEx. I have a package that needs signing for by your company director. I'm a bit confused because the address details don't give a name."

The receptionist replied, "That'll be Mr. Zhukov. Just bring the package to our warehouse. I can sign for it on his behalf."

"No, ma'am. It says it has to be his signature. Is he at work today?"

"He's out of the office. Back tomorrow."

"Shoot. Is he in D.C. today? Maybe there's another address I could deliver it to?"

"Yes, he's in the city. But the only other address we have for him is his home address. I'm not at liberty to give out that information without his permission."

I wasn't going to ask for that. It could make Zhukov suspicious. I feigned frustration. "Listen.

I've got a ton of deliveries to make and I'll get my ass handed to me if I don't get them done. Is there any way he can come into work and sign?"

The receptionist's tone was angry. "He told me that he can't be disturbed today unless it's urgent. There's nothing more I can do for you. Please bring the package in tomorrow." She hung up.

The thought of losing a day worried me. As every minute passed, the risks to Tom's safety increased. But something the receptionist said gave me an idea.

I went back on to LongTrade's Web site and browsed the promotional pictures showing smiling workers, assembly lines, trucks being loaded by men wearing safety helmets, and external shots of the warehouse and its surroundings. I loaded a map of that part of Washington, memorized the route to get there, and drove.

Two hours later, my car was stationary on a side road off New York Avenue. The area around me was industrial, with numerous warehouses and other company buildings. I couldn't see any security. There were a few workers, some on foot, others in work vehicles. None of them took any notice of each other as they went about their duties.

I had a direct line of sight of LongTrade on the other side of the avenue. Its driveway was used by multiple warehouses close by. This was excellent. I could pose as an employee of one of the other companies, or an associate paying LongTrade a visit.

I reached into my bag and got what I needed, then walked across New York Avenue and entered the complex containing LongTrade. If challenged by anyone, I'd say I was lost and had a meeting with a company called Globalite. It was the name of a real company I'd spotted from the avenue. But I couldn't see anyone. Presumably workers in this part of the industrial zone were all inside. That included LongTrade's.

I could see a hive of activity through Long-Trade's windows. I circled the building, ensuring I was at least forty yards away from it. I didn't know exactly what I was looking for—just something that would help me create a disruption.

There were no windows at the rear of the warehouse, next to a parking lot. Nor could I be seen from other buildings, because they were too far away and had no windows facing this direction. The only vehicle in the lot was a van that had Long-Trade's name and logo painted on its side. Farther away from the building was a large fuel tank, with pipes leading into the warehouse. It was fixed to the ground and made of metal sufficiently secure to protect its contents from fire or lightning strikes.

I glanced around.

The first time I'd done something like this was when I was assigned by GCP to France's intelligence service DGSE, which sent me on black ops missions.

The time to move was now.

Speed and confidence were crucial.

I walked fast to the van, rolled underneath it, used tape to fasten an item to the gas tank of the vehicle, rolled away, and walked quickly back to my car.

I'd used a small piece of the dynamite Michael Stein had supplied, together with one of the timer detonators he'd included in the package. I couldn't see the van now. But I could hear the bang that ignited its gas tank.

Zhukov's cell phone rang. The number on his screen showed it was the switchboard of his company LongTrade. "I told you I didn't want to be disturbed today."

The receptionist calling him sounded in shock. "Sorry, sir. It's just there's been an incident, and . . ."

"An incident? What happened?"

"One of the company vans just caught fire. Right outside the warehouse. Nobody's hurt, but . . . but . . ."

"Spit it out!"

"The fire department is putting out the flames. They say paperwork needs to be completed."

Dealing with this was the last thing Zhukov needed. "What caused the fire?"

"The fire chief doesn't know. He thinks it must have been an electrical fault. Because no one was hurt, he says he won't spend time investigating the accident. That's an insurance company matter. But he's concerned that it blew up so close to our fuel supply. That means extra paperwork, apparently. The staff is very shaken up."

"Oh, for fuck's sake." Zhukov checked his watch. "Okay. I'll be there in an hour. Maybe less if traffic's okay. And tell my employees that if they don't get back to work, heads are going to roll."

I watched LongTrade through Tap's camera, which had a high-powered zoom lens.

All was chaos around the warehouse. Workers were outside, some of them gesticulating wildly at each other. Fire crews were moving back and forth with hoses. A fireman with a different-colored helmet from the rest, the chief, was holding a clipboard and talking to a woman. Maybe she was the receptionist I'd spoken to. Black smoke was visible over the top of the warehouse. And employees from other business units were standing outside, watching everything that was happening.

If anyone asked me what I was doing, I'd avoid the question by asking if they knew about the fuel explosion over there. I'd say I was taking photos for my kids. But compared to the bustle around the warehouse, it was dead quiet on this side of the avenue.

I'd checked the six non-fire-crew vehicles that had come and gone during the forty-five minutes after the explosion. None of their drivers behaved like they owned LongTrade and were taking charge. If my plan to bring Zhukov to his place of work failed, there was nothing left for me to do other than go to the police. I'd hand them the teddy bear and tell them I thought the voice in the recording belonged to Viktor Zhukov. I hated that option. Before the police got to Zhukov, Tom would likely be killed.

Another vehicle slowed on New York Avenue and made the turn into the driveway that led to LongTrade. I couldn't see the driver. I kept my camera trained on the car. It stopped outside the front of the warehouse. A man got out, his back to me. He spoke to the woman and the fire chief, then walked quickly to the back of the building. Five minutes later he returned, his face toward me.

I zoomed my camera.

I was looking at the face of the man I'd seen in the back of the police car leaving the Granges'.

Motherfucker.

I memorized his license plate number. My heart was beating fast, and for the first time I could remember, I had a feeling that something had gone right for me.

The man I was watching had to be Zhukov. He had an air of command. I could tell by the way employees were reacting to his presence. He was writing on the fire chief's clipboard, his mouth moving fast. The woman next to him looked scared. Perhaps Zhukov was chastising her. The Russian handed the clipboard back to the fireman. Nearby, a group of employees were loitering. Zhukov walked over to them and swung his arms while shouting. I bet he was telling them to get back to their jobs.

His face livid, he got in his car and drove out of the complex.

I followed him.

Mobile surveillance is tradecraft I'd honed in hostile cities around the world. And I had plenty of experience adapting the technique for rural areas. As I followed Zhukov through D.C., I kept three cars between him and me. But as we got to the outskirts of the city, I dropped back. My eyes were darting between Zhukov's car and the map application in Tap's phone. Even though I knew D.C. well, I didn't know every inch. I was using the phone to check out parallel routes to the road we were on. This was in case Zhukov suddenly changed direction and I lost sight of him.

Thirty minutes later, we were heading north in the suburbs. I dropped farther back so that it would be impossible for Zhukov to recognize the make of my vehicle, let alone read its license plate. Traffic was considerably thinner as we drove along route 124 through rolling countryside. Thankfully, there were still enough cars to prevent me from standing out.

Zhukov phoned Edward Carley. "Sorry I missed your call. I had a stupid matter to take care of at work."

Carley's tone was cold. "I told you that you are *not* to be attending to any of your business affairs today. Only focus on the package. What time are you dealing with it?"

"I'm nearly back at the house. My guys are doing all final preparations." Including cleaning the place to eradicate any traces of their presence there. "It will take about another two hours. Then we'll deal with the package."

"Don't give me specifics, but do you have an idea where you'll dump it?"

"In the early hours, I'm thinking fairly central in the city."

"Excellent. Once that's done, the project is finished and you will have earned your pay." Carley ended the call.

I slowed down as I saw that Zhukov was signaling a right turn.

I checked the map on my phone, which didn't show another road where he was turning. I used two fingers to zoom in on the spot. All I could see on the map was a thin white line where Zhukov was driving. It must have been a private road, and it ended after five miles. There were no other roads in or out. I stopped my vehicle on the side of the main road, hazard lights on as if I'd suffered a mechanical breakdown. It was a huge risk, but there was no way I could chance following Zhukov along such an exposed private drive. I had to hope my map was correct and that Zhukov's destination was at the end of the road.

I waited ten minutes, started the car and entered the private road.

A slight rise half a mile ahead meant I couldn't see any farther along the road. Zhukov's car was nowhere to be seen. I drove along the track, empty fields either side of me. I was preoccupied with the possibility that the Russian was heading to his home and that Tom Koenig was being kept elsewhere.

At the top of the rise a sign was posted next to the road.

BADEN LODGE. AVAILABLE FOR
SHORT-TERM RENT. INQUIRIES TO
MASON & CO. REALTORS.

Zhukov wasn't heading to his home. He was going to a place that he'd secured for a week or two.

I drove over the rise and now could see for miles down the road. There was nothing on it save the speck of a speeding car. I stopped and used the camera to zoom in on the image. Yes, it was Zhukov. This was as far as I dared go. There were no trees or other features that would help me hide my car. That left me no choice. I drove off the road onto the field to my right. My car juddered as its suspension tried to compensate for the uneven ground and its tires slipped over mud. I stopped the car in a hollow, sure it couldn't be spotted from the lane.

From my backpack, I took out the MK23 pistol with sound suppressor. It had eight bullets. Not knowing if that would be enough, I put in my jacket the two dead detectives' SIG Sauer P229 pistols and four spare magazines. Everything else, I left in the car.

Moving on foot, I crossed the field at speed, my MK23 in my hands.

Thirty minutes later, I threw myself to the ground and observed the solitary clapboard farmhouse at the end of the road. In front of it was Zhukov's car, along with seven others. Beyond the house were more open fields. The house looked to be over a hundred years old, and was sizable but dilapidated. Presumably that was why its owner rented it out—to raise some cash for repairs. I doubted it got much business. It was too remote, the countryside too bland.

But it was a perfect place to imprison a kidnapped child.

All of its curtains were closed. My idea had been

to watch the house for an hour, then move in. I'd have to go in blind.

It started to rain. The light faded as black clouds took over the sky.

If I called for a SWAT team and hostage negotiators, the first thing they'd have to do was establish whether there was a felony. And even if Zhukov and his colleagues refused to leave the house, that didn't prove anything other than lack of cooperation. So negotiations would begin. They'd take hours, maybe days. And within that time frame Zhukov could execute Tom. The one thing SWAT would not do if they turned up now was seize the element of surprise and storm the place.

I had no desire to negotiate with the occupants of the house. Pure speed and aggression were what mattered.

It's the only way to deal with desperate situations like this. And it's what I'd been trained to do as a soldier and a spy.

But there was the possibility that some of the occupants of the house were innocent. Zhukov could be here for another reason entirely. Maybe his associates were legitimate business colleagues gathered for a work retreat.

I'd soon find out.

I tried the front door handle. Locked.

I shot a silenced bullet into the lock and kicked the door open.

A woman was in the hallway.

Her eyes and mouth went wide as she saw me. She quickly withdrew a pistol from her waistband. I shot her in the head and stepped over her dead body.

Oblivious to what was happening, a man sauntered out of a room. A duster and spray polish were
in his hands, a gun fixed under his belt. He dropped
the cleaning products a split second before my bullet entered his brain. I opened the door to my left.
Inside was a living room containing two men in
paper coveralls and medical face masks. They were
on their hands and knees scrubbing the wooden
floor. Their heads quickly swiveled toward me. I
shot one of them, rushed to the other, and put my
gun under the man's chin.

"Where's the boy?" I hissed while ripping off
the man's mask.

"Fuck!"

"I'm not here for you. Just the boy."

The man looked terrified as he responded, "Basement. He's in the basement." His face smacked the
floor after I pulled the trigger.

I checked the other rooms on the ground floor,
all empty. At the end of the corridor were stairs
leading up and down. I had to clear upstairs first,
in case there were more hostiles there who'd try
to stop me from leaving with Tom. The stairs had
a right angle halfway up. As I took each step with
my pistol at eye level, a man turned the bend in the
stairs. He tumbled down past me with my bullet
in his eye.

"You okay?" called out a man from somewhere
upstairs.

I reached the top of the stairs.

A man was walking along the upper corridor,
a quizzical look on his face. Seeing me, he spun

around and managed to cry out one syllable before I killed him.

I ran in the direction the man had turned. I was near the end of the corridor when a big male poked his head out of a bedroom. I fired, but the man instantly disappeared back into the room. I was out of silenced rounds. I dashed into the room just as the man was pulling a handgun from a bag. I jabbed my knee into the man's back and smashed the butt of my handgun onto his upper hand, causing him to drop his weapon. But the man was still on his feet. He dropped low, turned, and stepped forward while delivering two punches. One powerful blow connected with my chest, forcing me back. The man had skills in unarmed combat. So did I. I ducked as another blow came my way, shifted my shoulders, punched him in the gut, kicked his ankle, and sent another punch into his face. The man's eyes closed and he fell sideways to the floor like a tree that had been felled. He was either knocked out or dead.

To be sure of the latter, I gripped the man's chin and the back of his skull and twisted his head like a corkscrew. I dropped his head after hearing his neck snap.

Though the basement was relatively soundproof from the rest of the large house, Zhukov could hear the sound of his team doing heavy lifting over Tom's sobbing. They were preparing to leave the house this evening and were clearing all traces of their time here. The technical equipment in the basement had been removed, destroyed, and its broken parts dropped in the center of a lake two hundred miles away. Two of his team were cleansing the house of DNA, room by room, though they'd all worn rubber gloves and covers over their shoes throughout their stay here. They were placing all their personal belongings in the trunks of their cars. And there'd be no paper trail to Zhukov from the booking process to secure the rental. He'd used cash and a false ID.

He looked at Tom. The black hood was over his head and his hands were tied behind his back. He was sitting on a wooden chair underneath the solitary bare lightbulb hanging from the ceiling. The child was still wearing the red pajamas he'd been in when Zhukov had snatched him.

"Crying won't help you." Zhukov smiled. "In a few hours, it'll all be over."

He looked at his watch. It was time to check how his team was progressing.

He walked up the stairs to the ground level. He froze. One of his men was facedown on the other set of stairs. He heard two loud bangs and felt unbelievable agony in both kneecaps.

"I'm assuming you must be Viktor Zhukov." I strode up to him, my gun pointing at his head. With my other hand I rummaged through his pockets. "After what my bullets did to your knees, you're going to need a lot of reconstructive surgery. Even then, it'll be a miracle if you walk again."

I took out Zhukov's cell phone and only weapon—a handgun. Zhukov was going nowhere.

I went to the other four bodies on the floor and removed their guns and phones. I placed all of them on top of a cupboard in the kitchen. No way would Zhukov be able to get there and reach them.

The Russian was screaming as I stepped over him and made the descent into the basement. I tucked my gun into my waistband and rushed to the boy in the center of the room.

Ripping off his hood, I cried, "Tom, Tom!" and hugged him. "It's okay. Everything's going to be okay."

Tom was in shock and confused, his eyes wide, red face dripping with tears. "Uncle Will? What . . . what . . . ?"

I was moving fast behind his back. "I just need to untie these knots. Hold still."

"What's happening?"

"Just hold still, little man," I said soothingly. I managed to get Tom out of his shackles and crouched before him while gently holding his arms. "You're safe now."

Anguish, rather than relief, was evident in Tom's expression. "Why did you do the bad things?"

"I didn't. I'll explain everything. First I have to get you out of here. But there are some unpleasant things upstairs I don't want you to see."

I went to lift Tom.

The boy recoiled.

I knew why. Tom thought I'd gone on a murder spree instead of adopting the twins. In Tom's eyes, Uncle Will was a bad man who'd let him down. But here and now, resolving that had to wait. I lifted Tom onto my chest and buried his face in my jacket so that he wouldn't see the dead bodies and what I'd done to Zhukov. After I carried him up the stairs, Tom flinched again as he heard the Russian's scream.

"It's okay, it's okay," I said in Tom's ear.

Zhukov was leaving a trail of blood behind him as he attempted to crawl on his belly to the front door. I stamped on his head.

Outside, I placed Tom down and said, "Wait here. None of the people who kept you here can hurt you now."

"Not true!"

"It is true. I promise." I bent over at face level with the child, my hand on his shoulder. "I need to get some things from inside. Just wait here, by the cars."

I went back inside and collected the five cell phones from the kitchen. Then I searched the three dead men upstairs and took their phones as well. Downstairs I watched Zhukov still using his arms to move himself inch by inch toward freedom.

I kicked him onto his back and placed a boot on his chest. "Stay still."

The pain in Zhukov's knees was making his eye involuntarily twitch.

I crouched beside him and tapped the barrel of my SIG Sauer on the Russian's forehead. "Who's your boss?"

Zhukov spat in my face. "I'm my own boss."

There was no mistaking his lisping accent. He was the man who'd grabbed Tom.

I replied, "I've never met you before. And your name's not known to me. Bit odd for you to go to all this trouble to frame a complete stranger. I want to know who gave you the idea to set me up."

"Go fuck yourself."

I moved my gun. "You're a foot soldier. One of many. I bet it wasn't even you who killed my sister."

Zhukov laughed, though his face was screwed up and blood was coming out of his mouth. "You mean the woman I held down in the bathtub? The one I shot twice in the brain?"

"Yes." I stood up and shot him in the ankle.

Zhukov writhed on the floor.

"What matters most to you right now? Protecting your boss or your life?"

Gasping for air, the Russian replied, "You're going to kill me anyway."

"I want to keep you alive. For now."

"I don't believe you!"

I smiled as I circled the prone man. "Work it out. I want you alive because you can tell the police what really happened. If I kill you, I kill my ticket out of here."

"Go to hell."

"I am in hell. You put me here." I pointed my gun at Zhukov's thigh. "If you tell me who set everything up, I'll walk out of here. The alternative is I keep shooting until your body goes into massive shock and kills you."

Zhukov gritted his teeth, sweat pouring out of his face. "How did you find me?"

"A recording device in Tom's teddy bear. It was very clever of him to activate it just before you took him." My eyes were unblinking. "Soon, you'll be begging me to put a bullet in your head. Who is he?"

I could see that Zhukov's pain was becoming intolerable.

"He paid you to do all this, yes?"

Zhukov nodded.

"In which case, don't let me kill you for the sake of money you can't spend."

Resignation was in Zhukov's eyes. "Edward . . ."

"Edward who?"

"You won't kill me?"

"All I want is his name and my freedom!"

Zhukov wiped blood from his lips. "Edward Carley. You know who he is."

I did. He was the brother of Jack Carley—three years ago I'd exposed him as a high-ranking CIA traitor working for Russia. Six months after beginning his life sentence in a maximum-security American prison, Jack Carley had killed himself. His brother was a powerful businessman and former surgeon. He'd testified at the inquest, saying that he held the intelligence officer who'd exposed Jack as responsible for his death.

Edward Carley had somehow identified me as that person.

He'd waited three years for his revenge.

And this was his dish served cold.

"Where is he?" I asked.

Zhukov didn't answer.

I shot him in the leg. "Where is he?"

Zhukov was sobbing. "Stop. Please . . . stop."

I stared at him.

"He's . . ." Zhukov had blood all around him.

"Yes?"

"Montauk Yacht Club, Long Island. Luxury

cruiser. He will leave in two weeks. Don't know where he's headed, but it will be away from the States."

There was one last thing I needed to know. "With your help, Carley made my life miserable. Worse than that, you kidnapped Tom Koenig. When were you going to kill him? Tonight? Tomorrow? Dump his body in a prominent place in D.C.? The final nail in my coffin?"

Zhukov shook his head. "No. You got that wrong."

"I doubt that."

The Russian's body was shaking. "My orders were to take him into the heart of the city tonight, and let him go unharmed."

"Liar!"

Zhukov said, "I'll tell the police everything. I swear."

"If you do, cops will arrest Carley. I don't want that to happen. More likely you won't tell them the truth." Zukhov moaned in agony. "That said, I did promise you that if you gave me your boss's name, I'd walk out of here. I don't break promises. But that is all I promised you."

I shot Zhukov twice in the brain and walked out of the house.

TWENTY-EIGHT

Tom was nowhere to be seen.

Urgently, I sprinted around the house, scouring its surroundings for the boy in his red pajamas. Nothing. No doubt the sound of gunfire in the house had scared him away.

Where would he have gone?

The road leading away from the house.

I ran as fast as my exhausted legs could move, covering half a mile before I saw Tom in the center of the road. The ten-year-old's arms were flapping as he ran over gravel and stone that must be punishing the bare soles of his feet. The poor boy had simply had enough. And in his eyes, Uncle Will was a murderer.

I caught up with him and lifted him by the waist.

"Let me go! Let me go!"

I held firm, fixing him into a fireman's carry and brushing debris off his feet. "We're going to the police now. You can tell them what the Russian man did to you." I walked quickly to my car. "And I'm going to tell them what he did to me."

Though I'd make no mention of Carley.

Placing Tom in the front passenger seat of my car, I said, "You're a witness to the fact that I didn't kidnap you. That doesn't automatically prove I'm innocent of the other crimes they think I committed. But it will give the police a huge starting point and motivation to look at things differently. They'll investigate the house you were kept in." I drove the car onto the road. "But meeting the police isn't going to be straightforward. We've got to do this carefully."

Tom was silent, hugging himself. No doubt he was desperate to be reunited with his brother and for the nightmare to end.

We were soon back on the main road. I was driving south toward D.C., searching for a place in the surrounding countryside that suited my purposes. I turned the car off the road and stopped. I looked at the number stored in the communications intercept device Tap had been carrying.

Using one of the cell phones I'd taken from the house, I called the number.

A woman answered.

I said, "Detective Painter. My name is Will Cochrane. I'm innocent of the crimes you believe I've committed. I have Tom Koenig. I want to give him to you and hand myself in. But I know that emotions are running high. I don't expect you to come completely alone, but I also don't want to meet you backed up by half of D.C. law enforcement. One of them might put a bullet in my head. We have Tom's safety to consider if bullets start flying. Only you and Joe Kopański must come. I mean you no harm. I just want this matter dealt with calmly. Drive north on route 124. I'll call you from another cell with further instructions."

She asked, "How did you get my number?"

I hung up. I removed the battery from the cell so that any attempts to trace its location would fail, and tossed it out of the car window. I looked at the intercept device and waited.

Painter and Kopański were rushing to their car in the basement of police headquarters in Washington.

Painter was on the phone to the city's chief of police. "Maybe Cochrane's finally had enough. But this could also be a trap. I need a SWAT team, a hostage negotiator, a medical unit, and an undercover firearms unit."

Within ten minutes, the basement parking lot was a hive of activity, SWAT officers climbing into two black trucks and thirty plainclothes detectives and three paramedics entering their vehicles.

Painter fixed her police radio in place and spoke into her throat mic. "Okay. Joe and I will take point. Everyone stay right on our asses."

She called the chief of police, updated him about their status, and concluded, "We're ready to go. I'll keep you posted."

The convoy exited the parking lot.

* * *

I heard the calls Painter had made. I waited fifteen minutes and used another cell to call her. "Detective Painter. I wanted to do this calmly. No drama. You'd do well to assume I'm watching you. Lose the SWAT, detectives, and medical units. Only you and Kopański. Otherwise we don't have a deal."

As they were driving at speed through the northern zone of D.C., Painter looked around urgently. At her side Joe expertly navigated his way through heavy traffic.

In her radio mic, she said, "Cochrane says he's watching us. He must be on our tail. I want three unmarked cars to drop back by five hundred yards. He must be between that point and us. Work that gap."

Three police cars at the rear of the convoy did as they were instructed, slowing down until they were five hundred yards behind. They took turns driving closer to the convoy, scrutinizing each car in the gap, before dropping back again.

I called Painter. "Whatever you think I've done, I'm not a cop killer. I won't lay a finger on you or Kopański. But you need to make a decision—do this my way, or maintain the heavy-handed approach. If it's the latter, you won't see me."

Painter felt utterly conflicted as she asked Kopański, "What do you think?"

Like his colleague, Kopański wasn't sure. "He could be playing with us. He's assumed we'll bring backup. Or he's not playing with us. Maybe let the undercover boys behind us see if they can flush him out."

"And if they can't?"

Kopański glanced at Painter. "If we meet him alone, there's a strong possibility he'll shoot us simply because he's worked out that we're the lead investigators in his case. It's his payback."

I said to Tom, "I'm going to fix everything and make things up to you and Billy. I know this must be scary for you right now. Soon, this will all be a distant memory."

I stroked his cheek.

He winced.

It deeply saddened me to see the boy like this. But I knew he was traumatized. Specialists would help him overcome the trauma. Right now, nothing I could say to him would help.

I picked up another cell and called Painter. "Have you made a decision?"

Painter responded, "That's not how these things are done."

"Then change how things are done. If you think I'm trying to lure you and Kopański out here alone, just so I can hurt or kill you, you're wrong. I've got bigger interests at heart. And the biggest of them are to ensure Tom is handed over to you and my innocence is proven. Make a damn decision."

Painter drummed her fingers on the dashboard as she and Joe reached the outskirts of the city. "Shit!"

Kopański said, "He didn't want to kill me and the other cop on the Amtrak. But we think he killed plenty of cops since."

"We *think*?"

"Yeah. We *think*."

"But you and I have kept an open mind."

"That principle's been tested to the limit."

"I know!"

The detectives were consumed with their own thoughts for a few moments.

Kopański broke the silence. "I say we give Cochrane one more chance to prove his innocence."

"I agree."

Painter ordered the convoy to stand down but remain static in the area in case it was needed. There were objections from each unit's commanders, but she overruled them.

She wondered if she and Joe were making the worst mistake of their careers.

Twenty minutes later, I called her from another phone. "Have you made a decision?"

She told him she had. It would only be her and Kopański coming to the meeting.

I replied, "I'd like to believe you, but I still need to be cautious. I'm going to guide you to a place where any backup you may have will stand out a mile. If I spot that backup, you'll never hear from me again. I'll find other means to get Tom into your care."

I gave her very precise instructions. I grabbed

my bag. Looking at Tom, I said, "We need to get out of the car and go for a walk."

Outside the car, I removed my jacket and placed it over Tom, its hem touching his toes.

I smiled. "The teddy bear I bought you was what told me you were alive. You were a clever boy to record the Russian man's voice."

Tom didn't smile.

We walked for twenty minutes, for the most part me carrying Tom.

"This'll do," I said. "Now we just need to wait."

We were on an escarpment of open fields. Three-quarters of a mile away there was a solitary farm track. The layout was near identical to the surroundings leading to Zhukov's house. No trees, no other features. Just the track that probably led to another farmhouse, though it was not visible.

I called Painter and gave her further instructions. "Remember—I'll know if you break your word."

"Are we doing the right thing, Joe?"

"Damned if I know the answer to that." Kopański turned the car off 124 at precisely the place Cochrane had told him to exit. They were on a single farm track that went on for miles, according to the GPS. The fields on their right were flat, and those on their left rose to a small hill about three-quarters of a mile away. "You know that if Cochrane kills us, we'll have a fancy full honors funeral. But all of East Coast law enforcement will rightly think we were dumb to stand the convoy down."

"I know. Not sure that concern is high priority for me right now."

"Me neither."

Painter's phone rang.

I was watching the blue car through the zoom lens of Tap's camera. It was about two miles off the 124. Nothing was behind or ahead of it. I conducted a 360-degree examination of our surroundings. The location allowed me superb visibility over miles of land, despite dark clouds hanging motionless in the sky. Thankfully, the rain had stopped.

When Painter answered my call, I said, "I'm assuming that's you in the blue car."

She replied that it was, asking where they should meet me and Tom.

"Nice try, Detective. Keep driving." This time I kept the line open instead of hanging up.

The blue car continued onward.

I waited until it was directly opposite me. "Stop the car and get out."

A male and female got out of the car. The female was in a black pantsuit and white blouse, her black hair pinned up. The tall male was in a suit. I recognized them both from the confrontation on the Amtrak.

I said to Painter, "Put your handguns on the roof of the car. Any backup weapons as well."

Painter said, "No way."

I said, "My handgun is in a pack on my back. If you put your weapons on the roof, Tom and I are going to walk to you. It will take us about fifteen minutes to reach your location. If things go wrong, you'll have as much chance of reaching your guns as I will of unslinging my pack and reaching mine. But without the weapons in our hands, we stand a much better chance of having a constructive dialogue."

Painter said she was putting her cell on mute while she discussed this with her colleague. I stayed on the line, watching Kopański shake his head and Painter raise her hands.

Both put their handguns on the roof of the car.

"Satisfied?" asked Painter when back on the call.

"Yes. And as we approach you, if you see a gun in my hand I will fully respect your decision to reach for yours." I ended the call. "Come on, Tom. It's time to get you home." I placed the camera into my pack, ensuring a gun was on top.

I lifted Tom into my arms and walked quickly down the escarpment until we were on flat land. At this distance, Kopański and Painter were mere specks.

Fifteen minutes later, I could see them standing side by side. Their car was behind them, guns still on the roof.

They were two hundred yards away, motionless.

I kept walking, saying to Tom, "I'm sure these are good people. Everything's going to be fine."

One hundred yards.

I said, "We'll sort everything out. I'm going to be in trouble for what I had to do to rescue you. But I think the police will understand it was all necessary."

Fifty yards.

"No guns!" I called out to the detectives. "I'm keeping my word. We take this steady."

Tom and I were now five yards in front of the detectives.

"Detectives: so nice to meet you."

Painter and Kopański were silent, their guns six feet behind them.

I lowered Tom to the ground. To the detectives, I said, "I'm going to tell you what I'm guilty of and what I'm innocent of. I assaulted you and a uniformed police officer on the train. I badly hurt a large man in a diner in Lynchburg; he was trying to stop me leaving the establishment. I disarmed two police officers in the same city, and am guilty of causing damage to their vehicle. I am guilty of not handing myself in earlier. And I'm guilty of having to use maximum force to rescue Tom." I gave them the location of Zhukov's house, while placing my hands on Tom's shoulders. "But I'm not guilty of kidnapping this young boy. Nor did I kill my sister, the Granges, or any other innocent people. I've been framed and I would like to tell you how I think it was done."

I crouched beside Tom and said to him, "Go to these people. They'll take you to Billy and Aunt Faye. Tell them who kidnapped you and that I had nothing to do with it."

I stood.

Tom looked at me, a look of fear and disbelief in his eyes. His lips were trembling and tears were rolling down his cheeks.

"Go on, Tom. There's nothing to worry about. I

wouldn't ask you to go with them if I thought they were unsafe. Isn't that correct, Detectives?"

Kopański nodded.

And Painter held out her hand. "It's okay, Tom. We *will* take you straight to your family."

To my relief, Tom ran to them.

The boy then pointed at me. "He ... Uncle Will ... he kidna ... he stole me. Put me in the house. He was there sometimes while they kept a hood on me."

Shock sucker-punched me. "What are you talking about, Tom?"

"Your voice. I heard your voice. You were in the room with me. The man with the funny voice asked you questions. I heard you answer him."

They must have made covert recordings of me speaking during the preceding months. And used elements of those recordings in ways that sounded natural in Tom's prison. It was the only explanation. Tom would know if someone was trying to impersonate me.

Knowing that didn't do anything to alleviate my shock. "That was part of the plan. The man who took you told me that he was going to release you unharmed this evening in the city. I didn't believe him. I was wrong. He wanted you to tell the police what you've just told me. In their eyes, that would mean there was no doubt I was a kidnapper."

Kopański took a step toward his gun.

But I was quicker and had my pack off my back and in front of me. "Don't! Just don't. Notice that I haven't pulled out my weapon. Let's keep it that way."

The look in Tom's eyes and the expressions on

the detectives' faces told me they didn't believe I was innocent. "They used recordings of my voice. Maybe they got them at the Waldorf. More likely they got them many other places."

Painter said, "With everything stacked against you, we can't accept that possibility."

Emotionally overwrought, I said to Tom, "Whatever *anyone* tells you about me, I want you to grow up remembering what I'm about to tell you. I didn't do the things they say I did." Using the words *grow up* made me realize that I was telling myself that I'd probably never see the twins again. Under other circumstances, that realization would have reduced me to tears. "I wanted to look after you and Billy after everything that happened to your mom and dad." My eyes were burning. "Look after yourself, Tom. Work hard at school." I asked the detectives, "Is Faye going to look after them? Is she strong enough?"

Kopański answered, "Yes, to both. She'll cope just fine, and that's the way we want it. We didn't want the boys to go into . . ." He was about to say foster care, but held back finishing the sentence because of Tom.

I knew what the cop had been about to say. "Good. I'm no danger to the twins or Faye. I suspect you've got Billy and his aunt in protective custody, in case I go after them. Whatever you think I've done, nothing changes the fact that I've handed Tom over to you. Let him and his brother lead normal lives, live in Faye's house, and attend their school. I would *never* interfere with that. Reassure me, please."

Painter said, "You could go crazy again. You say now that you mean them no harm. That might change in a few months."

I took a step closer. "Let me ask you this, Detective Painter—do I show any signs of being crazy or having temporarily recovered from a bout of lunacy?"

In a measured tone, she answered, "You're not crazy."

Kopański added, "I agree. You know exactly who you are and what you're doing. But in the eyes of the law, that'll get you fried rather than a life sentence in a secure hospital for nut jobs. You understand?"

"Fully."

Kopański said, "The dice didn't roll your way."

"No, they didn't." I felt cold and focused as I started backing away. "Tom's safety was my priority. But I also hoped bringing him to you would make you think I might be telling the truth. That's been taken away from me as well. No doubt you'll want to keep looking for me. Don't bother. I'm going to vanish." I kept backing off.

"We won't stop until we get you." Kopański took another step.

But Painter put her arm on his. "No, Joe. Too risky."

My heart was broken as I said my last words to Tom. "Good-bye, little man. I love you and Billy. Please tell Billy I said that. I let both of you down. I'm so very sorry."

One hundred yards away, I turned and sprinted off.

TWENTY-NINE

It was late afternoon when Philip Knox received an SMS from Simon Tap's cell phone.

> WE NEED TO MEET THIS EVENING. POLICE HAVE FOUND TOM KOENIG, UNHARMED. SEARCH FOR COCHRANE CONTINUES, THOUGH POLICE BELIEVE TRACKING HIM IS NOW GOING TO BE INFINITELY TOUGHER. WE NEED A NEW STRATEGY. I HAVE AN IDEA, BUT NEED YOUR HELP.

The SMS gave details of where and when they should meet.

Since the huge police operation in Lynchburg, the media had maintained headline coverage of the Cochrane manhunt. But most of it was conjecture. They relied on police updates and live developments, but Cochrane had seemingly gone to ground after what had happened in Virginia. An hour ago, Knox had heard on CNN that the police were giving a press briefing in two hours about a new significant development. That would be about the rescue of Tom Koenig.

Tap was right. Monitoring Detective Painter's phone had been useful, but had ultimately failed. He wondered what Tap's idea was. He was extremely resourceful and never gave up. And he was the only person capable of going up against Cochrane.

In the parking lot outside CIA headquarters in Langley, Knox started his car. He had at least a one-hour drive north to the three-thousand-acre Liberty Reservoir in the countryside northwest of Baltimore. It was a venue much adored by anglers due to the size of the water's carp and other species. Tap had given Knox an eight-digit grid reference to pinpoint the exact location of a fishing bench on the side of the reservoir where they'd meet. Grid references. Military guys like Tap seemed to live by them. Under the circumstances, that was wise. For Knox and Tap to meet in D.C. would now be too dangerous.

In the police safe house in Roanoke, Billy and Tom were hugging each other, speechless inside a twin bedroom that was as functional and drab as the most basic of motel rooms. Joined by love and grief, their biggest fear was what might happen next. Yet another new school? Would they ever see their friends Johnny and Paul again? Why had nearly everyone they knew abandoned them?

In the adjacent living room were the detectives who'd reunited the twins—the sad-looking woman who walked funny and the big man who looked like he'd put half his face against a stove. They were talking in hushed tones. Normally, the twins would have eavesdropped on the conversation, as it was almost certainly about them. But they were too numb for that now. Everything was taking place around them; they had no voice, no say in matters, and they were wholly resigned to that plight.

Too much had happened to them. In their eyes, the grown-ups had either failed to protect them or died trying.

But Aunt Faye was different now. She didn't cry anymore, seemed busy like normal grown-ups, said strong words, told them off when they were naughty, and gave them hugs right after.

She came to them now and sat on Tom's bed. "Tom, the police detectives next door are going to need to talk to you some more about what happened to you. But I told them that has to wait until morning. They agree. I also told them something else. Both of you—do you mind if they come in here and speak to you? It's your room, so they wanted me to ask first."

"It's not our room! It's a horrible—"

"I know, and it has everything to do with that." Faye glanced at Painter and Kopański, both watching her through the doorway. "Boys—I'd like them to come in."

The boys nodded, thinking that whatever was coming next would be yet one more blow to the stability they so cherished.

Kopański stood before them. "I've got a daughter. She's twenty-seven. A bad thing happened to her when she was eighteen. Not going to say what it was." He looked at Painter. She looked back at him, wishing to go up to the proud man and hug him. "But you guys know all about bad things. They hit the innocent, the people who've done nothing wrong. Other innocent folks get hurt in the process. So we have to rebuild."

Painter looked at the boys. "Aunt Faye wants to take you back to her home." In Roanoke, close to their school. "We agree. Your uncle Will is no danger to you. We know that from what he told us and from the expression in his eyes. But we need to know you're fine with that."

Billy and Tom exchanged glances. Their young minds raced on many superficial levels—considering the chance to play with their Nintendo games, meet their friends, eat Aunt Faye's delicious desserts, sleep in comfy beds, so many other things—though those superficial thoughts were grounded in something far deeper.

The need to feel safe and loved.

They smiled. Living with Aunt Faye was exactly what they needed.

"You don't need to sleep here anymore," said Kopański. "You can go to Aunt Faye's house this evening. That's your new home, and it will stay that way for as long as you like."

Tom said, "Uncle Will isn't crazy and he'd never have done what you think he did. Not what I said. Not . . ." It was a new thought, and blurted without prior cognitive process. What he said surprised him, though he wholeheartedly believed he was right.

Billy added, "We know he can kill people. But the right people. You're saying he killed the wrong people. And you're wrong about that."

The declaration gripped the seasoned cops.

Painter said, "The problem we have is that we have to deal with evidence. But I sort of agree with you. I didn't see a bad man earlier today. That's why you're going home."

Ten minutes later, as Faye and the twins prepared to depart, Kopański and Painter stood outside the safe house. It was dark now, and a fine rain was spattering Roanoke. The helicopter that had brought them and Tom Koenig here was a few blocks away, ready to take the cops back to Washington. There, they'd relinquish all equipment loaned to them by the D.C. PD and return to Manhattan.

Cochrane had done as he'd pledged and vanished.

There was no point in their staying away from New York any longer.

A sickle moon cast meager light into the night sky over the reservoir. Fishermen, Philip Knox imagined, would revel in the peace and solitude of this spot. Some time away from the stresses of marriage, child care, jobs, all adult responsibilities, as they opened flasks of coffee, tucked one leg under the other, and breathed the night air.

But they weren't here tonight. At least, if they were, they were not to be seen by the portly CIA officer whose shoes and suit trousers were sodden from tramping through the wet grass to get to this isolated place and sit on the lakeside bench. It was like Tap to choose such a rugged venue to meet. He had no fondness for cities.

Knox checked his watch. Tap would be watching him now, as he always did, ensuring that it was safe to proceed. That didn't bother Knox. If anything, it reassured him. Knox had a career to protect. Mixing with someone like Tap would sully his professional reputation.

Water lapped close to his brogues. Over the reservoir a heron glided to its nest. Toads and frogs were croaking. Insects were emitting sounds like rusty bedsprings. And bats were darting close to the waterline.

The CIA officer looked at his cell phone. Nothing from Tap. That was usual. He always went dark before meetings.

He wondered what Tap's new plan was to kill Cochrane. It needed to be good. All that mattered was getting Cochrane off the planet.

Three hundred yards away, on the other side of the reservoir, I watched Knox through the scope of the sniper rifle I'd taken from Tap's car. I was wearing gloves; the only prints on the weapon were Simon Tap's.

Knox had wanted me dead. I was certain his colleagues had no idea that he'd instructed Tap to kill me. Last time I'd encountered him when I was working for the Agency, Knox was a powerful man with a large budget under his control. Much of that budget was unaccountable. Almost certainly he'd used CIA cash to pay Tap. That was unforgiveable. And I had enough problems as it was without having to look over my shoulder in case Knox deployed another assassin.

Among many good qualities, I could honestly say that I was a man of dignity and humility, a fine lute player and a lover of baroque and flamenco music, an accomplished chef, and a person whose instinct was always to help others.

But I couldn't, hand on heart, say I wasn't a cold-blooded killer.

And if anyone had it coming, it was Knox.

I pulled the trigger and watched as my bullet entered Philip Knox's head.

THIRTY

A week later, Dickie Mountjoy returned to London in a coffin.

The American authorities had been superb, having conducted a prompt postmortem and established he'd died of a massive heart attack. David had coordinated with them to repatriate his body to England. His connections as a mortician had enabled him to pull strings and expedite the process. He and Phoebe wanted the old man home as quickly as possible so they could bury him next to his wife.

Now he was in an open casket in a funeral parlor next to David's place of work. David checked on him and went into the reception area, where Phoebe was waiting. She hadn't seen Dickie yet.

"He looks peaceful," said David. He hugged his girlfriend. "You don't have to do this if it's going to be too emotional."

Phoebe had a handkerchief by her eyes. "I want to say good-bye."

He led her into the parlor. As they stood over the old man, Phoebe's grief poured out, her boyfriend holding her and kissing her forehead.

"Why did he have to fly? He should never have gone to the States."

David knew it was the grief talking. He said, "The doctors said it wasn't the trip that killed him. His heart was a ticking time bomb."

Phoebe touched Dickie's hand. "But why did it have to happen there?"

David stared at the major's face. He seemed contented. "I believe it was meant to be. He's always been a soldier. Did his duty, no matter what the risks. And he did his final duty by telling American cops what sort of man Cochrane was." He placed his hand over Phoebe's. "After that was done, he could let go."

Phoebe nodded. "He *was* always a soldier. And he died a soldier."

At the Montauk Yacht Club, some of the plutocrats whose vessels were berthed in the harbor were reveling on deck, taking advantage of an unseasonably balmy evening. Wine flowing, laughter bouncing off calm waters, canapés passed from one beautiful person to another, candles giving the playground a religious ambiance, all illuminated by the dock's all-seeing lighthouse.

Edward Carley dined alone on his luxury cruiser. His crew were ashore, downing their last beers for several weeks. Tomorrow he was leaving America, so tonight he'd decided to take advantage of the East Coast's finest cuisine—a lobster from Cape Cod, cockles farmed in Barnstable, asparagus and truffles brought to him by boat from New Haven, melted New York Adelegger cheese infused with lime and cracked pepper dripped over the crustacean, and a thirteen-hundred-dollar bottle of saturated ruby Harlan Estate 2000—a California wine, but purchased from Manhattan's Le Dû's Wines.

The tall and slender former army surgeon paid deference to the cuisine by ensuring he was immaculately dressed. It seemed to him to be sloppy to dress in anything other than a shirt and tie whipped into a schoolboy knot, and a suit that had been handcrafted in Savile Row. The sixty-three-year-old's green eyes and silver hair complemented the color of his attire. Behind him was a window overlooking the illuminated black harbor. The music system was playing J. S. Bach's "Come, Sweet Death."

He ate carefully, each morsel inserted into his mouth with precision and pleasure. His yacht bobbed a little, the gentle swell a remnant of a fierce mid-Atlantic undulation that had now abated enough for experienced seafarers to cross the ocean safely. His passage to the port of Sines, Portugal, would be smooth; and he would travel onward to Jakarta when conditions allowed.

He knew from news reports that Tom Koenig had been freed, Will Cochrane had escaped, and Zhukov and his team had been murdered. None of that mattered.

Cochrane was still on the run and in hell.

* * *

I walked along the thin wooden jetty toward the large yacht, my future desperate and without direction. Everything had been taken away from me except one thing: revenge. But that alone was enough to make me focused and resolute. Any hostile who tried to stop me on the jetty would have died. A policeman trying to arrest me would have been knocked unconscious. A concerned citizen who tried to apprehend me would have turned and fled if they saw my face.

But no one knew I was here.

And no one prevented me from walking up the gangplank onto Edward Carley's yacht.

I'd been watching it for three hours, confident that only Carley was here.

Dining alone.

As I entered the vessel, I didn't feel anger about what had been done to me. Instead, I was here because of Sarah, James, Celia, Robert, and Tom. They deserved retribution. It didn't matter if it went bad for me. My life was irrelevant. Theirs weren't.

When Carley saw me, he smiled.

This surprised me.

Carley placed a bite of lobster into his mouth and wiped his hands with his napkin. "Mr. Cochrane. You've come to kill me."

"I have." I walked to his dining table, my right hand pointing my SIG Sauer at his head, my left hand gripping the table. I knew what I had to do. Antaeus had given me the means to do it.

"You stole that weapon from one of the detectives

protecting the Granges, no doubt." Carley placed his hands next to his plate.

"No doubt."

"So, you're now a thief, among so many other things."

"Yes."

Carley shrugged. "In the eyes of the law, there aren't many crimes you haven't committed."

"Thanks to you."

"Yes, thanks to me." Carley laughed. "It must grate on you that I dragged you to this level."

"Now we're both at that level."

Carley's expression turned cold. "Tell me what you suspect has happened to you."

I told him that I guessed it took Carley months to financially cripple my sister and her husband, though I didn't know the details. But I explained everything else I thought had happened.

Carley nodded. "Clever, Mr. Cochrane. Are you wearing a police wire? Here to get a confession out of me?"

"What do you think?"

"You're pointing a gun at my head. You don't want police involvement." He chose his words carefully. "I'll give you a hypothetical scenario. It's not a confession. I have to be careful in case you *are* here to incriminate me. A story—to bring Sarah and James to their knees involved fake letters from the taxman, money filtered out of their accounts, expenditures made in strip clubs that James had never attended, and a pony in the middle of the road that made James swerve and crash his car. Everything else you've said is accurate. Your sister was beyond desperate when I called her pretending to be a headhunter and invited her to interview for a well-paid job in New York. I made that call within days of your trip to the States, and had been watching you longer than Sarah. I knew all of your plans. My men recorded your voice using long-range audio equipment, and they used some of those recordings in the basement where they held Tom Koenig. They followed you when you arrived at JFK. And they watched you check into the Waldorf Astoria. What happened next was precisely as you described—the sleeping gas in the hotel room, the injection to knock you out, Sarah's murder in the bathtub, contaminating the crime scene with your prints and DNA, and at every stage thereafter ensuring you were set up to become a mass murderer and kidnapper of people who you were supposed to love and protect."

I placed my finger over the trigger.

Carley said, "Don't be stupid. I know you killed my men. No doubt you tortured one of them; probably Zhukov, though I've no idea how you got to him. Do you honestly think I'd just wait here for you to show up and shove a gun in my face?"

I didn't reply.

Carley said, "The correct answer is yes, I did hope you'd show. I wanted to see how wretched I'd made you. Seeing you now doesn't disappoint. But I'm in no danger. I have a bigger gun. A man, not too far from here, is watching you through a telescope attached to a rifle that is designed to bring elephants to their knees. You kill me, he kills you."

I was motionless.

"But I don't want either of you to pull your triggers. I want you to live."

"A life of hell?"

"Yes." Carley picked up an asparagus spear and bit its head off. "Or you can take the coward's way out, shoot me, and commit suicide. You choose."

I gripped my gun tighter. "Your brother was a traitor to America. I did nothing wrong by highlighting that fact."

Carley stared at me. "My brother was stupid, greedy, and vain. But he was still my brother. He's dead. Your sister's dead. Now you know how I feel. I suggest you get off my property."

My every instinct was to pull the trigger. But I knew Carley wasn't bluffing about having a sniper watching me. And Antaeus had predicted the same in his note to me. Someone like that will always have people watching over him.

I lowered my gun. "One day, you'll die."

Carley smiled. "As a former medical man, I can tell you your statement is wholly accurate. The mystery is always when it will happen."

My gun bobbed as anger coursed through me.

"Good-bye, Mr. Cochrane. Welcome to the life I've gifted you."

"What you did to my family and friends is unforgiveable." I spun around and walked off the yacht, knowing my every movement was being scrutinized through crosshairs. I exited the jetty, and ten minutes later was in Simon Tap's vehicle. As I drove away from the harbor, I took an erratic route, to ensure that the sniper had no chance of keeping me in his sights.

Two minutes later, the bomb I'd placed under Edward Carley's dining table erupted and sent more than a thousand pieces of Carley's brain and body into the sea.

THIRTY-ONE

Three hours later, I was in New York City.

Back where it had all started.

I'd parked my car on the outskirts, leaving my backpack inside. I'd only taken one hundred dollars of the money Antaeus had given me, one SIG Sauer, and a couple of spare magazines. The other handgun, rest of the cash, and everything else I'd left in the vehicle. The chances of me getting back to the car were probably nonexistent.

But there was one more thing to be done, and I had to see it through.

No matter what the cost.

I got on the subway and headed for lower Manhattan, wearing my hood over a baseball hat that was tilted over my eyes. My head throbbed, partly from stress and partly from spending the last week driving in daylight and sleeping in my car at night. If I could, I'd willingly give half of Antaeus's three hundred thousand dollars just to get a bed for the night and undisturbed sleep. But that luxury would have to wait, if indeed I would ever experience it again.

After alighting from the train at Park Place, I walked up Broadway. Traffic was slow moving and heavy; throngs of people were still on the street despite the late hour. Many of them looked like tourists—smiling, laughing, carrying shopping bags, having a good time. Never in my life had I felt so removed from the people around me. I guessed that was how it would always be now. Me versus everyone else. No friends or colleagues. The last remaining member of my family allegedly murdered by my own hand. A leper apart from society.

A wanted fugitive.

I had to make that end.

My destination was nearby, but I couldn't get too close yet. First, I had to turn lower Manhattan into chaos. Everything had to look natural, as if I'd been found out and pushed to the brink. But if I survived that chaos, the thought of what would happen next made me want to vomit.

I needed a trigger to set things in motion. I scoured the crowds around me. There. Two cops on foot, about seventy yards away. They were slowly walking in my direction, oblivious to their proximity to America's most dangerous criminal. I stopped and turned my back to them, using the reflection of a store window to watch behind me. I couldn't see them now, only the nearest people moving around me. If the officers were no longer coming toward me, I'd soon find out. If that happened, I'd find them or other cops and repeat the drill until my plan worked. Getting caught off guard was key. It didn't have to be perfect. Appearing momentarily careless was fine. All that mattered was that I got law enforcement's blood boiling and rushing to their head.

I saw them.

Sauntering ten yards behind me.

If I were a religious man, I'd probably have made the sign of the cross over my chest. It wouldn't have helped me.

Five yards.

Time to make this happen.

I removed my hood and baseball cap, turned while rubbing my hair, froze, and shouted, "Shit!" as I stared straight at the officers.

For two seconds they didn't seem to know what the problem was.

Then they recognized me.

And reached for their pistols.

"Get your hands on your head!"

I whipped out my handgun, fired two shots over their heads, and ran across Broadway, leaping onto the hood of a car, jumping down and swerving around other cars, my gun still in my hand. People were screaming and shouting, drivers leaning on their horns. I yelled at people to get out of my way and spun around. The two cops were halfway across Broadway, guns unholstered, one of them on his radio calling for backup. I fired two more shots into the air.

They sent all of lower Manhattan into a frenzied panic.

* * *

Kopański ran into Painter's midtown precinct office. "Sighting of Cochrane on lower Broadway. One hundred percent it's him. Shots have been fired."

She immediately got to her feet. "I'll slow you down. Get out there. I'll coordinate units from here."

As Kopański ran to the basement parking lot, Painter ripped down a wall map of lower Manhattan and picked up her police radio.

I switched direction, moving south down Broadway, dodging petrified pedestrians. The cops were still behind me, screaming at me to stop and hit the ground, yelling at people to get out of the way. Two more cops were ahead of me, in body armor, sweeping their arms left and right to tell people to move out of the line of fire. People complied. There was a forty-yard clear channel between me and the cops. Time to up the ante. Without slowing, I shot them both in the chest, causing them to crash to the ground. They'd live. I ran over their supine bodies and swerved left onto Worth Street.

"I want a helicopter in the air, now." Painter was leaning over the map on her desk. "Where is he?"

An officer on the radio responded breathlessly, "We're pursuing on foot on Worth Street. Heading east. He's just shot two of our men. They're okay. Vests saved them."

What the hell was Cochrane doing back in New

York? she wondered as she ran her finger over the map. She asked for the location of mobile and foot patrols in the immediate vicinity and then gave each patrol specific instructions.

"Block off the east end of Worth Street. Two mobile and one foot patrol follow in from the west. On-foot units head to Worth from Lafayette, Centre, Baxter, Mulberry, Mott, and Elizabeth Streets. Mobiles head north to Worth along Centre Street."

Painter called Kopański. "Where are you?"

"Driving down Broadway. I'm getting updates on the radio."

"If you can, take him alive. But if you see any threat to civilian life, go for a head shot."

"Abso-fucking-lutely."

A police car turned onto Worth Street and came hurtling toward me, its lights flashing and sirens wailing. I stopped, took aim, and fired four shots. All of them entered the engine block and stopped the vehicle. But the cops were out of the car quickly. One of them had a shotgun. Shit. I had to change direction. Glancing back, I could see twelve cops on foot, running toward me. The only reason they hadn't opened fire was because there were too many pedestrians around me, all of them crazed with fear, their movements erratic and confused.

I glanced up a side street. Other cops were coming down it, guns in hand. Police were converging from all directions. My plan had gone seriously awry. It was time to improvise.

A small Chinese restaurant was to my left. It

was at capacity, diners staring out of the windows. No doubt they were wondering what all the sirens meant. I ran in.

A man shouted, "Oh my God, he's got a gun!"

I shouted, "Anyone tries to leave—I shoot!"

People dropped their cutlery. Some screamed.

At the far end of the restaurant, a middle-aged Chinese woman in black tunic and pants looked like she might be the restaurant owner. She had her hand to her mouth; her eyes were wide.

"Are you in charge?"

She nodded emphatically.

"Lock the front door."

Customers were begging me not to hurt them as I pointed my gun at the proprietor's head. "Do it now!"

Outside, stationary police cars were everywhere, officers on foot and using the car doors as protection while they aimed their weapons at the restaurant. I could hear a helicopter drawing closer. Its searchlight bathed the police units. The back of the restaurant would have similar coverage.

I was completely surrounded.

"Close the curtains."

The restaurant owner was speaking to herself in Cantonese as she complied, her hands shaking.

"Mister, we don't want trouble," said one of the male diners.

"Shut up!" I paced back and forth, deliberately looking like I was a desperate man capable of anything. It wasn't far from the truth.

There were twenty-two customers in the restaurant, three chefs in an open-plan kitchen that was visible to all diners, and two waitstaff. In total, there were six children and nine women.

I pointed at a back door and asked the proprietor, "Does that lead out onto a street?"

She nodded.

In a loud voice I said to everyone, "Are any children here only accompanied by a male?"

No one replied in the affirmative.

"Give me your set of keys," I said to the proprietor.

She did as I asked. "All right. Listen up. All women, including female members of staff, plus all children are to leave by the back door. Now!"

Mothers ushered their kids, all of them shooting horrified looks at their male partners.

"Move! Now!"

The kids were crying, mothers and female waiters sobbing, as I waved them toward the back door.

"When I open the back door, move fast."

They were in a line, ready to go.

The restaurant owner was in the back of the line. I asked her, "Which key locks the back door?"

She pointed at one of the keys on the bunch.

"When you leave, you slam the door behind you. Got it?"

"Yes, yes."

I put my back flush against the wall adjacent to the back door, my gun pointing at the center of the restaurant and the men. "Right. Get out of here."

The woman at the front of the queue whimpered, "Please don't hurt my husband," as she opened the door and exited.

Five seconds later, they were gone. I locked the

door and said to the remaining thirteen men, "Put your hands flat on the table. Keep calm. Do exactly what I tell you to."

One of them stuttered, "What . . . what . . . are you going to do to us?"

"That depends on you and the police."

Another asked, "What's going to happen now?"

I replied, "Now we wait."

Kopański was at the back of the restaurant. Alongside him were twelve squad cars and thirty officers. The front of the restaurant had an even bigger police presence. And the helo above him wasn't going anywhere, its searchlight fixed on the restaurant. The released hostages were farther up the street, being cared for next to a large police truck. Next to them was a SWAT van. Ten officers from the unit were interviewing the hostages, getting an exact layout of the Chinese restaurant. One SWAT sniper was already in situ, watching the back of the restaurant through the scope of his rifle. Another was covering the front.

The detective called Painter. "He's holed up. Ain't going anywhere. You'd better get down here." He walked over to the SWAT commander and asked, "What's your assessment?"

The commander took off his helmet. "I don't like it. Thirteen male hostages in there. So far we've no visibility of where they're positioned. Only two ways in and out. And the room's quite small, so the chances of collateral damage if we go in are significant."

"Do you have any other options?"

"Nope. If we get the green light, it'll be door breaches and flashbangs. Still, the chance of our bullets going through Cochrane and hitting hostages is significant. Let's see how the negotiators get on first. One thing's for sure—dead or alive, there's no way out for Cochrane."

The SWAT commander motioned to one of his men. Together they lifted a heavy piece of machinery out of their vehicle. It contained gas canisters, tubes, and a drill. Kopański knew it was a very sophisticated piece of equipment that could drill holes silently while suctioning all debris. Pinhole cameras could then be inserted through the holes. This was SWAT's means to take a peek inside the restaurant.

"Stand up—all of you." I told the three chefs to join the hostages. "I want you to upend tables and put them against the walls. There should be enough of them to completely cover the perimeter. But leave a six-inch gap between wall and table."

One of the men asked, "Why do you want us to do that?"

"Pinhole cameras."

A TV was in the corner of the restaurant. I turned it on to a news channel. Live reporting showed the restaurant from the air. It was surrounded by an army of cops and a sea of flashing blue lights. Above the restaurant, a police helo was hovering. I flicked through other media channels. They too were covering the siege, some from the ground, others from the air. The media was scrutinizing the event. This was good, because it meant the police had to play by the rulebook. And that meant they had to be seen to try to negotiate me out of the situation. Providing I didn't start killing hostages.

And I wasn't going to do that.

The tables were now in position, leaving empty floor in most of the room.

I said, "Get in a circle, close to the tables."

"Why?"

"Just fucking do it!" When they were in position, I said, "Now start walking around in a circle. Don't stop unless I tell you to."

"This is crazy."

"For you, maybe. But not for me."

I didn't want SWAT to pin down the location of the hostages before storming the place.

In the building next door, the SWAT officer got off his knees and whispered to his commander, "That's the third hole I've drilled. There're barriers in the way of all of them. Something wooden."

"Tables?"

"Looks that way. The bastard knew we'd try to use cameras. You want me to go in from higher up?"

"Too risky. Try from the other side of the building. But if it's more of the same, we'll have to make do with thermal."

But the thermal imagery wouldn't tell them who was Cochrane and who wasn't.

The telephone at the reception desk rang. I just knew it was the police.

I answered. "Yes?"

"Am I speaking to Will Cochrane?"

"You are."

"This is Lieutenant Ames, NYPD. I'm the guy outside the building who wants this to end peacefully. I'm your friendly voice."

"You're a hostage negotiator?"

"Correct."

"Your priority is the safety of my hostages. My welfare comes a big second. That hardly makes you a *friendly voice*."

Ames laughed. "Well, we can get to know each other and work around that."

"Listen, Mr. Negotiator. There's only one law enforcement official I will speak with. Her name is Detective Thyme Painter."

I hung up.

Painter arrived at the scene and approached Kopański. "What's the latest?"

Kopański replied, "SWAT tried to put in covert cameras through the walls. But Cochrane's blocked their view. They're now trying to go through the ceiling. Cochrane will be looking for them." He held out a cell phone. "You need to take this."

"Why?"

"It's a hotline to the restaurant. Cochrane won't speak to the negotiator. Only you."

"But I'm not a trained negotiator."

Kopański shrugged. "Guess we don't have a choice."

She took the phone.

I watched the men continue to circle the restaurant. Two of them were my height.

I tapped them on the shoulder. "You two stand in the middle of the room."

"Please—"

"In the middle of the room." When they were there, I said, "Remove your outer clothes."

They looked confused.

"Now!"

They got undressed.

I kept my gun trained on them as I removed my jacket, boots, and pants. "Now we're going to mix and match." I smiled. "The end result will be that not one of us will be wearing identical clothes to those we wore coming into the restaurant."

One of them said, "But . . . you can't change your face."

I ignored the comment. "What size are your shoes?"

"Twelve."

"Same as me." I tossed him my boots. After getting dressed and ordering the men to get back into the mobile circle, I pulled one of the Chinese chefs aside. "In the kitchen, do you have bags?"

He looked quizzical. "Bags?"

"Grocery bags. Preferably paper."

The chef nodded.

"And rope? Or strong string?"

"For hanging chicken and duck. Yes, we have that."

I told him to retrieve the items and that if he picked up a meat cleaver when in there I'd shoot him in the head.

The phone rang.

I picked it up, silent.

"Will Cochrane?"

"Hello, Detective Painter. May I call you Thyme? It would be so nice to jettison formalities."

"I'm liable to say the wrong thing to you."

"Because you don't have a certificate saying you successfully completed an NYPD hostage negotiating course? Tut-tut, Detective. You do yourself a disservice."

"Will—there's no way out of this. It's the end of the line for you."

"I don't expect a way out of Manhattan. You know why I came back here?"

"I thought you'd stay away from major cities. No, I don't know why you came back."

"Think, Detective."

Painter was silent for a few seconds. "It's where your sister died. For some reason you were drawn to be close to where that happened."

"Correct." I was lying. I had no idea where Sarah's body had been taken. Being here would have given me no closure—whether I was a grieving brother or her murderer. But I had to disguise the real reason I'd returned. "I had to take a risk. And now look what's gone and happened."

"Are you going to let the hostages go?"

"As long as the police don't do anything rash, yes. All of them. Unharmed."

She said nothing.

"SWAT will be trying to get a look inside here. I might have fucked them on pinhole cameras, but they'll be using thermal imagery. It'll show them that I'm keeping the hostages constantly on the move."

"I guess you know all about storming buildings."

"Of course." I added, "If SWAT's told to end this, they'll breach both doors, toss stun grenades, and teams will enter front and back. They'll be armed with Heckler & Koch submachine guns, and will have handguns as secondary weapons in case there's a malfunction. Probably they'll kill the lights a split second before entering. Their guns will have flashlights attached. Half of them will cover the left side of the room, the rest the right. When they see me, they'll shoot to kill. But I'd say the chances of them hitting a hostage are above fifty percent. Do you know what they'd prefer to happen?"

"No."

"They want me to try to escape. That way a sniper can take me out. Or I just walk into a volley of NYPD fire."

Painter sounded genuinely concerned when she said, "You can't escape. Don't try that. You've killed cops. The guys out here will be justified in shooting you if you try to get away. But while you're in there and not killing anyone, we have a chance to cool things down."

"It's a bit late for that. But I need to decide what to do. I hadn't planned for this to happen. Call me back in sixty minutes."

The chef placed brown paper grocery bags and several balls of twine on the kitchen workbench. I moved behind the bench, facing the restaurant. Placing my handgun down, I grabbed a knife from the kitchen, cut the string into equal lengths, and started braiding it into rope.

* * *

Painter said to the SWAT commander, "He wants sixty minutes to decide what to do. Providing he does nothing before then, I say we give him that time."

"That's fine by me."

A thought occurred to Painter, prompted by something Dickie Mountjoy had said to her in the Manhattan interview room. She called Detective Inspector Toby Rice from the United Kingdom's Metropolitan Police. After explaining what was happening, she told him what she had in mind. "Can it be done? Urgently? We've got less than sixty minutes."

She walked to Kopański. "Why the hell doesn't he give himself up?"

Kopański was leaning against a police car, his gun trained on the restaurant. "I don't think he wants that. He just hasn't decided yet how he wants to die."

Thirty minutes later, the restaurant phone rang.

"I said leave me alone for an hour."

But the woman on the phone wasn't Painter.

"Will—it's Phoebe."

"Phoebe?"

Her voice was hesitant. No doubt she had police with her in her London home, or she'd been picked up and taken to a station. "They told me what's happening. They want you to give yourself up. They've said that if you do that and don't hurt any hostages, they won't shoot you."

I hadn't expected this to happen. Despite being in an unbelievably shitty situation, hearing

Phoebe's voice was like getting a call from an angel. "Phoebe," was all I could say.

"You must give yourself up, Will. There are no alternatives."

I felt myself getting emotional. "There are. I could just walk outside and get my head blown off. Better that than spending the rest of my life in prison, or going on death row."

Phoebe was sobbing. "I didn't have to call. They couldn't force me to. But I wanted you to hear from me that there are people out there who still love you. No matter what they say you've done."

"There are only three people left alive who love me—you, David, and the major. And you might as well be on Mars for all the difference that makes to me right now."

Phoebe was silent.

I breathed deeply. "But I do appreciate the call. However this ends, it's so good to hear your voice. How are you all?"

"Will, it's . . ."

"What?"

"It's Dickie. He flew to the States to put in a good word for your character. It was the last good deed he wanted to do."

I had a sinking feeling. "The last?"

She was now openly crying. "His heart gave out. They flew his body back. We buried him today."

"Oh, dear Lord." I gripped the reception table.

I had a mental image of Dickie. We were trying to fix a leak under his kitchen sink. The job complete, he'd said, "Let me fix us a nice cup of tea and bore you about why people of your generation are soft compared to my lot."

I'd made my excuses and left.

Now, I wished I hadn't.

That was the last time I'd seen him.

"Dickie," I whispered.

Phoebe said, "He knew you're a good man. We all do. Whatever you decide, can you keep that in mind? Maybe do something that would make Dickie proud."

"I will. Good-bye, Phoebe. Look after David. Take it easy on the champagne. And whatever happens, always remember that I'm an innocent man."

I hung up, full of grief.

But that emotion had to be put to one side. I had work to do. Phoebe was right. I owed it to Dickie to go out in a way that would make him proud.

Twenty minutes later, Painter called the restaurant. "Have you decided how you want this to end?"

Cochrane answered, "I have."

"Please tell me it's the right choice."

"That depends on your point of view. It'll happen in five minutes, in the front of the restaurant. And remember that I'm holding a gun and it's pointed at someone's back."

Urgently, Painter said, "The sniper will go for a head shot."

"That's his call. Just make sure it's the right one."

It was time to move.

I said to the thirteen assembled men, "Hands in

pockets at all times. If anyone breaks the rules, you not only risk your life, you'll be risking everyone's life. There are a lot of twitchy fingers out there. If you do this exactly right, I guarantee you'll soon be free and unharmed. Okay. Let's move!"

Kopański and Painter were at the front of the restaurant, standing behind the fleet of squad cars. The helo was still overhead, its searchlight positioned on the door. Over fifty uniformed cops and SWAT officers were on Worth Street. A sniper was on the top of a building opposite the restaurant. If Cochrane did anything wrong, he'd be gunned down in a second.

Other helos belonging to media were in the air. On the ground, news crews were catching the action from behind cordoned-off areas farther down the street. Everyone was expecting something big to happen. And this was making prime-time television.

The restaurant door opened.

All officers braced themselves, their firearms trained on the door.

One by one the occupants of the restaurant came out.

All of them were tethered together by rope around their waists.

Their hands were bunched inside their jacket pockets.

And on their heads they had brown grocery bags that only had tiny holes for their eyes to see through.

"Don't shoot! Don't shoot!" shouted Kopański into his radio mic.

Painter checked her notes of what Cochrane had last been seen wearing. Three of the men in the line matched his height. But the clothes had been mixed up. The police sniper had an easy head shot. But he risked killing a hostage if he got it wrong. And somewhere in the group was a man holding a gun.

There was only eight inches of rope between each man. None of the hostages could make a run for it. And with their hands in their pockets, it was impossible to know who was holding a gun.

Slowly, the fourteen men walked away from the restaurant. All the cops could do was watch.

The cops, and millions of TV viewers.

SWAT officers rushed the restaurant. It was empty. Cochrane was in that line of men.

The line walked east down Worth Street, the police helo matching their pace and keeping its spotlight on them. Police on foot followed on either side of them, guns trained on each man.

They were headed to a cordon one hundred yards away, behind which were other cops, members of the public, and media.

Kopański raced ahead of the hostages, shouting, "Move that cordon! Now!"

For the first time in her career, Painter was able to keep pace with a fleeing perp. They were walking so slowly. Behind the group, squad cars were following with lights flashing.

"Detective Painter." The voice was Cochrane's,

though it was impossible to know who in the line had called out. "Clear a path!"

Painter didn't care that Cochrane could hear her as she spoke to the SWAT commander on her radio. "Stay ahead of the group at all times. He's going to have to go solo sometime. That's when you take him down."

Ahead, Kopański and other police were urgently moving the cordon back, barking orders at civilians to move their asses.

Cochrane and the hostages drew closer.

Then turned right down Centre Street.

Where are they headed? thought Painter. Cochrane must have known that he wasn't going to be let out of Manhattan. His plan was dumb. The group could only go as far as the weakest man in the group could go. Eventually, one of them would fall to his knees. And police would be around them at all times.

Patty Schmidt from NBC was in the air. Beside her in the helo were her trusted cameraman and audio technician. They'd flown from D.C. as soon as they'd heard about the siege. The last time she'd covered Cochrane in Lynchburg, he'd shot two cops in cold blood. Now, she wanted to capture his death on camera.

Hair coifed, attire immaculate, the seasoned broadcaster made an address to the camera.

"What you're seeing are fourteen men. They're tied together. Bags are on their faces to hide their identities. One of them is Will Cochrane. He's got a gun pointed at the others. The police can't open fire because they don't know which man is Cochrane. This is a real-life bogeyman, hiding under a mask. But here's the thing. He wasn't always like this. Once, he was a secret national hero. He didn't get any thanks or recognition for that. He worked the shadows. Our best always do. We should be asking ourselves how it's come to this. What broke him? And what did we do to let him down? Or maybe a better question is, what did our government do to drive him to this?"

This was a nightmare tactical scenario for the SWAT commander. In fact, there were no tactics suited to this situation. Cochrane and his hostages couldn't be let off the island. But if they tried to leave, that left some hard choices. Almost certainly hostages would die in the process.

His men were around him as he ran down Centre Street, ahead of the line of men.

Kopański was by his side, screaming at a police barricade. "Get that fucking thing taken down! They're coming this way!"

NYPD officers complied, lifting portable barriers and moving them to the side of the street.

Within five minutes, the line of fourteen men walked past them, every inch of their movement tracked by the cops.

Painter and dozens of uniform officers flanked them. She called out, "Let them go! You are not getting off Manhattan."

Cochrane didn't reply.

The noise was incredible—helicopters, sirens, cops shouting, civilians shrieking as they were pushed away from the moving kill zone.

Where is Cochrane taking the hostages? thought Painter. *And what in God's name is he hoping to achieve?*

Cochrane and the men turned.

Onto the Brooklyn Bridge.

"Mr. Cochrane," she shouted, "I'm not letting you reach the end of the bridge."

He didn't reply.

She was on her radio mic. "Shut the bridge down. No traffic on the bridge. And I want a heavily armed barricade at the eastern end. No matter what, they do not pass." She glanced at the line. "You getting all this, Cochrane?"

The SWAT commander and his men were sprinting along the bridge. Cars were exiting fast, nothing behind them because the far end had now been blocked off by a barricade, squad cars, and over one hundred cops.

This was where it was going to end.

The commander was under orders to apprehend or kill Cochrane. No matter what.

The route ahead was now empty. Four hundred yards away was a sea of blue lights and armed officers. There was no way through.

He reached the barricade, spun around, and aimed his submachine gun. His men did the same. In the distance the fourteen men were in sight. Which of them was Cochrane? Beside the slow-moving group were Painter, Kopański, and an entire precinct's worth of cops. Police and media helicopters were overhead, their searchlights on the group. Squad cars were behind them, lights still flashing.

Forward or back, there was no way off the bridge.

We were halfway across the bridge. I hadn't planned for the hostage situation, but maybe this was for the best. Inside the grocery bag over my head, my breathing was fast, the paper sucking in and out with each inhalation and exhalation. The men tied to me were shit scared. I wished it had worked out differently. I'm a killer. The men attached to me had just gone out this evening to grab some noodles with loved ones. They didn't deserve this. Didn't deserve me entering their lives.

Nobody deserved me.

The world thought I'd betrayed it; everything I'd done before now was meaningless.

I was scum.

This was how it had to end.

"Detective Painter." My voice was loud. "This is as far as we go. Move your officers back."

"I can't."

"You can."

We were still, the blackness of the distant East River beneath us. I thought about my American father. He was such a good man. A U.S. Marine; a CIA officer. Was he like me? I think so. He raised kids; I'd wanted to do that too. And he'd sacrificed himself for the States. Just like me.

I cut my ropes and said to the hostages, "Get out of here," as I clambered over the railing. I was on a precipice.

Facing the river, police, and media helos.

Standing on the side of the Brooklyn Bridge.

Death a fucking awful fall below me.

It was time to end this. I took off my bag and revealed my face to the world.

I knew cameras were on my exhausted face. I looked to the sky. Few people could survive this fourteen-story jump. People were shouting. Most of their words didn't register.

But I heard Painter say, "Please don't."

And Kopański say, "Stay where you are!"

The black river was below me, its tide a torrent.

Snapshots of my life raced through my mind. All of the hardship and pain seemed wanton. The sacrifices to no avail. The friendships sullied. The people who loved me disappointed.

SWAT was running toward me.

Was I a good or bad man?

I didn't know.

Others would decide.

I jumped.

THIRTY-TWO

A week later the president and his chief of staff were in the subterranean White House Situation Room. Opposite them were four people.

The attorney general.

Marty Fleet.

Thyme Painter.

And Józef Kopański.

Kopański said, "Suppose Cochrane was innocent of the crimes."

The chief of staff said, "I doubt that, but suppose he was. Philip Knox engaged his asset Simon Tap to kill Cochrane. We know that now. Capitol Hill is in no doubt that Cochrane killed them instead. Do you agree?"

The attorney general nodded.

To Kopański, the chief of staff said, "He attacked you and another officer. Agree?"

Reluctantly, Kopański answered, "Yes."

The chief of staff was on a roll. "NYPD officers severely assaulted. Thirteen men taken hostage at gunpoint. That alone would have gotten Cochrane the death penalty."

"But he didn't kill any of them," said Fleet. "They were just in his way."

"Lots of people seem to get in Cochrane's way." The chief of staff waved his hand. "Do we pronounce Cochrane dead?"

The attorney general answered, "Yes. Coast Guard says it was a fierce riptide that night. Even if he survived the jump off Brooklyn Bridge—and we think that unlikely—he would have been dragged out to sea. He's dead."

The chief of staff locked his eyes on the detectives. "You ran him to ground."

Kopański answered, "No. We followed him to a place of his choosing. He was in charge that night."

Painter added, "It was his swan song."

Marty Fleet was about to add his thoughts.

But the attorney general gripped his arm, fearing the young man would jeopardize his position.

Marty Fleet shook him free and spoke to the president. "Sir—you should have done more to help him."

"Marty!" said the AG.

Fleet stared at the president. "Once I thought I wanted to be like you. Then my sister fell out of the sky in a climbing accident. That changed everything. She tries to speak to me. She can't. She's just like Cochrane. Fucking dead. But here's the thing. I care for her."

The detectives were looking at Marty. He

was killing his career. Their respect for him was enormous.

Fleet stood and pointed at the chief of staff. "The difference between you and me is that I look after Penny. Always."

He stormed out of the room.

A man entered a diner in Kansas. He was elegantly dressed, his beard trimmed, his voice that of a southern gentleman. He ordered a black coffee and took a seat in a booth. The waitress thought he was cute in a throwback kind of way. He noticed that but paid it no mind.

"Do you have a newspaper?" he asked her. "Preferably a national one."

She said, "I can check."

He smiled.

The waitress hesitated. There was something about the big guy. It wasn't because he was handsome. Or built like he could tear apart the diner. It was his eyes. They looked so beguiling.

She brought him today's copy of the *Washington Post*. He glanced at the front page. It said that Will Cochrane had been dragged out to sea a week earlier.

He gave the paper back to her and said, "Thank you."

She said, "You in Kansas for a reason?"

"Yes."

For some reason she couldn't move. "Is it a good reason?"

He smiled. "I want to be here."

She left him. Always this way, he thought.

He was nothing as grandiose as a lone wolf.

As Knox had articulated to NYPD, he was a dog. No masters. No one to love him anymore. Kicked out of their backyard to fend for himself and be who he really was.

A scavenging mutt.

A besmirched spy.

A man who cared for his friends.

A soldier.

A fighter.

An American.

Will Cochrane.

ACKNOWLEDGMENTS

With thanks to my two brilliant mentors, David Highfill and Luigi Bonomi, and their second-to-none teams at William Morrow/HarperCollins Publishers and LBA Literary Agency respectively.

ELECTRIFYING THRILLERS BY

MATTHEW DUNN

SPYCATCHER

978-0-06-203786-2

Will Cochrane is the CIA's and MI6's most prized asset, and now his controllers have a new assignment: neutralize one of the world's most wanted terrorists, believed to be a general in the Islamic Revolutionary Guards. But on a breakneck race through the capitals of Europe and into America's northeast, the spycatcher will discover that his prey knows the game all too well . . . and his agenda is more terrifying than anyone could have imagined.

SENTINEL

978-0-06-203794-7

CIA headquarters receives a cryptic message from an agent operating deep undercover in Russia: *"He has betrayed us and wants to go to war."* Unable to make contact, the director turns to Will Cochrane. His mission: infiltrate a remote submarine base in eastern Russia, locate the agent, and decode his message—or die trying.

SLINGSHOT

978-0-06-203805-0

On the streets of Gdansk, Poland, Will Cochrane waits for a Russian defector bearing a document about a super-secret pact between Russia and the U.S. Under a hail of gunfire, a van snatches the defector away from both Will and a recovery team from the Russian foreign intelligence service. Now, it's up to Will and his CIA/MI6 team to find the defector before the Russians do.

DUN 0317